Anatoly Medlov:

Complete Reign

Latrivia S. Nelson

RiverHouse Publishing, LLC is registered in the United States Patent and Trademark Office.

.

All **RiverHouse, LLC** Titles, Imprints and Distributed Lines are available at special quantity discounts for bulk purchases for sales promotions, premiums, fund-raising and educational or institutional use.

Imprint: *RiverHouse Publishing, LLC*

ISBN: 978-0-9832186-1-6

This book is printed on acid-free paper.

For Adam, Tierra and Jordan.
Mommy's finally home...

Acknowledgments

Thank you God for your favor.

This book would not have been made possible without the following people: my dear husband and best friend, Adam Nelson, Kandace Tuggle (KanDesignGrafix.com), Novellette Whyte (authorgurunovellette1.blogspot.com), the women of the Anatoly Medlov: Complete Reign Blog (www.anatolymedlov.wordpress.com), my dear friends Markum T. Lenowski and Viktor Ivanov and every reader.

Prologue

Last chapter of Dmitry's Royal Flush: Rise of the Queen

Prague, Czech Republic

A beautiful sunset cast a tranquil glow over the Medlov chateau as the family prepared for a huge dinner. A month had passed since *the Dorian incident,* and things were finally back to normal.

Royal and Dmitry had committed to being completely transparent, and Anatoly had been off for a month selling his *inventory* around the world. Anya had even started to attend a school in town only blocks from the boutique that Royal and Dmitry drove her to and picked her up from every day.

Tonight, the feast was larger than ever. Food had been prepared all day, and the house was cleaned and opened in celebration of Dmitry and Royal's newest addition to the Medlov family scheduled to arrive in eight months.

The news had come as a shock only weeks after the two arrived back from Sochi in the form of brutal morning sickness for Royal. Dmitry was ecstatic at the prospect of *doing it right this time*, and they quickly headed to the doctor for confirmation and prenatal care.

Royal's enormous appetite had Dmitry cooking constantly. He prepared special meals for her every day at the restaurant and spent his nights picking out names and preparing the nursery. For the family, this was their third chance at a new life, and they intended to succeed this time.

The dinner had already started when Anatoly arrived. He came in with bags of gifts for everyone and doggy treats for Anya's puppy. The family had all but begged him to fly in.

Since Sochi, he seemed very much removed from everyone, always working and never spending time with the family anymore. Dmitry knew that it was because of Victoria. Only, every time that he dared broach the topic, Anatoly only withdrew more. It took Anya calling to invite him to the party for him to come. He could never resist his little sister.

His blonde locks mirrored his father's. They had both grown their hair back, only Anatoly had also grown a full beard. His tanned face was aged slightly, and he had a permanent scowl.

"Anatoly!" Anya screamed when she saw him. She ran across the foyer and jumped in his arms.

Dropping the bags, he quickly picked her up and swung her around, glad to see his favorite girl. "How are you, baby?" he asked, kissing her rosy cheeks. "I've missed you so much."

"We've missed you, too," she said as he put her down. "Where have you been?"

"Around," he said, rubbing through her hair. "I brought all these beautiful pink boxes just for you. They are full of gifts from around the globe, *even* from Disneyworld."

Her face lit up. "Oh, thank you. Thank you, Anatoly," she said, hugging him.

Royal rounded the corner slightly pudgy and glowing. She extended her arms and hugged him warmly. Rubbing his beard, she kissed his cheek and grabbed his hand.

"I was hoping that you would show," she said, guiding him to the dining hall. "Everyone is already here."

"I'm sure that no one came to see me," he said gruffly. "You look great. Big and pregnant."

"Shut up," she said laughing.

"No, the look fits you. You should stay knocked up."

They entered into the main dining hall to see all the staff from the house, the restaurant and the boutique along with acquaintances of Dmitry and Royal at the various tables eating, drinking and talking.

All eyes went to Anatoly as he walked through the door with Royal. As usual, the women swooned and whispered about him. A month ago, he would have taken a mental note of each and everyone one, but tonight he simply made his way to his father's table.

Dmitry stood and gave him a hug. They laughed and embraced each other, and then Dmitry offered him a seat.

"Good to see you, son. How's life?"

"Busy, papa. Good to see you, too."

Dmitry wiped his mouth with his napkin and gave a clever grin. He looked over at Royal and winked his eye.

"I have brought special wine from my last trip to Italy. Why don't you go into kitchen and grab it for me?"

"Wine? Papa, I'm boss now. Why do you send me to do these types of things?"

"Because it is from the new winery that I just purchased last week. I already have someone running it, but I'd like for you to sample it. Tell me if you like it."

"Alright," he sighed. "Where is it?"

"I left it on countertop."

"What is it called? I'm sure that there is more than one bottle in kitchen, old man." He was almost short with his father.

"It's called *donna bella*."

"Beautiful woman?"

"Yes, you like?" Dmitry's eyes were eager.

"That's not very original, papa" he said, standing up. "I'll be right back."

Anatoly made his way through the crowds of people, past the servers to the kitchen. He walked in and looked to the long island in front of the door and searched it. Sure enough. A bottle of *Donna Bella* was sitting there waiting for him.

He picked it up and looked at the bottle. It *was* sort of a catchy name now that he thought about it, and the label was impressive with gold foil and crimson and green colors. Okay, maybe he was being too hard on the old man.

"What are you drinking?" a voice asked from behind him in the corner.

Anatoly looked up from the bottle but wouldn't turn around.

"Wine," he clenched his jaw.

He heard the click of heels behind him, moving towards him slowly. He could feel the sway of her hips even before he could see her.

"Chardonnay? What year?" the voice asked.

Anatoly turned slowly to find Victoria standing behind him in a pair of skinny jeans that showed her bow-legs and stilettos that made her even taller. Her long hair was pulled into a ponytail, and she sported large diamond studs. She gave a big smile and blushed slightly at the look on his face.

She took the bottle from him and grabbed the two glasses waiting beside it. Pouring him a glass, she handed it to him.

"*I'm doing you the courtesy of not sneaking it to you like a fucking snake.* Now drink it," she mocked.

Anatoly took the glass and drank all of the wine then pulled her into him. They looked at each other for a long while in the silence of the kitchen. She ran her hands through his curly locks and down through his scruffy beard, and he held her close clenching her waist and thighs.

"I thought you were dead," he confessed.

"Your father has a very long reach. The woman who worked for Dorian was paid off the day of the event by Dmitry to get me to Kerch."

"Kerch?"

"Yeah, I'd never been there before. Anyway, this woman pulls a gun on me, then escorts me out the back of the studio after the transaction had been made. The next day, I ended up in Kerch. I was there for weeks, and then I went to Yalta." She shrugged her shoulders. "The Ukraine is really a pretty place."

"Some parts of it. My father told me that he had friends in Kerch."

"Yeah, some pretty heavy hitters, too. I stayed there until he sent for me, and then I ended up in Italy at a damned winery. Your father was there talking to some Italian guy in Italian. So, I didn't even know what they were saying. Then he offered me a job to work there, market his stuff, you know legit work. He bought the damned winery that day, and I got a sweet job. It's nice."

"Why didn't you call me?"

"I wanted to, but Dmitry and Royal insisted that I not. They said to get my life straight first, make sure the heat was off of that *last thing*, because it was all over the world news and everything, and then when it was time, I could see you again."

Anatoly looked down at the ground. "I should have never sent you there."

"It's the best thing you could have done for me. Really," she lifted his chin.

"So you're not a deviant anymore?"

"Oh, yeah," she laughed. "I'm just not setting up old rich guys anymore. I sell wine," she laughed. "But I've missed you."

He leaned against the island and pulled her to him. "Missed you."

"Are you hungry?"

"Not really."

"Want to get out of here? Maybe go to the condo?" she asked. "It has been a month."

Anatoly patted his pockets. "I've got my keys right here. Let's go."

"What about saying goodbye to your folks?"

"My father said goodbye when he sent me in here," he smiled. "I'll catch him in the morning."

The two left quickly towards the garage while the rest of the family ate dinner together and laughed and sang as the band played an upbeat Russian tune.

Snacking on a pickle, Royal looked towards the door to see if anyone was coming. "I guess he found the *wine*," she laughed.

"I guess so." Dmitry shook his head. He pulled her to him and kissed her lips. "I love you."

"I love you, too," she said, touching his face.

"What about *me*?" Anya asked.

"We love you, too," they both said, pulling her over to them.

Chapter One

Next Day
Prague, Czech Republic

The late morning sun's fiery blaze awoke Anatoly from his peaceful sleep. His blue prisms slowly opened to the clear skies shining brightly across the room. He squinted a bit, wiped his tired eyes and yawned. Why didn't his folks have real curtains in their bedroom? *How did they wake up to this every single day?*

Sitting up in the bed, he looked over at the black woman lying in bed beside him. Her dark skin gave dramatic contrast to the silver sheets that barely covered her long, slender body. A small grin colored her full lips. Long, dark, thick hair spilled over onto her pillow. She slept as if she did not have a care in the world.

Bending toward her, he looked at her chest slowly rise and fall. Peaceful bliss for her but not for him. Resting his head back on the headboard, he ran his hand through his blonde tendrils and gripped the back of his neck, massaging his aching bones.

Unfortunate for her, he had that familiar feeling again now that he had her – the urge to flee. At the very moment that she committed, he disassociated. It was cause and effect for him. He knew it as soon as he finished making love to her.

Sweaty and exhausted, he had collapsed beside her, feeling a million miles away from her body even though it was so close to his own. She had looked into his eyes and confessed her love for the first time in their pseudo-relationship. And he had whispered in Russian, "*Ya ne lyublyu tebya*," (*I don't love you*), in response.

She had gone to sleep smiling and oblivious. He had gone to sleep thinking about his dilemma – how to undo what he had done far too spontaneously. The tightness in his chest had started immediately, as soon as she spooned against him and closed her big, brown eyes. His father was right. It simply would not work.

Now, curled up beside him, wrapped in the sheets, she never felt him when he stirred, when he pulled his body from the bed and quickly slipped on his jeans.

Once fully dressed, he stood by the bed for a while, staring at her and thinking of all that he had put her through and vice versa.

Finally when he had reasoned enough, he grabbed his wallet and keys and slipped out of the bedroom.

The family could take care of her arrangements to get back to Italy to the winery. He knew that his father would *at least* – Royal may not.

All he did know was that he couldn't stay in the condo with her a moment longer. Now that he knew that she was okay, that she had not been harmed because of him, he could release her.

In fact, he had already released her, whether he liked it or not. She wasn't the one. It was sort of refreshing when he thought of it. To fall in love with Victoria would be too easy and far too dangerous. She was like him. Cunning. Forward. Greedy. His decision would be best for the both of them or at least for him. And that was all that mattered at the end of the day.

It would have been cruel to leave her stranded at his parent's condo alone, so he left the keys on the kitchen counter for the Bentley. But he didn't leave a note. That would be too much.

Words couldn't express what he was feeling right at the moment anyway. What was the use of trying? He'd walk for a while and clear his head. He just had to get out of the condo and way from her, had to get away from the commitment that was coming. The looming inevitability of a bad relationship choked him out of the space – drove him to flee.

Opening the front door to the house, he looked back one last time up the stairs and then left.

The sun was just as bright outside as it was in his father's bedroom. It shone down on him and fed him the energy he needed to get on with things. He took a deep breath, savoring the fresh air, slipped on his

Aviator shades and headed down the steps towards the walkway.

Looking around at all the well-manicured lawns, the expensive cars and the people walking up and down the sidewalk, he felt a calm that was not possible a minute ago.

This place was such a far cry from the life he had known when he was a boy. Everyone here was privileged. They had no clue what it was like to struggle, to fight for every crumb. But then again, neither did he anymore.

Life was good, but his was pushing him to get back to Memphis. His business could not run itself. There were things to do, people to see, money to make, guns to sell.

Catching a taxi a few miles outside of the upscale, gated community, he ordered the small Indian man to take him straight to the airport. He would bypass heading back to the countryside to his father's chateau. Dmitry would understand. His father was like that. He was wise in his years because of the women that he had gone through before meeting his wife, Royal. Only Victoria was not his Royal. There was nothing anyone could do about that.

Within the hour, he was on the tarmac of a private airstrip with a cup of tea and a cigarette, preparing to board his private jet and head back to the states from Prague.

Still smelling like sex from the night before, he threw his cigarette down and headed up the stairs to his plane. The metal clanged under the weight of his heavy boots as he quickly made his way up. When he got to the top, he turned around and looked over the airstrip.

Finally, so far away from the condo, he could breathe again. The tightness in his chest had subsided. But he did wonder if she was awake yet, if she had found the keys, put the pieces together and figured out what he didn't have the nerve to tell her. *Goodbye. Take care. Don't call.*

"Welcome back, Mr. Medlov," the flight attendant said, offering to take his nearly empty cup.

Turning away from Prague, he passed his Styrofoam container to her and took off his shades.

"Thanks, Karen," he said, feeling a sense of relief. "Let's get out of here, *da*."

Chapter Two

Memphis, TN

Anatoly raced through the city on his motorcycle from his father's old mansion to *Mother Russia* restaurant with his mind on the meeting that would take place in less than an hour. He gripped the handlebars and jolted down Walnut Grove past the people in their family cars obeying the speed limit. Their slowness annoyed him. Or maybe it wasn't them at all. Maybe it was his need for the fast life. *Fast all the time. Fast until death.* His new mantra was completely against his father's old school teachings, but he embraced it happily.

Reluctantly, his men followed as best they could a few cars back. He didn't really like bodyguards very much, even though according to the council *they were a necessity*. However, they made him feel more vulnerable than when he was alone.

Alone, he could take care of himself. He felt like the true recluse that he was. Plus, there wasn't much he couldn't handle with the heat he was packing under this coat. Cop or Thug. He could take anyone out, if needed.

Most days, he felt utterly invincible. Like today. He was roaring inside, but he didn't know why.

There was just something in the air. Something urgent was on the horizon.

He accelerated as soon as the stop light turned green. Digging in and pulling off hard, he was just about to switch gears when he felt a jolt from behind. A sudden jerk took his bike off the ground. He propelled forward in the air helpless to the power of the strike. Then his body hit the hard pavement with an earthquake-like thud. He rolled twice feeling chunks of flesh tear apart as he clumsily bounced.

On his back, he looked up at the sky and tried to breathe when the momentum slowed. His chest felt as though it would cave in. He heard cars screeching around him, trying to stop for the man lying in the middle of the street. Then he heard a car door open, heels pound the pavement and a woman screaming.

"Oh, my God! I'm so sorry," she squealed from afar. She ran up to him and dropped to her knees. "Can you move? Oh my God!"

Anatoly tried to move, tried to breathe. He reached for his helmet, to pull it off and inhale fresh air. She helped him remove his head gear. Her perfume greeting him as he emerged. Sparkles of white light blinded him. Sweat formed on his forehead from the pain. Then he heard familiar, Russian voices. His men. They came running and pushed the woman out of the way.

"Boss, boss, are you alright?" one voice asked.

"Call an ambulance," another voice ordered.

"I'm so sorry!" the woman said again.

"Help me up," Anatoly finally ordered as his vision came back to him.

"Boss, I don't know if you should move," one of his bodyguards said concerned.

"Help me up," Anatoly insisted, making his body move. If they wouldn't help him, he'd get up himself, then there would be hell to pay.

His men pulled him up while a few others picked up his bike. Anatoly looked around. Cars stopped, and people looked on with their hands on their mouths. *Great*, he had become a spectacle.

Limping, he went over to the sidewalk and sat down on its edge near a gutter. His men gathered around him as if he had just been shot. He wanted to scream at them, to demand some space, but he was too tired to bark. Instead, he slumped over and rubbed his bloody knees. He hated road rash. *This shit will leave scars for years,* he thought to himself. He winced as he touched the exposed, torn flesh mingled in denim jeans. *Fucking bad driving women*, he thought to himself.

As he looked across the street at the woman, who had evidently hit him, Anatoly could tell that she wanted to come over. She stood in her red suit with her cell phone to her ear talking to someone – probably the police – about the accident and staring at him.

"Should we get you out of here?" Vasily, his bodyguard asked.

"No, go on to restaurant. Tell McNamara that I'll be late for our meeting. See if he can reschedule for later this evening. Find out when his flight leaves and make any arrangements that he needs," Anatoly said, still looking at the woman.

"What about her? You want us to..."

"No," Anatoly said, looking back down at his aching knee. "*Just* go and do what I told you to."

"Yes, boss," he said, taking a few of the men with him.

The woman couldn't help herself any longer. She put away her phone and ran through traffic across the street to him. Her hair had fallen down out of its neat ponytail and her wide doe-like eyes were filled with tears.

Anatoly looked at her and automatically thought of Victoria. Her chocolate skin glistened with perspiration and her full lips curved into a pensive frown.

"Sir?" she looked over at the bodyguards who sat with him. Stepping back a few feet, she raised her voice. "Is there anything that I can do? I'm so sorry. I didn't look up in time. It was my fault."

"I know it was your fault. I couldn't have done this to myself," Anatoly snapped. "Do you have insurance?"

"Of course." She looked over at her Audi. "I can go and get my card. Are you alright?" She looked back over at him.

"Do I look alright?" Anatoly asked.

The woman sighed and put her hand on her heart. She wiped the tears quickly from her face. "I'm so sorry. I was...not paying attention." Her voice faded.

A police car pulled up with its lights on and siren blaring. Anatoly looked over and rolled his eyes. *Great. Now the pigs come.*

A fat, stubby, white officer pulled himself out of the car and slowly made his way over, wobbling with every step and determined to take his time. He looked at the odd group with a frown. *A black woman, a biker and a group of misfits in suits?*

He pulled out his notepad and pen as he got closer then stopped when he saw who was sitting on the sidewalk. Not just any biker. It was Anatoly Medlov. Turning around, he grabbed the radio on his shoulder and called in something.

The woman looked over at the officer then at Anatoly. "He sure is taking his time," she said offended. "Officer!" she called out. "Is an ambulance on its way?" She pointed at Anatoly.

"I don't need ambulance," Anatoly said gruffly, getting up without his men. They knew better than to help him in front of the cops.

"But you're bleeding and injured," she protested, putting her hand on her hips. "Excuse me, officer?"

The fat cop turned around and swallowed hard. He walked up to the group and looked at Anatoly. "Can anyone here tell me what happened?" he asked in a slow, southern drawl.

"We had an accident," Anatoly said, ignoring the pain. "We were just about to exchange insurance information and be on our way."

"Who was at fault for the accident?"

"Me," the woman said, raising her hand.

Anatoly eyed her. *Damned right it was her fault.*

"And what's your name, ma'am?" the officer asked.

"Destiny," she answered with a ring in her voice. "Destiny Palmer."

Anatoly looked over at the woman as she explained what happened to the officer. She had a Southern accent, sounded like she was from Memphis, looked like something out of a magazine with her busty curves and striking features.

Her thick, naturally arched eyebrows brought out her bright, brown eyes covered by wing-like lashes. Her cheekbones were high and rosy; her nose was carefully carved, and her lips were covered in a gloss that made them perfect for kissing. She wore a tailored red suit – red being his favorite color – that discreetly covered her well-kept body.

He trailed her arms down to her long fingers. Manicured nails. No rings. Not married. She wore red-backed, leather heels that highlighted her thick, muscular legs, and she clenched her Blackberry as if it was her only lifeline.

What was odd to Anatoly was that she smelled like sex. It was strange that woman dressed so conservatively would smell like something so lustful, but the perfume that she wore screamed words that were so provocative he was certain that under all the layers of fine clothing, she was wearing lace. He looked at her hips as she stopped explaining.

She and the officer looked over at him for his version of the story and caught him before he could take his eyes off her perfect butt. He smiled as he looked up - didn't even bat an eye.

***

Anatoly's bodyguard pulled up to his boutique, *Dmitry's Closet*, and dropped him off at the front door. Aching from head to toe, he limped inside, letting the door slam behind him.

The patrons looked up as he made his way through the store to the back office with his head down and his leg dragging.

In the corner by the dressing room, Renee, the store manager, watched him dumbfounded. Excusing herself, she left her assistant, Miriam, to see after the customers while she followed Anatoly to the back.

As she came through the door, she saw him wince and sit down behind the credenza. After making sure the door was locked behind her, she strode over to the office refrigerator and pulled out an ice pack, then walked over to the desk. He looked up at her with a *don't-even-ask* scowl.

Renee ignored him. With a smirk, she put the ice pack on his forehead, applying more pressure than needed to his reddened face.

"What gave me away?" he asked, putting his hand on hers as she applied the ice. He looked up at her with a boyish grin. His lip was busted and bruised, but he smiled anyway, forgetting the pain.

"You're all scarred up," she said quickly. "Pretty hard to miss. What happened?"

"I got hit by car," he explained. "On my bike," he continued.

"I told you that thing wasn't a good idea." She stood back up and crossed her arms. "Now look at you."

"Ugh. You are so afraid of everything, Renee. I had to buy you a Hummer to keep you from being afraid of road."

"That's the company car, *remember*? My name isn't on it," she corrected him.

"Well, you're the only one who drives it...so...," his cell phone rang. He rolled his eyes. *Who was it now?*

The pain shot through his arm as he reached into his pants and pulled out his phone. His bloody knuckles scrubbed against the denim and stained his pants.

Renee winced for him.

"I'm alright," he said more for her than him.

Renee didn't blink an eye. She didn't believe him. He needed a doctor, but he was too bullheaded to call.

Sitting back in the chair, he looked at the number for a minute. His face turned pale.

Turning away from Renee, his voice lowered, and he nodded as he spoke in Russian. There were a hundred pauses between his stuttered words.

Renee watched him from across the room in awe. She'd never seen him talk to anyone with such careful measure – not even Dmitry. He finally looked up at the ceiling, grunted, then finished his conversation and hung up.

Turning around, he slipped his phone in his pocket and bit his lip. Renee was compelled to stay and pry. Unable to obey her instinct to leave him alone, she cleared her throat.

"Bad news?" she asked.

Anatoly snapped out of his daze and looked up at her. He swallowed hard again and tried to shake something off.

"You could say that," he finally uttered. He gave a weak smile. "My...my mother just died." His eyes watered.

***

Like his father before him, Anatoly sat at the head of the Medlov Crime Family table in the basement of *Mother Russia* as the council talked. As he listened while they argued, his mind traveled back to the voice on the phone, a young, desperate boy of a voice – his little brother.

It had been so long since he had laid eyes on his family, so long since he had hugged his mother. When he left many years ago, his mother had told him to never return, to never look back. He had taken her advice. Even when he was in Moscow, only miles away from his childhood home, he never visited. His mother never answered his calls, even when she knew that it was him. Word had traveled to her that her son was a Vory, was a boss, was a *somebody*. But how could he ever remain, if people were to know where he had come from? So she disowned him out of love, and now she was dead.

Anatoly snapped out of his daze and cleared his throat. The loud room quieted. They were all sympathetic for the boy's loss, but they had seen him harden over the years. The quiet lion had grown from a cub to a king through crafty business deals and cold-hearted killing tactics. They knew that he would recover soon from his newest wound.

There would only be a few more evolutions before Anatoly was the exact replica of his father—an act of betrayal so cruel until he would never recover, the loss of a true friend or a lover, and the torn ties of family bliss. Each boss had experienced each pain in a different way, but the story was always the same.

They looked at him now, going through one of the three pains he was promised as boss. His mother had just died and with her any thought of kindness or conscience. The death of a mother was one of the two leg weights lifted off a man in Anatoly's position.

When his mother passed, what was left of his humility would shed like old snake's skin. The new man who emerged would always be tougher, more resilient and more dangerous.

The older men in the council had nearly applauded when they heard the news of his loss, realizing that the boy's alienation from outside people only made him more astringent.

"I'll be gone *at most* two weeks. There are a couple of meetings that were coming due anyway," Anatoly said, looking down at his pale hands. His voice was dry. "I'll make the best use of my time while I'm there."

"Before you leave, we should discuss one looming problem," an older man on the council, Yuri, said from the far end of the table. He sat forward and looked around. The other men looked on.

"Yes," Anatoly gave his permission to speak.

"Lieutenant Nicola Agosto," he said with a deep growl. The room tensed with the mention of the Italian police officer's name. "His investigation is getting closer and closer. We have only two options, turn him or kill him."

"Killing a cop at his level isn't that easy to do," Anatoly answered. "I have contacts in his shop. Let me reach out to them to see what can be done to neutralize him, but *per the request of my father*," Anatoly tapped his pen on the table, "We have been advised to tread very carefully with Agosto."

"Why?" Yuri asked.

"Because it brings far too much attention back to us in ways that we won't be able to hide. There are ways to muddy the waters for Agosto without actually touching him."

"Does he have something on us?" Yuri asked. "We do not negotiate with police officers..."

Anatoly snarled. "Don't mistake my youth for ignorance, Yuri. I know that we do not negotiate with officers, but we also do not expose ourselves and show our hand without cause." His hand hit the table as he looked around the room. "I'm getting really tired of being reminded of the code, like I do not know it."

"We meant no disrespect, Anatoly. We only wanted to address the issue with the pig," Yuri retracted.

"Agosto's a boy scout. I doubt that he has anything, otherwise, he would have already used it, but we have men close to him who know what he's up to and keep us ahead of him." Anatoly sat up in his seat. "So, nothing happens to Agosto or his family while I'm away." He stood up and stretched his aching back. "I'm done...anything else comes down the pike, pass it through Vasily. I've gotta get some rest."

***

The sun had finally set by the time that Anatoly walked outside of *Mother Russia*. The wind blew through his blonde locks and filled his nostrils. He took a deep breath and looked up at the stars shining down on him. A tight pain was growing again in his chest – too much stress. He bit his lip and slipped into the back of the car at the front of the restaurant waiting to pick him up.

His driver, Vasily, drove quietly through the streets without bothering his friend. He watched

Anatoly look out of the window, staring out into nothingness. He wanted to ask him if he was alright, but he knew better. A Vor thrived on pain, on anger. It only made him more powerful. Their type was bred on hopelessness, so when hope emerged, they knew where it came from.

***

Pulling up to the gated compound only minutes away from downtown, Anatoly was escorted back home in his Mercedes. The bodyguards stood guard in the hut, watching their boss as he was escorted up to the front of the large, plantation-style mansion, lit up at dusk with lights. In the driveway was a black Hummer.

Evidently, Renee was visiting.

Anatoly looked at the truck and gave a sigh of relief. He needed to see her face tonight.

Grabbing his backpack and his IPod, he walked up the stairs slowly. As Vasily opened the door for him, he smelled food drifting through the corridors. Anatoly tried to conceal a grin.

Dropping his backpack in the corner, he checked the mail on the table in the foyer and yawned.

"Do you need anything else, boss?" Vasily asked, standing with his hands clasped in front of him.

"*Net.*" Anatoly grabbed an envelope off the table and slipped it in his pocket. "Take the rest of the night off."

"*Spesiba*," Vasily said, bowing his head. He turned and headed down the back corridor to his room.

When his man was out of view, Anatoly headed toward the kitchen. He walked softly down the marble floors in the darkness of the house into the large kitchen.

Renee had the television going while she cooked up a small feast. With her back turned and her IPod attached to her hip, she sang as she put the final touches on the fried chicken that she placed on a silver platter.

Anatoly stood in the darkness of the corner watching her with his arms folded in front of him. He could watch her all night if she left him.

Outside of his mother and his step-mother, she was the only woman that he knew who loved to cook. She took immense pride in it, but because she was alone in Memphis, away from her large family in Atlanta, she only got to cook for more than herself when she came to see him.

In her favorite apron, she whirled around the kitchen moving plates and flatware to the island bar for the two of them. In between cooking, she drank straight out the wine bottle and sang Al Green.

"Are you just going to stand in the corner like a pervert, or are you going to help me fix the table?" she finally asked, without looking away from the mixed greens stewing on the stove.

Anatoly stepped out of the darkness with a clever grin. Quietly, he went over to the cupboard and pulled out two wine glasses. As he sat them down, he looked at the table and noticed the card by one of the plates.

"It's for you," she said, taking the ear buds out of her ear.

"What is it?" he asked with his back toward her.

"Open it and see." She turned off the eye on the stove and grabbed a bowl. "Fried chicken, greens, yams, beets for you, and cabbage...for you."

"What's the occasion?" He opened the envelope to find a sympathy card from Hallmark, *praying for his family during their loss*.

"I just felt like you needed something to cheer you up. You had a pretty shitty day," she said, putting the food on the table.

The bowls clinked on the granite table top. Placing the mittens down, she looked up at him.

As she walked off, he caught a whiff of her perfume. He had bought it for her in Jerusalem. He bought it because when he smelled it, he thought of her. She was his little pudgy friend –someone that he could talk to, confide in *to a point*.

Only tonight, he didn't want to talk to her. At that very moment, he wanted to kiss her as a way of thanking her and feeding his own need. He clenched his jaw and looked away. *This was Renee for goodness sake*. The bump on the head today had obviously been harder than he had first suspected.

As she took off her apron, he noticed that she wore a black silk sundress that showed a lot more cleavage than normal. He took his seat and put the napkin on his lap, then looked up at her and shook his head. Since she had lost *the weight* recently, she was starting to look less and less like an employee and more and more like a prospect.

"What's the dress for," he asked, pointing at her breasts. "Are you planning to feed a tribe of starving children tonight?"

Renee looked down and smiled. "I've got a date," she answered with a bright glimmer in her eyes. "They do look big in this dress, huh?"

Anatoly choked. "A date? With?" A territorial jealousy boiled in the pit of his empty stomach.

"A guy who came into the shop today. A basketball player. I almost said no when I first saw him. He looked like a freaking Medlov – only he wasn't Russian. He's from the east coast. He's here to check out the team."

"Why was he at the store?" Anatoly asked.

"He thought we sold men's clothing," Renee answered with a shrug.

She turned and went back to get the bottle of wine, instantly recognizing his jealousy but choosing to ignore it. Anatoly never liked anyone to have anything that he didn't already have or hadn't had. She didn't expect this to be any different.

"So, am I eating alone?" he continued, trying to put a guilt trip on her.

"No. He and I are just going to Beale Street to watch a band play later. I figured that you and I could eat dinner first and then..."

"Oh." Anatoly fixed his plate. "You wanted to get me out of the way first, *eh*?" His plate clinked.

"Basically," she said, sitting down. "So eat fast. I might get laid tonight, and a sister has been on a serious dry spell, you know."

Anatoly coughed into his napkin.

Renee laughed. "I'm just kidding, Ana."

"What did I tell you about calling me that? It makes me sound like...sissy," he laughed.

"We all know that you're no sissy."

"You know this how?"

"I'm the one who has to explain to these women that you're not *available* when they come lurking around my shop," she said, sneering at him. She stabbed the chicken. "They all think that I'm the devil." Her southern drawl thickened.

Anatoly grinned. "You are." He tasted the food and forgot his worries. *Man, did he love her cooking.* He sank his teeth in the crispy, golden, juicy chicken and planted his rigid elbows on the table. He winced again as he remembered his bruises.

Renee watched him in complete satisfaction. She smiled and placed the napkin on her lap.

"Is it good?" she asked, tasting her food.

"Better than pu..."

"Watch your mouth," she interrupted.

Anatoly grinned and quieted down. They sat in silence, enjoying their food as the *Food Network* played in the background.

***

His father had never opened the windows of the master bedroom. It was too much of a security risk, but Anatoly couldn't imagine anything better.

The wind blew in and rustled the curtains, cleansed the room and cleared his thoughts. He lay in bed awake with his hands behind his head thinking of his mother.

It was still early, barely nine, but as early as he had to wake to get a start on his day, there was no need to stay up all night.

In the darkness, he recounted his childhood, the smell of his mother's hair on Sunday morning before mass, the smells of breakfast. Even though they were poor, she still worked so hard to give them a happy childhood. Her attempts had not been successful, but it was the effort that he had always admired, especially after finding out that his father's mother had been a whore.

Her photo flapped in his hand under the powerful push of the ceiling fan above him. He looked at her, her thin lips, her pale skin, her bright blue eyes and hopeful smile. A tear formed in the corner of his eye, but he quickly pushed it back. *There could be none of that.* He simply wouldn't allow himself to mourn her. *Alexandria.*

Sitting up in bed, he reached over for the bottle of vodka on the nightstand and thought of his newly recovering step-mother and put the bottle down. *Was there no solace?* He had no friends, outside of the men who called him boss and followed his orders, outside of Renee who was on a date with a strange man, outside of Anya, who was a child thousands of miles away.

Even his last lover, Victoria, crossed his mind. He hadn't called her since he left her in Prague two months ago. The word from his father was that she had been extremely angry *to put it lightly*. The last thing that he needed to do was to talk to her.

So, he was alone. His father had warned him of the cost of being the boss. It was the worse form of solitude. Everyone feared him. No one would risk getting close to him, not even his own family.

A knock at the door disrupted his thoughts. He recognized the hard tap on his door. It was Vasily. He sat up, wiped his tired eyes and turned on his lamp - the turn of the knob audible through the door.

"What is it?" he asked loudly.

"There is woman at your door. She's from this morning, boss. She said that she needed to talk to you. Should I send her away?"

"What *woman* from this morning?"

"The one who hit your bike," Vasily explained.

"How did she..."Anatoly stood up by the bed and slipped on his jeans. "Tell her I'll be down in minute. Put her in living room."

The woman stood in the living room in the same red suit from earlier. Anatoly rounded the corner with a cigarette hanging out of his mouth. His faithful dogs followed behind him. Barefoot, he walked up to her with a frown on his face. She turned and smiled at him.

"Hi. I know it's late. And it took me forever to find you, but I just had to come by and make sure that you were okay," she said, offering a small box. "It's a little peace offering."

Anatoly looked down at the box and walked past her. "Don't they have some kind of rules against contacting people after you assault them?" he asked sarcastically.

She looked at the box and raised her brow. "Yeah, they do. Look, I know that this is...*odd*, but I can't tell you how horrible I felt about nearly killing you this morning." She placed the box on the table.

"Have a seat," Anatoly said, lighting his cigarette. "How did you find out where I live?"

"Well, up until this morning, I'd never heard of you, and then I went to work and told my co-workers what happened. I remembered your last name, and they told me about that incident that happened a few years ago with your dad. I Googled you, and there was few pictures of your house."

"I need to buy a new house," Anatoly said under his breath. He took a drag of his cigarette and slapped his knee. His dogs came to him and settled by his sofa. "So you saw all that shit that they said about us online, and you still came over here in the dead of night?" he asked intrigued.

"Well, it's only nine. Actually, I just got off work and...I wanted to leave this with your butler, but he said that he would come and get you."

Anatoly heard Vasily's footsteps moving away from the room. He looked back at the woman and shook his head. "I don't have a butler here. So, where do you work?"

"For *Memphis Metro Magazine*," she said, pulling out her credentials. "I'm a food critic. I just started with the magazine. I moved here from Birmingham about two months ago."

Anatoly reached out for the box. It was more of a test to see how gullible the woman actually was. She quickly picked the box up and took it over to him. He opened it and removed the wrapping. It was bike reflector. He looked back up at her and grinned.

"I thought you could use one," she smiled.

"I could probably use a sense of humor more," he said, putting the reflector back in the box. "What is your name again?" He already knew, but he wanted to hear her say it.

"Destiny Palmer," she said, standing up a little straighter.

Anatoly stood up. "I tell you what. If you really want to make this morning up to me, then come by the restaurant tomorrow and do great interview on my manager and my food, but don't show up at my door with reflectors and jokes like I'm someone to play with, *da*?"

"Okay," she said, taking the box back. "I just wanted to break the ice."

"*Ice* broken," he said, putting out his cigarette. "Vasily, show Ms. Palmer out of my house."

"Sorry," she said, realizing that she had offended him. "Maybe this was the wrong thing to do, but I just wanted to see you again." Her voice was softer now. She gave a nervous smile and turned to follow Vasily.

Anatoly watched her walk away and felt a little guilty for being so hard on the woman. In truth, he wanted to see her again too.

"Tomorrow at noon. Lunch with me alone," he said, rubbing his dog's head. "Then you do my interview."

She turned and smiled. "See you then."

Chapter Three

Nicola Agosto perched his feet up on the park bench and watched as a group of men filed out of *Mother Russia* into the high-end luxury vehicles awaiting them and drove off into the sunset. He found it very cinematic in a way. *The mafia always got away in the movies.* But this was reality, and he had a serious hard-on for the Medlov Crime Family. If it was the last thing that he did, he would put the lot of them in jail, where they belonged.

Folding his newspaper under his arm, he stretched his legs and pulled a couple of dollars from his pocket to give to the homeless man sitting on the bench beside him.

"Every time that you see them going in there, and you call me, you'll get a little more, Louie," he said to the old man as he passed him the money. "But it's got to be *those* guys."

"Hey, I'm homeless, Nico, not blind. I know what I'm looking for." He took the money and shoved it into his pants.

"You got good pockets in there? I don't want the money falling out."

"I'm going to buy beer and get something to eat," the man explained. "It won't be in there long enough to get lost."

"Alright, alright. I'm out of here, but you take care of yourself."

"Same to you," the homeless man said, standing up. "Say hello to the wife. Thank her for the food she sent down last week. She's a freaking saint, your wife."

"Tell me about it," Agosto said, rubbing his lower back. How people lived on park benches was beyond him.

He walked down the trolley line to his unmarked squad car, jumped in and put the keys in the ignition. Then, he paused. In a rush, he'd almost forgotten. He got out quickly and looked under the car to check for a bomb. Since three years ago, he'd learned his lesson about the mafia and bombs. One had nearly cost him his eye...nearly his life.

Jumping back inside the car, he turned the ignition and pulled off into the streets with the AC blasting. Adjusting the vents, he let the air cool his hot, sticky body. He couldn't wait to peel out of his vest and get something to eat. His stomach growled so loud it sounded like it would eat him. Plus, he'd seen what he needed to see. Something big was going down soon. Only this time, he didn't have a source inside – not yet.

He picked up his cell and hit redial. The phone rang a few times before it picked up. A woman's voice answered.

"Hello."

"Meet me in ten minutes in Mid-Town on Flicker Street."

"Isn't that a pretty obvious location?"

"It's *pretty* safe," he said, hanging up.

Ten minutes later, a red Audi A8 pulled up to the Memphis Police Department Training Facility beside Nicola's car and parked. The woman looked over at him as if she was short on time. He pulled off his shades and pointed inside of the building.

With her notepad in her hands, she grabbed her purse, slammed her door and ran inside quickly. After Nicola watched her go into the front glass doors, he looked around one last time and headed in after her in a slow, leisurely stride.

"You're going to blow my cover," she said as he walked into an empty classroom and closed the door. She was visibly frustrated with him. Pacing back and forth, she clasped her keys in one hand and rested the other on her hip.

"Easy there, *crazy horse*. This is your first investigation. I think that I've got a few on you. *You* let *me* tell *you* when you're blowing your cover," he said, sitting down on the desk at the front of the classroom while he *schooled* her.

"I had lunch with him today," she said a little proud of herself. "He didn't give me one good bit of Intel, but the point is that I had lunch with him."

"Bravo," his voice was flat.

Destiny was pissed that Agosto didn't seem the least bit impressed. "My first day on this case undercover, I went to his home..."

"After you intentionally hit him with a vehicle. That's assault," Agosto interrupted.

"The point is that I got in."

Nicola raised his brow. "A lot of people get in, Destiny. But did you get anything?"

"I saw him in both of his elements. He's a hermit at home. He's surrounded by bodyguards at work."

"Fits the profile of most mafia bosses."

"And I think that he's interested in me."

"Fits the profile of most men." He stood up off the desk and tried to smile. "I don't want you to be too overzealous. I know that you'll do well, but you can't read more into an interaction than what's there. At this point, you're just some hot chick who works for a local rag. I need more than that. You have to figure out a way to get in with this young guy without sleeping with him."

"I would never sleep with him," she said offended.

Agosto waved his finger. "You say you would never do a lot of strange things before you go undercover, but you wake up one morning and you've crossed everything, and I mean everything, off your list. Just remember, if you sleep with him, this investigation becomes inadmissible, and I become your worst enemy."

"I will not sleep with him, Lou. I just want you to see that I'm closer to getting inside than you think."

"Okay." He checked his watch. "We will see, *young lady.*" Hearing voices in the hallway, he turned without saying another word and left her in the room alone.

Destiny stood looking out the blinds of the classroom at the sun setting and rolled her eyes. *What did Agosto know about anything?* Like she said, she was close. The way that Anatoly talked to her, looked at her, he would walk her right into his operations before long. And then, Agosto would have to eat his words.

Grabbing her purse, she finally left with one mission in mind.

***

Anatoly's personal cell would not stop ringing. He looked at the phone and grunted. *Blocked number.* He already knew who that was. Victoria. She had called him every single day since he left her at his father's place. *Why wouldn't she just give up? How could she not have gotten a clue yet?*

He almost picked up and answered, just to tell her to get lost, but he decided against it. Instead, he hit IGNORE and kept eating.

"How was your date?" he finally asked. His deep blue eyes were menacing.

"Nice," Renee said frowning. She had avoided talking about it on purpose.

"I'm going to be gone for a while, so if you want to stay here..."

"I like the apartment," she said, pouring another glass of wine.

"What's wrong with you now?" he snapped.

"You missed Royal's birthday today."

He put down his fork and sat back in his seat. Every year since Royal's *passing*, Renee had gone to her grave site on her birthday with Anatoly and put down flowers. He played along because it threw the feds off, but he wanted so badly to tell her that his step-mother was alive and well in Prague.

He watched Renee brooding over his oversight and debated again if he shouldn't just tell her. She would never tell a soul. Plus, it would ease her pain.

"Sorry, I had...*stuff* going on." His voice was softer. Looking up at her, he watched her face change.

"You don't have to apologize to me. I just don't want you to...you know." Her voice ached.

"Want me to *what*?"

"Forget." She swallowed hard. "I don't want you to *forget* her, Anatoly. She was a very good woman. She didn't have any family. *We* were her family. It just seems right that we do what any family would do." She rolled her eyes again.

He picked up his glass of vodka and took a sip. "I know. I haven't forgotten, Renee. *Not hardly*."

"Good," she said, getting up from the table. Taking both of their plates to the sink, she turned to find him still looking at her. "What?" she asked.

"Nothing. I better get ready to leave. I'm on a plane out of here in an hour. The offer still stands. If you want to stay here, you can."

"Be safe," she said softly.

Anatoly didn't smile, but his eyes glimmered. Standing up, he walked over to her, grabbed her bare arms and kissed her forehead. It made him instantly think of his father and Royal, how they carried on for so long during their courtship. Is that what he was doing? *Courting Renee?* The thought disturbed him. Pulling back, he looked down her in her bright, brown eyes.

"I will," he said, walking off.

***

Victoria threw her phone across the room and watched it collide with the wall. In pieces, it shattered and fell onto the floor by the computer desk. That BASTARD!

She grabbed the open bottle of wine and took a big gulp. The excess ran down the side of her mouth and slithered down her chin. Breathing hard, she wiped her face and cursed.

If Anatoly thought that he could just play her, he had another thing coming. She didn't give a damn about the mafia, his father or even Royal at this point. If he wanted to just screw her and throw her away all while pretending that he loved her, have her let her guard down and then crush her, she would make him pay. And she knew just how to do it.

Going to her computer, she searched for the stories about the *Massacre in Memphis* three years ago and found that Lieutenant Nicola Agosto headed the investigation. Anatoly had always said that he hated Agosto more than any other cop in the world. Evidently, the man had to be a serious threat. And he was probably just who she needed to get Anatoly back without it coming back to her.

How hard could it be to find a cop?

Her lip quivered as she pulled up his contact information. His picture said a thousand words. He was a tall, clean cut, dark Italian man in his late thirties. *Handsome. Formidable. An Alpha male for sure.*

She could look at Agosto's photo and tell that he was a boy scout, probably ironed his underwear. When she told him about the big gun shipment a few months ago in Sochi and how Anatoly laundered his money through art and kept a large inventory in Memphis the only one who would be spending time would be Anatoly...*up state*.

Scribbling his number down on a notepad, she quickly turned off her computer and fell over into her bed. Her thoughts danced about her in the hazy daze of drunkenness.

Tears formed at the sides of her eyes, but she wiped them quickly and turned over to bury her face

in her pillow. Inhaling her perfume, she cried aloud.
How she hated him for what he had done.
Anatoly had made her love him.

Chapter Four

Kapotnya (Moscow)

Anatoly looked out the window of his Land Rover as it escorted him down the MDK beltline. It was a dreary Wednesday afternoon, and the smoke of the Moscow Oil Refinery billowed up between spurts of hot fire into the polluted atmosphere and darkened the gloomy horizon.

He and his men were headed to the Kapotnya district. It was a place that he had not visited in many years, and though it was one of the poorest and most crime infested areas in all of Moscow, it was his home.

Running his hands over the console, he let his window down and smelled the air. As thick, strong contaminants filled the back of the SUV, he closed his eyes and thought of his last drive down this stretch of highway away many years ago.

He had left hastily with a pocket of cash and a garbage bag of clothes.

His mother had given him all the money that they had in savings and begged him to go to the USA to find his father. "Find Dmitry," she urged in his box of a bedroom with a hand of waded-up rubles that were stained with smut from hiding them in the fireplace as she stood in a work smock. Lips twisted and eyes full of pain, she packed his things quickly and kissed him on his cheek before she sent him away.

He remembered that fateful night out in the courtyard of their impoverished apartment complex when he shot a man dead by the swing set. He was only 18 then and full of rage. His mother had worried that he would be sent to prison *or worse*. And while he did not fear his future, she did. Little did she know that he had been in a gang since he was ten years old.

To go to prison would have simply put him on a quicker path to the Vory and gained him more respect, but she told him that he would face a fate worse than being a Vor if he stayed. "You must go," he remembered her saying. "And you must never, ever come back, Anatoly – not even when I die."

She had always feared for her eldest son – a blonde, stout, quiet young man with eyes full of rage and a heart full of malice. And she did right to do so.

His first murder had been one of necessity.

The forty-year-old man he had slain had eyes set on his sister, a girl barely twelve.

When Anatoly saw the man rubbing his sister's hair on the swing and offering her a piece of candy to go up to his apartment for a while, he shot him.

It had been a quick, respectful death – more than the man had deserved. He never got a chance to tell his mother that part - that the man had been a letch.

Instead, like always, he kept his secrets. Besides, they all thought that he had gone mad. And maybe they were right, but that man would never have his sister.

Since he had come to the states, however, only one other murder had been a necessity. It was a shame that one had been his uncle. He looked down at his hands as he thought of the day that he put a bullet through Ivan's back in his father's mansion and watched the giant's body fall forward. That day, he knew that he was a murderer, because before then he had never enjoyed murder, but after that, he had.

"Boss, do you really want to go inside of apartment? There is a group there now. They cleared the hallways just in case for you. But the place is a real shit hole," Vasily informed him, looking back at his young boss sitting in a daze.

"Why *wouldn't* I want to go up there?" Anatoly asked. "I came all this way, didn't I?" His blue eyes were ice cold.

Vasily didn't respond. He simply looked over at the driver and nodded. Anatoly eyed them both for a moment, then averted his gaze back out of the window. He rode the rest of the way with a clear mind and thought of nothing.

***

The residents of the small, impoverished community gathered curiously as the convoy of luxury vehicles pulled in front of Anatoly's old apartment building.

Quickly, men began to file out and stand on both sides of the cars before Anatoly's door was opened. The grand show made him mildly embarrassed.

He paused as he looked out of the truck and then proceeded to step out and look around. Amazingly, nothing had changed. He wasn't sure how he felt about that.

Vasily stood by him looking around like a secret service agent on duty for the President.

Again, one more thing to further embarrass Anatoly as he and his entourage made their way through the crowds to the tall, bricked building that housed his mother's belongings.

Someone called out his name from afar, but he didn't bother to look up. He was certain that many people from around this place remembered him.

Many, before he left, had told him how he would never amount to anything. *Look at me now*, he thought. And they did look. Only even in their wonderment, they were afraid.

Word traveled fast, and the *word* was that the Boss had come to Kapotnya to pay respects to a woman whom he had abandoned in her final hours.

If his callousness had not been evident before, it was now. He didn't even care for family. A true Vor. Only true to the code.

The thought sent chills through his body. If they only knew that she would not have him, that she was so proud of what he had become until she didn't want him to ever look back at where he had come from, maybe then they wouldn't judge him so harshly.

Then words from his father filled his head. Without Dmitry being there to physically say it, he heard him. *"You don't owe these bastards an explanation. Pay your final respects and move on."*

He did just that. Lifting his head, he moved up the concrete steps with his men to the fourth floor with the speed of a lion.

It wasn't that he was afraid to be in a very vulnerable position of staircases and sure doom if caught in an ambush, it was simply that he wanted this over with...done and finished.

With halogen lights blinking and the smell of old urine in trash-filled corners, with people opening their doors and looking out of their peepholes, he passed quickly through the now guarded hallway to his mother's apartment.

The door was already open and his men stood inside and out with guns, protecting him from everything except his fear of what awaited him on the other side of the door.

Quietly, he walked inside of the dingy, dark apartment and ordered the men to leave. He stood in the box of a living room as they cleared the apartment and left. He didn't turn to see the door close, but he heard it, heard his men barking for the residents to stay out of the hallways, not to come any farther. He smirked, then turned his attention to his old home.

In the silence of the room, he heard the raggedy ceiling fan rattling only inches above him. The cool, stale air eased the sweat on his brow.

He slipped his hands in his pockets and surveyed the room. Not much had changed, except the pictures on small wooden tables. He kneeled down and looked. *Could it be?* His little sister had grown all the way up. She was beautiful, even more so than when she was a young child. Reaching out, he ran his hand very gently over the dusty frame and debated whether he should take it or not.

"I was 15 in that picture," a woman's voice said from the far corner. A smile nearly colored her broken accent.

Anatoly looked up from the picture at the wall. Standing back up, he was slow to turn around. He heard her feet walking over the old, stained shag carpet. Suddenly, he was no longer a boss, just a boy standing face-to-face with is little sister in his mother's house.

"It's been long time, Anastasiya," he said, preparing to hug her, if she would just move closer to him.

He committed her every feature to memory. Long, bone-straight, blonde hair. Pale skin only interrupted by rosy, high cheeks. Full pink lips curved into a heart shape. Bright, big blue eyes. Skinny frame. Petite. She had grown into a simple woman. She wore a long denim skirt and a plain white cotton shirt.

With no makeup, he could see dark circles under her angelic eyes. "You're still as beautiful as I remember," he confessed. He bowed his head in respect.

"I'm surprised that you remember anything," she said frowning. Leaning against the doorway, she held tight to the Bible in her hand. "The rest of the family is already at the church. No one wanted to wait for you."

Anatoly looked up surprised. "Why are *you* so angry with me?" He was dumbfounded by her reaction to his presence.

"It's not me who is angry with you, Anatoly. It is God," she said in a matter-of-fact tone.

"For not being there for *mat'*?"

She shook her head in disgust. "No. For doing the devil's work each and every day. But I'm praying for you, *brat*. I'm praying that God will help you, heal you. Right now, you think that you're really big man, because you have so many lost boys to follow you and die for you and *kill for you*. But soon, you will see the error in your ways. I only hope that after you do, you will fall on your knees and beg Him for His divine mercy."

Anatoly was speechless. Something humbled him. He didn't shout at her, tell her that his road started trying to save her. Instead, he simply smiled. "I'm glad to know that you are safe and well, *syestra*," he said, trying to mask his pain with sarcasm. "Since the family has already gone without me, I suspect that I should head over to the church for my mother's funeral."

"Yes," she said, walking closer to him. "This is for you." She passed him her brown, leather-bound Bible.

He took it in his hands, brushing hers as he did. They looked at each other for a moment, eye-to-eye.

"It is the same one that helped me find my way. I hope that it helps you find yours *in time*," she said, pulling away.

"Can I offer you a ride?" he asked, unsure of what to say.

"No. I said my goodbyes to *mat'* at hospital," she smiled. "I don't plan to go to funeral. I took care of her alone until her death. What is left at the church is only memories, and I do not care to remember her in *casket*." Touching his face gently with her cold, boney fingers, she gave a crooked smile and turned to walk to the door.

"But I have so many questions," Anatoly whispered. He looked down at the floor and tried to bare the pain of feeling the separation from her with every step that she took.

"There are no answers here for you, *brat*." With that and without looking back, she opened the front door and left.

***

The church was smaller than he remembered. This had been a place that he had visited many Sundays as a young boy, yet he felt like a stranger inside of it now. Begrudgingly reminiscing over his childhood and his saint of a mother, he sat in the front pew with his estranged sisters and brothers as the priest talked.

He was too strong and too proud to dare let a tear drop from his tired eyes, but his heart was heavy. And it was suddenly apparent to him how mortal he was and how unloved he was by so many that he genuinely care for.

Looking forward with his eyes focused on the casket, he would not lay eyes on his family, who stared at him in between their sobs like he was a leper.

He knew from his brief, painful moments with Anastaysia what they all thought of him. *Scum. Dirt. Thug.* He wondered now if their animosity stemmed from their lack luster lives that consisted of mundane existences his mother had inadvertently saved him from or because he had returned and reminded them of that fact.

In his mind, on the trip to Moscow, he imagined that they might at least be a little proud of him or at least happy that he had survived. Unfortunately, his imagination had not yielded realistic results.

His little brother, Immanuil, sat furthest from him stealing glances that didn't exactly mirror the family's consensus of utter hatred. Anatoly could tell that he so wanted to reach out to him. His mossy green eyes sparkled when he saw him as he entered the sanctuary, but his middle brother held him back with a firm grip and admonishing words that he hissed in the little boy's ear.

Arseny, his middle brother, was a constant reminder of why he hated this place. They barely spoke to each other, even after many years of separation, and in fact, he still did not call when their mother passed. *Arseny was a prick like that.* A devoted Catholic. A straight-laced, pussy with good grades and a bad physique who hid his shortcomings with sharp wit and a community-college degree that he held with the esteem of a Harvard cum laude graduate. They were complete opposites of each other in every way, and they both hated each other for it.

In the back of the church, the doors flung open, bringing with it the light of day. Attention turned from the lonely casket and the drawn up ceremony at the front to the parade of men in the back. Anatoly clenched his jaw and turned to see Davyd, his father's head bodyguard enter with his men and then a long, processional of Russian mafia elite, including his father, who carried his little sister, Anya, in his arms and his wife, Royal, on his arm.

Dressed in designer black and looking more regal than anyone else besides Anatoly in the entire church, they made their presence known. The whispers quickly turned into a low rumble by the small crowd as the pseudo-royalty proceeded to the very front with such audacity, it was perceived as pure entitlement.

Anatoly could feel the scowl on his brother's face, even without turning around, but how he enjoyed it. Even the priest stopped talking and looked on baffled. The seven-foot tall, blonde notorious boss of Moscow slipped into the pew behind his son with his family and members of council in tow and sat down, while his twenty-man crew disbursed around the church.

Leaning forward and ignoring the attention, his father put his hand on Anatoly's shoulder.

"Sorry that we are so late. Forgive my interruption. There was delay with my jet," Dmitry said gracefully. He looked down the pew at his son's brother and gave him a *how-dare-you-look-at-me* scowl and then turned his attention back to his son.

Arseny quickly averted his startled eyes to the front of the church again as his heart pounded out of his chest. He had never once seen the Boss in person, now to be so close was surreal.

"It is no interruption, papa," Anatoly said, patting his father's hand. "I am happy that you are here." He turned and looked at the man in his face. He wanted his father to know his sincerity.

"What did you expect? We support our own, especially during bereavement." Dmitry did not say it, but he knew that something had gone awfully wrong in his absence, and he intended to rectify any misperception that he would allow any disrespect of his son or the Vory v Zakone.

"Hi, Anatoly," his little sister Anya waved, unable to hold her peace. "Can I sit up there with you?"

Anatoly smiled. He was relieved in ways words would simply not describe. "*Da*, come here," he said, reaching for her. Picking the small three-year-old up, he pulled her across the pew and put her on his lap. She rustled around in her black lace dress and put her brother's arms around her. Resting her head on his chest, she ran her small fingers up and down his arm and kicked her legs happily.

"Be good, Anya," Royal warned barely above a whisper. "Remember what we talked about in the car. This is your brother's time...not yours." Dmitry's beautiful young wife's Southern American English accent drew even more attention.

It wasn't enough that she was a breathtaking black woman dressed to the hilt with an air of entitlement that rivaled Putin's, but she also flickered with every turn due to the many diamonds that her husband had adorned her with.

"I will, Mommy," Anya answered obediently. She bent to her brother's ear and whispered. "Mommy brought you a present to make you feel better."

"Did she?" Anatoly humored her. "Well, we'll get it after, *eh*?"

Anya nodded her head and turned her attention to the priest.

Suddenly, Anatoly did not feel alone anymore. His *real* family had finally arrived and in undeniable style.

***

At the burial site, as Anatoly came to grips with final thoughts of his mother, he wiped his tears and looked up from the lowering casket to see his father with his eyes planted on an individual across the small crowd.

Because of Dmitry's height, he could see over the people directly to one man of comparable height across from them. Their eyes were deadlocked on one another with menacing stares – a conversation taking place without words. He looked around to see Dmitry's men making their way to the man, slowly and undetected by the others. A sense of sudden urgency overwhelmed him. A sense of anger filled him.

Was he not even allowed to grieve, to just be a regular person at his own mother's funeral? Was there ever a day that he could just be? The answer was obviously no. There was nothing normal about a Vory, especially a boss.

As the priest told them to go in peace, Anatoly's thoughts went to the gun in its holster under his suit jacket. He motioned for his men to follow his father and was mildly angry that he had not spotted him on his own.

The crowd disbursed, and Anatoly's estranged family moved quickly from his presence and disappeared into the cars lined up along the cemetery road. He did not even get a chance to say goodbye. It would have been frivolous anyway. Instead, he followed his father, who bolted across the burial site to the man and grabbed him by his arm.

"Who are you," Dmitry demanded in a low deep growl.

The man looked up with a mischievous smile. He didn't have to look too far up, because he was almost Dmitry's height and size. He pulled away carefully and cleared his throat.

"Gabriel," he said in an American English accent.

Gabriel's men gathered around, along with Dmitry's men and Anatoly's men. They were making a spectacle, preparing for war.

Royal, Dmitry's wife, grabbed her young daughter and was escorted by her bodyguard, Davyd, back to her car. She knew a problem when she saw one after many years of being married into such a complicated family.

Dmitry looked back as his limo pulled away with his wife. *Clever Royal.* He smiled, relieved that his wife knew his place and relieved because in her absence, his cuffs were off.

"Gabriel *who*?" he said, pointing for the man to walk as they talked. Their small entourage followed behind them.

"Medlov," the man answered. "Gabriel Medlov." A smile colored his lips. With a twinkle in his eye, he turned on the Medlov charm.

"Impossible," Anatoly scoffed, looking up at the man.

"Hardly," Gabriel answered Anatoly. His voice was a deep, hollow baritone that carried in the wind. He stopped and turned towards the two confronting men. "My father was Ivan Medlov...your brother, I believe." He looked at Dmitry. "And your uncle," he said, looking at Anatoly.

Dmitry stopped and looked the young man in the eyes. They were mossy green with sparkles of deep blue hidden under long, dark lashes. His hair was wavy, short black. His skin was pale, only colored by the redness of irritation. He had striking features like his father – prominent cheek bones, a wide chiseled jaw, a perfectly slender nose, thick, naturally arched black eyebrows and perfectly white, sparkling teeth clenched under full lips that narrowed at the bottom. A hint of freckles colored his face. And most shockingly, he had his father's smirk.

Dmitry believed Gabriel. He believed that he was looking at his nephew, at his brother's son, even without proof, but he went through the formalities. It would be just like some police agency to send a look-alike to infiltrate his organization.

He stepped back a bit and looked at the man, sized him up. The boy was about six feet, seven inches tall. He had a wide, bulky frame that he hid under a black, tailored suit. And he had the Medlov stance – confident, cocky, unmoved.

"Why haven't I heard of you before?" Dmitry asked.

"My father didn't think that it was smart to tell you about me," he said, looking at Anatoly. "Wow, the apple truly did fall far from the tree that time, didn't it?" He looked at the shorter, stocky blonde boss and suddenly felt a bit of superiority. Anatoly was barely six-feet tall. To call him a Medlov was almost blasphemous.

Anatoly grinned. "I'll have your head for dinner if you say one more fucking word." Opening his coat pocket, he flashed a shiny blade. "Your papa ever show you how one of these works? You put in to the neck and slice."

"Easy boys," Dmitry said amused. He turned to Gabriel. "Why are you here?"

"I heard that the family had a loss. I'd never really laid eyes on you. I couldn't help it. I had to come. I was already here on business."

"What business are you in?" Dmitry asked.

"Are you serious?" Gabriel asked.

"Boy, do not think that I will cut you this much slack," Dmitry said, putting his thumb and index finger together. "Now answer me." His voice was firm. "What is your *business* here?"

Dmitry's men prepared to pull their guns. Anatoly's men had already pulled theirs.

Gabriel looked around and decided to defuse the situation. There was no sense of dying on the first meeting. He looked at his men and lowered his hand, ordering them to put away their weapons.

"Down, boys." He turned and looked at his uncle. "Primarily, identity theft. But I'm dabbling now in guns and..." he laughed. "Meth." He hunched his shoulders. It was known that the Medlov's did not deal in drugs or human trafficking.

"Bad cocktail," Dmitry said, shaking his head. "Where are you based?"

"New York," Gabriel answered.

"Fucking Liar. If you were there, I would have heard about it," Anatoly said appalled.

Gabriel looked at Anatoly and raised his brow. The guy had a real chip on his shoulder. "I've been *there* for quite a while, but we don't run our operations like the old Vor – no disrespect or anything. All of my men have college degrees and professions outside of their professions, *if you know what I mean*. No one is doing it the old way. We've found a new cover, and it works better. It keeps the...cops off of us and our product."

Dmitry didn't blink. A million thoughts processed instantly. *A college degree*? He's always wanted Anatoly to go to college. He was glad that someone had been able to do both. Relaxing his tense shoulders, he looked over at his son and smiled. "Do you have dinner plans tonight, Anatoly?"

"*Da*," Anatoly said snarling.

"Cancel them. You're going to have dinner with your cousin tonight," Dmitry ordered.

"What about me? I've got plans," Gabriel said interrupting. He had his father's wit.

"No, you don't," Dmitry said, turning back around to Gabriel. "And if you don't check out tonight by seven with *my men*, your smart ass won't leave this country alive."

Gabriel swallowed hard but wiped the smirk from his face. "Oh, I'll check out. Call New York. They refer to me as *college boy*. They'll tell you my whole story." He slipped his balled fists in his pockets. "So where's dinner, unc?"

Dmitry's eye flinched at Gabriel's statement. "My hotel. Seven."

"Okay. Where's that?" Gabriel asked, pulling out his Blackberry to type in the address.

"*If* you're running shit like you say that you are, you'll find it on your own and be there on time. If not, I'll find you, and I'll be *there*," Dmitry said, turning to walk away with his men.

"Nice meeting you," Gabriel called out as the men left. He could not help but grin to himself.

Chapter Five

Dmitry ran his hand over his wife's bare stomach and kissed her navel that poked slightly out above her bulge. Trailing the dark line from her belly button down midway of her lower abdomen with his fingers, he curiously stared at the young being developing safely in her womb.

In his mind, Dmitry hoped for a boy. It was one of his sincerest dreams to have a young man that he could raise from birth, instead of only having a chance to influence his seed after adulthood, like he had done with Anatoly. Plus, he already had a perfect little girl. His Anya was asleep now in an adjoining room, dreaming of unicorns and lollipops.

Royal lay in the bed topless with a smile on her lips watching her husband as he marveled at his newest creation. He seemed to be fascinated by their pregnancy and even more fascinated by her ever-changing body, even though this was their second child. She found it ironic that a man so accustomed to taking life was equally obsessive about giving it. For that, she was thankful.

Nuzzling her head deeper down into the pillows, she giggled when she felt him tug at her panties.

"Didn't you say that you had a meeting with your *new* nephew?" she asked, raising her hips obediently.

He carefully removed her black lace underwear and licked his lips. It had nearly been a full day since he had felt the warmth of his young wife. He needed her now.

"*Da*. I have meeting later," he said gruffly, concentrating on her body. "I don't know. I think pregnancy becomes you. Maybe I keep you pregnant for a while. You need to give me a few more sons and a few more daughters."

His dreamy, blue eyes flashed towards her and caused a skip of her heartbeat. She bit her lip as his finger slid in between her steaming thighs.

"The job of populating the Medlov ranks is not so bad, you know. I enjoy my responsibilities." His thick, Russian accent sounded even sexier when he was aroused.

"My goodness, Dmitry. You're such a freak. And the fact that you would *abuse* a pregnant woman makes you even more of a deviant, you know. " She closed her eyes and moaned as he fondled her.

There was a part of Dmitry that quietly appreciated the fact that her statement didn't bother her. He remembered a short time ago when discussing sex, abuse and pregnancy, even jokingly, would have had a serious and disturbing reaction that would have instantly drudged up old memories of his long-dead brother, Ivan.

But over time, his beautiful Royal had healed from her emotional wounds and now allowed herself the ability to have fun.

He smiled at the thought of finally getting through that dark portion in their marriage. "Au contraire. I am not a freak. I *am* master of all freakdom," he corrected in a husky baritone. "And you are my willing slave."

"Careful with that *slave* stuff," she said laughing. "You forget that I'm sensitive about my *heritage*."

He shook his head and grinned. On his knees, he pulled off his dress shirt and undershirt and threw them on the floor beside the bed. "Before I make you remember why you are *my slave and why I am master of all of freakdom*, can I ask you question?" His voice changed. A hint of serious concern laced his words.

"Yes," Royal said, now up on her knees helping him unbutton his pants.

"I told you what happened between the two boys today. What do you think about it?" His belt jingled as she tugged at it. "You never said. And you *always* say."

Royal stopped and looked up at her husband. His muscles rippled through his torso under the many tattoos that colored his massive body. His cologne intoxicated her. His hands made her quiver and turn to clay. Dmitry was the sexiest man that she had ever laid her eyes on, even as an older, more seasoned gentleman. But conversations like this could ruin any mood regardless of beauty.

"What do *I* think?" she finally asked.

"*Da*, what do you think, *zhenshchina*?" He looked down at her with a raised brow. His question sincere, he awaited an answer from his trusted wife.

There was a tense pause in the room.

Royal removed her hands from his black trousers that barely hid his steely erection only inches from her face and sat back in the bed against the headboard. Pushing her long hair from her face, she pressed her bare lips together and pulled the sheet over her exposed breasts.

"I just don't trust him. *Gabriel, I mean...not Anatoly.* And I don't think that you should trust him either, Dmitry. I can see it in your eyes even though you're trying to hide it. You're excited that there might be *one* more opportunity to fix things between you and Ivan, because you loved him so much, *even though he was rotten bastard*. My opinion is this...if that *boy* is anything like his father, it's best that you just kill him tonight and save yourself the trouble. No one will think ill of you for it. I know that I won't. In fact, I would be proud of you."

Silently, Dmitry watched her with an unreadable look in his crystal blue eyes that were accented by tiny, intricate crow's feet that were truly pronounced now as he slightly furrowed his brow.

He was shocked at her candid advice, but grateful for her truthfulness.

Since the incident in Memphis and the incident in Sochi, Royal had become more guarded than ever before. She was starting to be as cold and calculated as he, only without being involved in any illegal activities. This fact reminded him to tread carefully with his wife, his new equal.

Sitting beside her in the bed with his knees up, he planted his hands behind his head and looked up at the ceiling.

"*Ahh*...you know me well. When I saw him, I did have a hopeful...I was hopeful," he stopped his sentence. Turning to her on his elbow, he grabbed her caramel face and ran his thumb over her pink lips. "Have I really made you so jaded, Royal Stone?" His minty breath tickled her nose.

"*Da*," she answered with an equally stone face. "I only hope that I haven't made you soft." Running her hands through his blondish, gray locks, she leaned in to receive his kiss.

Hungrily, he pulled her to him with one hand and tore his pants off with the other. Opening her legs and balancing his weight as to not hurt her, he pushed inside of her warm body with one long, vicious, coiling stroke.

"As you can feel, my love, I don't know the meaning of soft," he whispered into her mouth as he devoured her.

***

Anatoly sat on the couch in his hotel suite talking into the black, Apple laptop on the table in front of him. Now comfortable in a pair of jeans and bare-foot, he drank his scotch under dimmed lights, trying to calm himself from the day's events and prepare for the evening.

With a platter of pickles in his lap, he slouched over and listened attentively as the men debated the latest issues.

Over the last few months, Anatoly and his men had moved more guns internationally than his father had moved in years. He used all of his contacts, met with as many bosses as possible and constantly pursued the all mighty dollar.

As he promised his father, after the operation in Sochi, quietly he had concreted the Medlov Crime Family at the top of the organized crime food chain. And where at first, many had assumed that he was unable to fully step into his father's lofty shoes as boss, now only a few questioned his reach and his eagerness.

He was building an impenetrable force of men, who were willing to do the hard work in seedy places of the world where no one wanted to go and willing to do the most unspeakable acts in the name of Vory.

As he sat listening to the men, he went through each of the deals meticulously and went down his notepad of questions, just as he had seen his father do time and again as boss.

Tapping his pen against his knee, he reached over for his cigarette and waved his hand to quiet the men.

"Enough, enough," he said, taking a drag. The smoke billowed up into a hazy cloud above him. "This is what we will do." His deep, baritone growl grew deeper. "Have Yuri call the dealer back and tell him that we will cut his percentage. I don't want him running this deal. It's too important, and he is less than reliable."

"Then, who will run it?" one of his men asked as they sat around a small meeting table in front of their computer.

"We will," Anatoly answered. "We'll send one of our men with him to facilitate. It's not rocket science, but it's starting to cost like it. I want more returns and fewer expenses. It's *our* product. So, it's our way or no way."

"We'll choose someone from Memphis," another man said. "It's too risky to trust anyone else. This is the last shipment, boss. If we can get rid of it properly, then we don't have to worry about the guns being traced back to us at any point."

"Don't you think that *I* know that? After all that I did, *myself*, to get this shipment, I won't allow anyone to screw it up." Anatoly put down his paper and pen and pulled the laptop closer to him. "Did you find Donovan?"

"*Da*, he was holed up in Chicago. We brought him back kicking and screaming. He was in basement of his mother's church."

"Good. Keep him alive until I get back. I want to see his eyes fade for his deceit," Anatoly steamed. "He's cost us millions up there talking to the pigs."

"Will do, boss."

"Anything else?" Anatoly asked.

"No," his men answered collectively.

"Good. Goodnight, gentlemen," Anatoly said, closing his laptop.

As he rested back on the couch, the background noise of the television in the other room clouded his thoughts along with his men talking among themselves about Gabriel. However, he could still see his sister's face and his mother's casket flashing every time that he closed his eyes.

Fortunately, he was now past tears or hurt. Instead, anger had filled his heart, anger at his family for being callous and anger at Gabriel for simply *being*. Something about his new cousin just rubbed him the wrong way and he intended to find out why.

As he drank the last of the scotch in his crystal tumbler, his cell phone rang. Looking at it, he rolled his eyes. Victoria. *Again.* He should have never gotten involved with the woman. His father had warned, but as usual, he had ignored him thinking that the old man had gone soft. Now, she was a thorn in his side. He started to answer it and threaten her, but he felt any attention would be too much.

"Vasily," Anatoly said, hitting IGNORE. "As soon as we get back to the states, get my number changed and get it to everyone *except* Victoria."

"Yes, boss," Vasily answered, standing behind him in the far corner of the room.

Anatoly looked behind him and raised his brow at the man. Vasily was a loyal solider of the Vory, never faltering in his responsibility. A young man, barely thirty, he was nearly as quiet as Anatoly but if possible, more serious and gravely tempered. When needed Vasily had been quick and deadly but also a friend to his boss during times when the young man had no one to confide in.

"Vasily, what do you do when you're not here?" Anatoly asked, motioning for him to come around the sofa and face him.

"I sleep...eat...workout," Vasily answered. "And occasionally...get laid."

Anatoly smiled. "It sounds like I can only help with one of those. Would you like drink?" He offered the scotch.

"Thank you," he reached across and grabbed the bottle.

"What do you think of Gabriel?" Anatoly asked, motioning for the man to sit down on the couch across from him

Vasily pulled at his slacks and sat down. His large muscular body bulged in the black suit, showing his guns tucked carefully under his jacket and his pants leg.

"I don't trust him," he answered in a low, thick accent. He spoke quietly to ensure no one could hear their conversation. "The code should never be compromised." There was a silent agreement between the two on that fact. Vasily continued, "He has job in society. A day trader. So, he lives double life. A man like that cannot be trusted, because he could also have double allegiance."

Anatoly was glad that he was not the only one in his camp who felt the unease of Gabriel's presence, and he was doubly happy not to have leeching *yes* men around him. Noting the man's observations, he moved on. "Did you do what I asked?"

"*Da*. It's being done now."

"Good, I want to see his face at the meeting with papa when he discovers it." He chuckled and toasted the man. "Thieves-in-Law."

"Thieves-in-Law," Vasily said, turning the bottle up.

Resting back on the couch, Anatoly grabbed the remote and turned the television on when his pocket began to vibrate. Reaching for his phone, he looked down and smiled. It was Renee.

"I've got to take this. Take drink and share with the men, *eh*," he said, dismissing Vasily.

"Thanks, boss."

When he was alone, Anatoly quickly answered before she hung up. "What's up?" he asked coolly, looking around. His voice lowered.

"Just checking on you," Renee answered. "And calling to let you know that Lt. Agosto came by here looking for you yesterday."

Anatoly paused.

"Are you still there?" she asked curiously.

"*Da*," he said quickly. "What did he want?"

"Said he was looking for you."

"Probably nothing. What else is going on?"

"Thought that would be enough."

They both were silent. Anatoly knew that Renee wasn't nearly as blind to his affiliations as Royal had been to his father's. Instead, they both never brought it up. However, before now, Agosto hadn't shown up in quite some time. His stomach turned in knots at the thought of what the *Italian* might have up his sleeve.

"And *Destiny* came by to see you. She brought a copy of the story she did on *Mother Russia* to drop by...only she didn't drop it by the restaurant. She brought it here. Don't you think that's odd?"

Anatoly agreed silently but wouldn't answer her aloud.

"Was the funeral tough?" Renee finally asked to change the subject. His silence had spoken volumes for her.

"No. It was just a funeral," he said, doodling on the paper as he talked. "My family is a bunch of idiots."

Renee laughed before she could catch herself. "I'm sorry. I didn't mean to laugh but so is everyone else's," she replied. "You ought to meet my folks."

"Can't be worse than mine."

"Yes, they are," she confirmed.

"I've never seen your family. They don't come up to Memphis to visit you."

"Well, we might fix that one of these days. Then you'll see that you're not alone. My drunk uncle, my crazy granny and my Vietnam daddy make a hell of a combination."

It was odd, but Anatoly was calmed by Renee's voice. She was so simple and so normal – two things that were far from his reach. Just knowing that she had thought enough to call and check on him made him feel better. His tough exterior was nearly broken until he realized how her charms were working on him. He quickly clamed up.

"Well, I have to go," he said, hearing the men in the other room. "But thanks for calling. I'll check in on you tomorrow." He stuttered. "And don't worry about Agosto. Like I said, I'm sure that it's nothing."

"*Okay*," Renee did not believe him but chose not to push it. "Bye."

He hung up without any more pleasantries. Lighting another cigarette, he digested their moment like food for his soul. Whether she knew it or not, he needed that. He needed to know that there was normalcy in at least one place in his life, and he didn't have to fake who he was to get it, like his father was forced to do at the onset of his relationship with Royal.

Then, there it was again. *The thought of a relationship with Renee.* He shook it off. Now was not the time to analyze himself or whatever was going on between him and his shop girl. It was almost time for his meeting with his father and Gabriel.

Chapter Five

Gabriel and his men stood in the elevator patiently awaiting its arrival to the penthouse of the hotel and staring blankly into the reflection of themselves in the mirrors of the door panel. It had taken a near act of God to find out where the Medlov's were staying and even a greater act of God to get through security downstairs.

Upon arrival, they were stripped of their guns, checked for weapons, bugs, poison and razors out in the rain behind the hotel by a large group of armed bodyguards. Then, they were ushered inside of the building after their pat downs and made to wait in the kitchen hallway among crates and boxes in the dimly lit corner as plates clanged and servers moved about quickly with meals and beverages. In silence, they waited and were watched, feeling as though at any moment they would be lined up and executed if one thing did not check out.

After many minutes passed, they were sent up, and although they all were frustrated by the ordeal, they were all happy that they had survived. One would have thought that they were meeting with a national dignitary not a crime boss, but as many knew, to meet a Medlov was the closest any of them would ever get to meeting pseudo-royalty.

As the elevator buzzed, the doors opened to another large group of well-dressed, heavily armed men. Gabriel shook his head and gave a leisurely smile before he opened his jacket to let them search him again.

"It's amazing that you all ever get anything done with all the searching that you do," he said as a man patted down his leg. "Easy," he jerked away. "That's *not* a gun."

The man looked over at door and nodded for Gabriel to gain access to the boss. He was escorted inside, but his men were not allowed to proceed. Instead, they were ordered to wait, and he alone was led to a sitting room that gave a beautiful view of downtown Moscow.

In a different world than the one outside, Dmitry and Anatoly were sitting across from each other talking and having a drink in the calm of a very luxurious room decorated in fine linens and upholstery, bejeweled with priceless art and classic lamps.

The men looked over at Gabriel with curious eyes, accessing him, watching him, making him feel like he was the elephant in the room.

He cracked a smile, pushed past the discomfort and pulled his balled up fists from his pockets.

"Good evening, gentlemen," Gabriel said as the butler walked up and took his jacket.

"Good evening," Dmitry said, placing his glass carefully on the end table. With his legs crossed and his back towards the view of windows, he extended his large arm and pointed at the seat near Anatoly. "Have a seat," he ordered in a deep, menacing voice. His eyes watched Gabriel as he made his way across the room.

Anatoly did not bother to speak. Instead, he finished his drink in one gulp and stood up, wanting to be as far as possible from the man who claimed to be his cousin. He made his way over to the window and leaned against the table with a sneer on his remarkably young face.

"You're on time," Dmitry noted, looking at his watch.

"I was forewarned," Gabriel replied, taking his seat.

He looked around, tried to make sure no one was behind him. Suddenly, he was acutely aware of his mortality now that he was in the room with two of the world's most ruthless killers.

"We don't like small talk. What do you want from us?" Anatoly asked, rolling his eyes.

Gabriel could see that the only thing keeping the young man civil was his father's hidden grip. He could feel the repression from across the room. It was as if Dmitry was standing behind his son with hands on his shoulders cooling his hot heels, but in fact, the man controlled the environment from afar. Dmitry sat relaxed in his chair, dressed in a new suit and visibly intrigued by Gabriel's presence.

"I've made a name for myself now. And I felt like it was time to introduce myself. I've been waiting in the wings long enough, gentlemen. Imagine growing up your whole life knowing that you had a family that you had been kept from *just because*," Gabriel said, looking at Anatoly.

"Now with sob stories..."Anatoly gaffed.

"We are only recently accustomed to sympathy, my boy. Your story might be lost on us," Dmitry said, wanting the man to skip the theatrics.

"My father was a methodical man," Gabriel explained. "I'm sure he had some reason for keeping me away. Whatever reason it was, it wasn't my fault or my choice."

"Your father was a raving lunatic," Anatoly interrupted. "He had to be put down like mad dog."

Dmitry looked over at his chair at his son but did not admonish him. Instead, he turned and smiled at Gabriel. In a gentle manner, he lifted his long hands and put his fingers together. "As you were saying," he urged.

"He kept me out of the way for a long time," Gabriel continued without looking at Anatoly. He locked eyes with his uncle. "He was a good father most of the time, although very absent. He took very good care of me from a far financially. After college, I wanted to get into the business. It took a lot of persuasion and even a few hundred thousand dollars of bribe money. That's when he started to give me a little work. It was tough, but once I proved myself, I started to pull together my own men, and he left a portion of his New York business to me when he came to Memphis."

"That's a lot to sum up in a few sentences," Anatoly said unconvinced. "That still tells us nothing about you."

"What would you like to know?" Gabriel asked, opened to the discussion and the confrontation looming between him and the young boss.

"Any kids? Wife? Other family? How *distant* was Ivan? Why? What kind of work did he throw your way? Why did he hide you? I could go on." Anatoly ran his hand down the windowsill and lifted it to look at the dirt. "You call this a suite, papa? This place is filthy."

Dmitry didn't bother to respond to his son. He kept his eyes on Gabriel. His gentle manner was slowly changing. His bright blue eyes narrowed. Like a predator, he locked on to Gabriel's every cryptic word as they fumbled out of the man's mouth. He was looking for just one untruth, because while he and his men dealt in secrecy and guns, they did not deal in lies.

"Let's do *one* something first," Dmitry said, motioning at the door.

An older man with a black bag appeared from the hall. He was short and balding, dressed in a three-piece black suit and limping slightly. Slowly, he walked over to the table beside Gabriel and placed his bag down. Then reaching inside the leather satchel, he pulled out a small vial and separated it to reveal a long, slender white object.

"He's going to swab your mouth. Open wide," Dmitry said, uncrossing his legs. "Then you can continue with your story."

All eyes were on the doctor as the old man approached Gabriel with a buccal swab in his shaking, glove-covered hands. Lifting his head, Gabriel opened his mouth obediently, and the man slipped his thumb inside his jaw and clenched it with his index finger to pull it away from his teeth.

Swabbing the inside of his jaw, the man looked Gabriel in his eyes with a unreadable frown then pulled the swab out and placed it inside of the container. Pulling his gloves off his hands, he dropped them inside of the garbage can beside the table and left as quietly as he had come.

"Continue," Anatoly said with a smirk on his face. "And remember that in less than 24 hours, we'll know if you're lying about anything that you say."

"No need to lie," Gabriel said, looking over at the bottle of vodka. "Do you mind?" he asked Dmitry.

"No," Dmitry said with a clever smile. "I don't, if that is what you need to help you."

Gabriel made his way over to the table and poured himself a hefty glass of vodka. Turning it up, he swallowed one large gulp then turned to the men. He touched his chest and smiled.

"I know what you think," Gabriel said. "You think that I'm some fraud. But look at me. *Really*, look at me. I'm the real thing." He hit his chest. "My father was a good man. I know that's hard to believe, but he was. He had a few *issues*. My mother knew it all too well. He fell in love with her or no...he slept with her when they were both just young kids. They met in London. Both went their separate ways but kept in touch. My mother moved to New York and my father followed after. passed.

"During his marriage to his only wife, Ari, he took on a less than active but more than absent role in my life. But he was proud of me. I don't know why. I wasn't an alpha male or anything like that. I was a boy scout. I made good grades and played baseball. But he was there, and he did a lot for me.

"When I told him that I was going to NYU, he paid for it. When I graduated and said that I wanted to be like him, he gave me some other options. He wanted me to be better than him. When I proved myself, which mind you wasn't easy to do, he left me his business. He said that he was going to Memphis to handle some unfinished business and wouldn't be back. I didn't want him to leave but he did. I thought that he was running away from me because we had gotten too close, but he claimed that he could start over there."

"He finished *there*," Anatoly said.

Gabriel slowed his explanation. "He was still chasing Ari even though she was dead – still chasing the memory of her. That is what sent him to his end. That is what kept him from my mother. That is what drove him from me. If anything this is all the fault of a woman whom I never even laid eyes on."

"So, you know how he met his end?" Dmitry asked, finally standing up.

"He loved you," Gabriel said, biting his lip to maneuver around the question. "I know that it's hard to believe, but he did. He talked about you all the time. But he just couldn't let *her* go."

"And how does that make you feel?" Dmitry probed. He knew how it made him feel. Defeated.

"As about as sad as it makes you. We both lost him to her, you." Gabriel clinched his jaw. "I wanted to reach out to you when it first happened. I wanted to share the pain with you that you must have surely felt for what you were forced to do, but my mother passed during that same week. I felt like it was a sign. I needed to prove myself first. And I think over the last few years, I've done that."

Anatoly watched from a far as his father approached Gabriel. They looked more like Medlov men than he as they stood face-to-face. They both were unmistakable giants in stature, muscular in size, and most of all beautiful. Their features appeared to be carved from the most stunning stone, every careful definition of their faces perfect and startling.

These were the type of men that people wrote about, the type of people marveled over and worshipped. Anatoly hated that. It was hard enough to live up to his father, now he had this bastard here vying for his attention, begging to outdo him. He stood up from the windowsill and cleared his throat.

"Vasily, bring in the computer," Anatoly snapped.

Vasily walked in quickly and set up the large laptop. Typing something in, he adjusted the camera and nodded at his boss.

"Recognize anything?" Anatoly asked, walking over to the computer. Both men took their eyes off of each other and met him at the table. "This is your home. I had *our* men in New York record this just for you."

All three watched as a masked man kicked in the door of Gabriel's high-rise penthouse in Manhattan and tear through each room. The camera the man held gave a clear view of the young man's private life. There were pictures of his mother, his grandparents and even his father. He gave them close up shots of the degree on the wall, the closet space, the bed, the kitchen. The man and his crew tore through the house, through his dressers and his bathrooms.

They searched the entire house for any sign of anything unusual.

Gabriel watched—mortified. His condo was being trashed and the little shit standing beside him was visibly enjoying it.

Gabriel leaned further into the computer and tapped the monitor. "Can you tell him to please stop ruining my shit?" he asked in a growl.

Dmitry watched, amused that his son had thought to be so clever but also torn by the clear destruction going on in front of him. He would never undermine his son's authority and order it stopped but to watch the event unfold was almost painful. The men flipped the mattresses, tossed the files, looked through his computer, took down his paintings, opened his vents, unscrewed his phones, everything.

"Don't worry. If they don't find anything, I'll send maids to make it perfect before you return home. It will look better than new," Anatoly said, turning from the computer happy with himself.

"What exactly *are* you looking for?" Gabriel asked.

"I don't know. What exactly *are* you hiding?" Anatoly turned to him.

"I didn't come here for this shit," Gabriel said, standing up to his full height. He looked Anatoly up and down and then gave a clever smile. Dmitry could instantly see his dead brother in his young nephew. "But if you want to play games, Anatoly, fine. I didn't *record* it for you, but I did have a very interesting date with the manager of your clothing store the other day. Renee's a sweet woman, and she can hold a great conversation, but I didn't pump her for a single piece of information on you, and I'm sure that she'll tell you that I'm no Ivan. Is that testimony enough."

The room became silent.

Ahh. There it was. Revenge in its purest and most malicious form. Dmitry didn't need the test results to see his brother's seed. He turned from the young duelers, refusing to become a part of their juvenile tactics. He had a lot to teach them both.

As the butler entered the room with hors d'oeuvres, he grabbed a cracker and caviar off the platter and waited for the eruption.

"You are checking up on me?" Anatoly asked. "You must have death wish."

"Obviously, I was, but I didn't trash your shit."

"Renee is *my shit*," he said, before he could catch himself.

Dmitry didn't blink. *So, it was Briggy first, then Victoria, now Renee.* He really liked Renee. He was hoping that she would avoid his son's clutches. Evidently, however, she wasn't as smart as she looked.

"Alright, enough men. I do believe that I called this meeting for my own purposes. You all should schedule time aside from this to sort out your differences about women, *eh*," Dmitry said, returning to his seat. "Besides, I think that Gabriel, if you are a true Medlov, regardless of your rivalry with your cousin, we should work something out. Throw you some more business."

Gabriel's focused shift.

Anatoly stood flabbergasted. *Throw this bastard more business?* He found the thought preposterous. He looked up at the towering man and rolled his eyes.

Why did he have to be a spitting image of Ivan? Things could have been so much easier if he didn't reek of his father.

"I look forward to it," Gabriel said, bowing his head a little.

"Oh, it will only be with Anatoly's blessing, which he will give *if* you prove yourself," Dmitry said, looking at his son. "Regardless of what you have heard, I am no longer boss. My only son has taken over that role, and he's done exceptionally well. I am only here in *mentoring* capacity."

Gabriel bit his lip and hid his fever-pitched anger. If he had to wait on approval from this prick, he'd never get in good with his family. However, Gabriel was a salesman. He knew how to bridge broken relationships and make people happy. Maybe he could put his skills to use on his cousin.

At the top of the stairs appeared the little girl from the funeral. With caramel smooth skin that was only interrupted at her rosy cheeks, she appeared to be a living doll. She stood barely three feet tall, a slender 50 lbs. with liquid, long black hair and startling blue, hypnotizing eyes.

Clutching a teddy bear in silence, she watched the men as they talked with a clever grin on her face as if she knew exactly what was going on.   Gabriel peered over at her, unable to take his eyes off the beauty.

"Daddy, can I come and sit with you?" she asked. Her clear voice carried across the room like a song, stilling the quiet chaos that ran feverishly through the men's pensive stares.

Dmitry stopped his conversation in mid-sentence. Eyes lighting up with every step that she took toward him, he extended his arms, received her with a homecoming hug, and pulled her into his embrace. Gabriel watched in amusement.

Such a small child commanded such reverse between the two men. He looked over at his cousin and realized that even Anatoly had switched his focus. While just a moment ago, he was adamantly opposed to him being in the room, he had all but forgotten him long enough to admire the young girl. And his uncle was completely entranced. It was evident without saying so that she was his reason for retirement.

"As I was saying, we are all family," Dmitry continued, kissing his precious daughter on the crown of her head. "And it is important that we work together in concert with each other instead of against each other. If I had my way, Ivan would still be alive, and we all would be working towards a more powerful empire."

"How much more powerful can one empire get?" Gabriel asked.

The men turned his way with greedy stares. He could tell in their looks that they both desired more. It was the most prominent gene in their collective DNA. Greed.

"A great deal more powerful, my boy," Dmitry said, still doting on his daughter. Rocking her on his knee, he bounced her playfully. "Once you check out, we'll show you how the Medlov's really do business, and you can walk away from this *day job* that you so religiously cling to. It's against the code. It's against your blood."

"But you ran a restaurant," Gabriel debated.

"Where I was the boss. Are you boss at your day job as day trader?" Dmitry asked.

"No."

"In that lies the problem," Anatoly finished.

He broke his trance and walked over to the butler to retrieve a small hors d'oeuvre. "We are about absolute power, not a piece of it. A piece of anything will never get you anywhere. You must discipline yourself to see supreme reign."

They locked eyes.

Gabriel questioned his temporary tutor. "And do you consider yourself to have complete reign, cousin?"

Anatoly gave a lazy smile and slipped the caviar in his mouth. Patting his hands together to wipe off the crumbs, he looked up at the giant man and shook his head. "I won't allow myself to have anything but complete reign, *brat*. That is what makes us different. I would never settle, where you already have."

There was something cataclysmic about the reference of the word *brother* for Gabriel. For a moment, his cousin, his superior, had allowed their differences to be removed long enough for him to share his philosophy of life and of business. And most of all, he had been called *brother*. The look in Anatoly's face was that of absolute certainty like God himself had assured him of his place on earth. It was odd that a man of such evil would have such a look – to be so sure of himself and so focused on his goal. Gabriel shook the thought off. He would think about that more when he was alone.

Their philosophical moment was over; however, when the black woman whom Gabriel assumed was this family's Helen walked into the room. She strode in with her eyes locked on him like he was a leper. With eyebrows spike and hands slipped into the pockets of her pants, she made her way over to Dmitry and stood behind his chair. Placing her hands lovingly on the back of the chair as if to protect her small family, she broke her silence.

"I was wondering where you had run off to," Royal said to her daughter.

"Daddy's having a meeting," Anya informed her mother. Looking over at Gabriel, she smiled. "Who is he, daddy?" she asked in a near whisper.

Gabriel thought that it was clever that the young girl had not asked the question when she had first come into the room. Rather, she waited until her question would carry the most weight and garner the most attention before she posed it. *Already methodical.*

"This is Gabriel," Dmitry explained. He would not clarify his presence any further, at least until he had irrefutable proof via DNA that the man was anything more to him.

"Like the angel," Royal said with a crooked smile. Her eyes gazed over him for a moment, summing the man up. "Are you an arch angel, Gabriel?" she mocked. "Have you a message from God?"

Gabriel could tell that she didn't like him, but he knew that she was his key to getting into this family. The men couldn't love the daughter as they did without loving the mother.

"I guess that it is ironic that a man like myself would be given the name," he agreed. "A Medlov could hardly ever be a messenger of God."

"So you believe in nature versus nurture, do you?" Dmitry joked. He raised Anya carefully off his knee and guided her to her mother. "Love, let us finish this, *da*. I'll be in for dinner in a moment."

"Alright, baby," Royal said, taking her daughter's hand. Walking past Anatoly, she rubbed his back. "How are you?"

"Fine," Anatoly said, understanding her concern for his loss earlier. He touched her hand.

"Will you have dinner with us tonight?" she paused. She insisted quietly.

"*Da, da*," Anatoly answered softly.

"It was very interesting to meet you, Gabriel, *the arch angel*," Royal said before she left the room. She gave him a dirty look. "You look very much like your *late* father. Let us hope for your sake that that is the extent of your similarities."

"I'm sure it is, ma'am." He bowed his head a little to bid her good evening, although he was unsure why. There was something about the woman that made him feel the need to bow, to be careful and most of all behaved.

An older man was standing in the corner looking at them the entire time, listening to their conversation and watching Gabriel's every move. He was stocky with a head of blondish gray hair tapered carefully around his pale face and startling blue eyes.

In a pair of black slacks and a black shirt, he brandished two very powerful weapons in holsters under his massive arms. As Royal approached the stairs, he turned his attention and followed her and the child back into the other rooms of the suite.

Gabriel automatically assumed the man must have been their bodyguard as he could feel emanating across the room another aura of protection.

Once Dmitry was sure that his wife was gone, he focused his attention back to the young men. He had been calm the entire time, choosing his words carefully and keeping the conversation light for the most part. Gabriel found it odd that he was so gentle. He had expected a brooding man full of threats and words laced with violence. Instead, he had been greeted by a man who had been all but forgiving of his father and respectful of everyone around him.

"You'll be staying with us until those results come back," Dmitry said, leaning his sharp elbows against his knees. "A room has been arranged for you on our floor and your friends have already been sent off."

"You want me to stay in this suite with you?" Gabriel asked dumbfounded.

"No. Royal would kill us both," Dmitry chuckled and looked over at Anatoly. "I've arranged for him to have a suite on this floor, if that's fine by you, Anatoly."

Anatoly rolled his eyes. He wouldn't deny his father his wishes, even though he wanted to do so. Instead, he tried to maintain his fleeting composure. "That will be fine, papa."

"Good," Dmitry said pleased. "Anything that you need, our men can provide for you. But you won't be allowed anyone in or out until the doctor visits us tomorrow evening. I'm sure that you can understand that you can't just waltz in here and make your introduction without a proper background check. In interim, be available should Anatoly or myself have questions for you. And if you check out, then be prepared for further instruction."

"Look." Gabriel shook his head. "I'm okay with checking out with you guys and having my mouth swabbed, but I'm not cool with being *quarantined* like I'm some kind of virus. I have businesses to run myself."

"What Vor does everything himself?" Anatoly asked.   "You have soldiers for that. If you don't, you *are* a failure."

Gabriel didn't respond.

"This is not negotiable, Gabriel," Dmitry said, standing up. "The men at the front will show you to your *temporary* housing. I'm sure you'll find it more than acceptable. But for now, you must excuse us. We have dinner waiting."

Walking out, closed to any discussion, Dmitry and Anatoly left Gabriel in the sitting room to await his next escort.

Chapter Six

The moment encapsulated Anatoly. He relished in the short letter that was hand-written by his baby sister. She had left it in the Bible for him, knowing that he would read it. And although he had contemplated throwing the *Book* away, he had kept it close because it had come from her, from her fingers, from her thoughts, from her presence. Now as he read her words on the flight home, he fought hard to keep the tears from breaching the sanctity of his eyes and rushing forth onto his hot cheeks.

My dearest brother,

Love is a fickle thing. I've found myself wrapped in turmoil because of your current position, but whatever you may choose as your profession, I want you to know that God is always ready to receive you, forgive you and love you. I pray for your safety and deliverance. I pray for your eyes to open to the life that you lead, and I know that one day you will find the peace that you were denied trying to protect me. When you have arrived at that moment, I will be there to welcome you to the world that you were denied.

Love forever,

Anastaysia

**

When his foot hit his doorstep, calm came over Anatoly unlike any before it. The smell of home filled his nostrils and resonated down in the core of him. Dropping his bags in the foyer, he whistled for his dogs. They both came running, nearly knocking each other down as they rounded the corner. Dropping to his knees, he stretched his arms open to receive them.

Vasily watched as his boss, very briefly, exhibited human behavior. Anatoly loved his dogs like they were people. He fed them only the best foods, allowed them to live in the house with him, unlike when his father lived at the mansion, bathed them himself, walked them, loved them.

Allowing the dogs to lick his face, Anatoly gave a hearty laugh and ran his fingers behind their ears. "Have you been good boys?" he asked.

"Boss, I'll take your bags to your bedroom," Vasily said, bending down to pick up Anatoly's luggage.

"No, I do it," he said, standing up. "Why don't you get out of here for awhile? You've been under me for like a week. I know you need some time, Vasily." Anatoly walked with his dogs following behind him down the hallway to the kitchen. He could smell food. "Is Renee here?" he asked the maid, who followed quietly behind them, unheard and nearly unseen.

"Yes, sir. She's in the guest bedroom."

"Did something happen?" he asked.

"There was a storm. Her power went out, so she came here," the maid replied.

Walking into the large kitchen, his voice echoed, "Vasily, go," he insisted. "Take some time."

Nodding his head, Vasily left with a grin on his face. It wasn't so much now that his boss was concerned about him resting, it was that woman upstairs that Anatoly wanted to go to.

After eating a full meal of steak, mashed potatoes and broccoli and sharing the leftovers with his dogs, he headed upstairs to his room. He kept waiting for Renee to appear in the kitchen, but she never did. He assumed because of the hour, she had gone to bed.

As he walked down the long corridor to his own quarters, he stopped at her door. It was completely shut and probably locked. Turning the knob, he was relieved to find it unlocked. The light shone in on her as the opened the door. Instantly, he thought of his stepmother. It was strange how many years had passed, and yet some events were etched indelibly in his mind.

Renee stirred. Sitting up in the bed, her large brown eyes locked on him. She pulled the covers over her and yawned.

"You're finally back, huh?" she said, reaching over and turning on the lamp.

"*Da*." He walked inside and closed the door. "Thanks for dinner. It was good."

"No problem. The power went out downtown. I didn't want to stay there in the dark."

"No, I wouldn't want you to." He sat down on the edge of her bed and leaned forward. With his hands on his knees, he wiped his tired eyes. "It's been a long trip."

"I bet. You normally stop in New York for longer when you go to Russia."

He smirked. "I didn't want to stop in New York this time. There is someone there...". He didn't finish his sentence.

"Someone like a girl?" She cut her eyes at him.

"No. A cousin," he explained. "Ivan's son came to funeral."

Renee bucked her eyes. *Was it possible?* Another generation of Ivan Medlov was too much to think about. Thoughts of a murdered friend crossed her mind and sent chills down her spine.

"Is he like his father?" she asked.

"Hard to say. He looks like him."

As she pushed the covers from her body, Anatoly saw that Renee had on shorts and a tank top. She sat beside him, boiling with anticipation.

"And," she urged him to continue.

"Why did you cover up when I open the door? You're fully dressed under there."

Renee shook her head. "What difference does it make? Tell me what happened in Moscow."

Anatoly reached over and pulled off her satin night cap to find her hair in large pink rollers. "I can't look at you with that thing on your head," he said, throwing the cap on the bed.

"This isn't a beauty contest," Renee rolled her eyes. "Now, what happened?" She instinctively touched her head.

"I can't tell this story without cigarette, either. Let's go downstairs and sit on patio," he insisted.

"You just want to play with those dogs," she said, getting out of bed.

Anatoly and Renee made their way outside into the cool night's breeze. Turning on the pathway lighting, he watched Renee as she sat on the swing and looked out at the vast lawn. It amazed him how comfortable she was with him – a man capable of the most heinous crimes. As the crickets chirped and wind blew past her, she looked over and smiled at him.

He whistled and the dogs came running to his side. Kneeling down on one knee, he rubbed his dog's ears. Lapping his face with its meaty tongue, the dog kissed his master and made him smile.

"Have you had your vitamins?" he asked the canine.

"Yeah, I gave both of them their dosages this morning," Renee answered.

"*Da*? Good," he said, standing up. Reaching into his pocket, he pulled out his cigarette box, hit the bottom, pulled one out and lit it. The smoke billowed up into the air and stretched across the sky.

Slipping the cigarette in between his fingers, he walked over and sat down beside her. He felt more relaxed now, relaxed enough to tell her what happened.

"So," Renee said, curling her feet up around her. "Spill it."

"I was at the burial site and my father noticed a man who was tall as he was from across the way. He looked like Ivan. So, he went to confront him and when he did, the man claimed to be Ivan's son. Later that night, we had a meeting with him, had the doctor swabbed him and then the next day, we found out that he is a family member. They used my father's DNA to confirm it." Anatoly took another drag of his cigarette and turned his face up to blow the smoke in the air. "He looks just like the fucker."

Renee shook her head. "Man, that's deep. So, did your father have him killed or something?"

Anatoly smiled. "No. He wants me to work with him."

"What?"

"Can you believe it? I couldn't. We're meeting in Prague next week."

"For what?" Renee squinted in disgust.

"After my father checks up on him a little more, he wants to find out what use Gabriel could be to the family."

"Just the thought of it..." Renee bit her lip. "I don't know. It's not my place to say, but you know how evil Ivan was." She tried to shake off the notion of Anatoly having to work with the likes of him.

Anatoly laughed aloud and looked over at Renee with an incredulous grin in his face. "Renee." He touched her shoulder. "We're all evil. Every Medlov who ever breathed or will breathe is...even me." The smoke from his cigarette circled his face and his cold blue eyes.

Renee swallowed hard and looked at him. "Some of you are more evil than others, Anatoly. Plus, you have the potential to do some good in the world. You don't have to use your power for evil. There is a way. There are so many ways. But you have to have balance."

"You know, when you look at me, when you talk to me, you make me almost forget that I don't have a soul." He smirked. His eyes flittered in the smoke of his cigarette.

"You do have a soul, Anatoly. And that's what I'm worried about. I don't want you to lose it over a few dollars."

"You know I don't deal in a *few dollars*."

"But is any amount enough to continue on like this?"

"What are you, my mother now?"

"No, I'm your friend. And I'm not as gullible as poor Royal was. So, I'm not going to just pretend and turn a deaf ear and blind eye when something I say might just resonate."

"This is a choice. My life is what I make of it. And I choose this, Renee. This is what I'll be for the rest of my life, no matter how bad it is and no matter how long I live. I would have expected you to know that by now."

"Well, a girl can hope," she said, rolling her eyes. "Someone has to pray for you."

"There you go with that again. Why is everyone worried about my *soul*? My sister wrote me an entire letter about it. Here," he said pulling out the small paper. "Read this shit."

Sitting back on the bench, she carefully unfolded the letter and quietly read the delicate words written for the man who was as rigid as concrete beside her. When she was done, she looked over at him and tilted her head.

He felt uncomfortable under her gaze and finally shifted a little. "What?"

"How did it make you feel when you read this?" she asked, passing him the letter back.

She watched him carefully put the letter back into his pocket. He looked away from her and thumped the cigarette across the patio. His dogs sat up as he did, looking at him, somehow sensing his mood.

"It infuriated me. She judges me. Even though it was all for her." He clenched his wide jaw. "Why is that women always want more, always want every- thing? They want to leave you with nothing. They want to break you down and have you fall at their feet with your sacrifices before they accept you. And they only accept you then, after they've put you through hell."

"That's love, Anatoly. Love makes you sacrifice everything."

He barely blinked. Looking at her lips as she said the word that curved around her full mouth, he shook his head and stood up. "That's not love, Renee. *That's* stupidity. Anyone who loves you would never ask so much from you."

"You're just frustrated right now. Gabriel. Your mother. It's been a hard month for you."

"Now you make excuses for me, when just a minute ago, you were worried about my soul?" he snapped. "The only thing that comforts me is the fact that I know that my family and my family's legacy will live on because I'm a strong enough man to not be sidetracked by idiotic notions of love and of women."

Renee looked down at the ground away from his angry scowl. She wasn't the least bit afraid of him, just disappointed. In silence, she rubbed her hands over her skin.

Anatoly immediately wished that he hadn't snapped at her. None of this was her fault, but it baffled him why she tried to make everything her problem.

Feeling guilty, he sat back down and put his arm around her. She tried to pull away, but his hands gripped her bare skin. He put his head to hers and gruffly sighed.

"I'm a lost cause, Renee."

"No, don't say that," she said in a pained voice. "You've just never had a chance."

***

Gabriel touched down at JFK airport and was taken directly to his high-rise apartment in Manhattan. He watched the city lights pass by as he sat quietly thinking. So much had happened so quickly – so much to digest. His head ached, his questions multiplied and no answers were within reach.

With shades on in the dead of night to hide his tired, red eyes, he pulled his exhausted body out of the back of the black town car and out into the rain. With luggage in-hand, he walked past the doorman.

"Good evening, Mr. Medlov. Happy to have you home," he said with a smile.

"Happy to be home, Oliver," Gabriel said, taking off his shades as he entered the lobby.

Running his hand over the elevator button, he sank into the corner and waited to arrive at the penthouse. It was then that he thought about how his place had been ransacked by Anatoly while he was Moscow. *Prick.*

As the elevator chimed and the golden doors swung gracefully open, he grabbed his key and unlocked his door expecting the worse. The click of the lock unhinging made his heart constrict. He didn't mind killing people much, but he hated messy houses. However, it was a complete surprise to find everything in order. Anatoly had promised that if he checked out, his home would be restored. He guessed that the little shit had kept his word.

Throwing his bags on the floor, he closed the door behind him and peeled out of his jacket. He took a deep breath, savoring the smell of his home – a mixture of expensive leather and cleaning products.

Walking slowly from room to room, he checked to see what all had been misplaced, discarded, destroyed. He could find nothing. In a way, he was relieved. While it did not take away the feeling of being invaded, he was glad that the most important things had not been abused – pictures of his mother and his father. He stopped by his bed and looked down at the nightstand to see a picture of him when he was four with Ivan, sitting by the Christmas tree at his mother's home in Manhattan. *Those were happy times.* That was before he found out what his father was and vice versa. It was amazing to him how blissful ignorance could be, how it could shelter one from being forced to actually live and plug into reality.

He set his keys down beside the framed photo of his father, slumped on the side of his bed and wiped his tired eyes again. Checking his watch, he realized that it was already well past nine o'clock at night.

What he really needed was a shower. He had been traveling for days. The clothes he had on reeked of airports, cigarettes and Russia.

This had been his first trip to Moscow. He had prepared for it for many months, and in his mind, he knew exactly what he was going to say to the men who had murdered his father. Several times, during their many discussions in the short period of time, he thought about just shooting them and getting it over with for all of them. But that would have been too easy.

Walking into his bathroom, he casted off his clothes in the corner and stepped into the shower. Rubbing his hand over the cold surfaces of the shiny knobs, he turned on the hot water and let it soothe his tired body. Hot steam rolled off his skin, carrying with it the scent of a long day. In a daze, he ran his hands over his body, over his tattoos, washing some of the excess ink into the water.

"Shit," he said, realizing that his marks were fading.

It would be necessary now to avoid too much soap until he could get to his faux tattoo artist at the shop. The thought mildly disgusted him, and he quickly washed and stepped out into the cold air.

With a towel wrapped around his waist, he stalked into his bedroom, grabbed a pair of jeans and slipped them on, along with a gray t-shirt and a pair of worn boots. Hair still wet, he checked his phone and realized it was time to get to the massage parlor for his meeting. After slipping on a skull cap, he dashed back out into the rainy evening.

He loved Manhattan best at night. It was unlike any other place in the world. Full of life. The people here did not care about weather or time. They roamed through the city going from one destination to the other with ease.

As he bundled up in his leather coat, he took in his surroundings, thinking of what it might be like to just be a guy with a normal life. A couple passed him, holding each other close and avoiding the rain with their large umbrella. They seemed happy. While he didn't know them, the look on their face portrayed peace. That was something he had been without for most of his life.

Being raised by a mother with trust issues and a father who was by all accounts socially dysfunction-al, he had spent most of his life seeking something. Peace was a word that was foreign to him. He had no recollection of what real happiness meant, what really family was supposed to be or what simplicity entailed. His life was a mirage of bad memories, even though he had been the recipient of more money than most and privy to a world that most thought only existed on television. There was supreme nothing-ness in what he had found. He didn't belong – not to the Vory, not to the government.

Ducking into a shabby store-front massage parlor out of the rain a few miles away from his penthouse apartment, he took off his jacket and stomped his feet on the mat.

A small Asian woman escorted him through the small lobby lit by red light bulbs and decorated with faux plants to a small room with a massage table. Quietly, she closed the door after him and locked it.

Digging into his pocket, he took out a thumb drive and placed it on the table across from him and sat down in the corner on a small stool.

Minutes later, the door in the back of the room opened and a tall Chinese American man appeared. Agent Lee was a middle-aged cynic who lived for his job with a no-nonsense, permanent scowl and a cop-style crew hair cut to match. He locked the door behind him and quickly got to the discussion.

"How was Moscow?" he asked, grabbing the thumb drive and stuffing it down into the inner pocket of his wool coat.

"Cold," Gabriel replied. "But also productive. I passed the test. I am who I say I am. I've got a meeting with the entire Medlov family in Prague at Dmitry's home in one week."

"Impressive," Lee said, sitting across from him. "And what of Anatoly."

"Oh," Gabriel smiled. "He hates my guts like we thought he would. The only problem that I can possibly see is Royal. The wife is a real piece of work."

"How so?"

"Well, she obviously doesn't trust me. I guess her history with my father doesn't help. But I have to win her over. I get the feeling that her opinion of me will determine just how long I live."

"She's supposed to be dead, you know." Lee put another thumb drive on the table and slid it across to him. "But she's small fries. She's never been involved in anything illegal, but faking her own death, from what I can tell. And it's going to be nearly impossible to get her back to the states and from under Dmitry's protection to do anything useful on her. At this point, I would just try to stay on her good side. Any mention of drugs at all?"

"Not one mention of anything illegal, but I'm sure that's what the meeting is for."

"How long do you expect them to keep you there?"

"As long as they want. I don't get the feeling that these men function on the same timetable as the rest of the world."

"So, how do we keep your cover concrete is the question? Since you left Russia, there has been a serious investigation on all your background with the New York families and inquiries from some of the oldest and more notable mob figures from all sorts of families from half way across the world."

"What can I say? I'm popular."

"Let's keep it that way. We're wiring more money for you. You need to be a little flashier. We've also got a back story for you on a few murders you were involved in last year. You can read through the thumb drive when you get time. Your place has been bugged, tapped, everything else since the break in. You'll need all new computers and everything. Remember to be extra careful. No communication with anyone who is not involved with the Medlov family and only communicate through me from here on out until you're pulled from undercover."

"I know the drill. I don't think we should treat Royal with kid gloves though. I'm telling you, I have to get her on my side."

"Well, what would you suggest?"

"I was reading her file, and she's an orphan right?"

"Yeah."

"Well, since I'm supposed to be an identity hacker, I need to pull a few strings and get some information that would definitely be sealed."

"Regarding whom?"

"Royal, of course." Gabriel pulled a piece of paper from his back pocket and passed it to Agent Lee. "This is what I could come up with myself, but I need more."

Lee looked at the paper and then folded and put it away. "Is this all?"

"This may be what I need to win her completely over and break through the barriers to really get the family to trust me."

"Or it could prove you're a cop."

Gabriel smiled. "I would think that it would prove that I'm the latter. Trust me, I'll be convincing, but I need it before I go to Prague."

Chapter Seven

Agosto heard his phone ringing from across the office. Cutting his conversation off with one of his subordinates, he quickly jetted through his door and grabbed the phone from across the desk before it could go to voicemail.

"Lieutenant Agosto, Memphis Police Department," he said, pulling the phone's cord towards him to cut the static.

"Hi, this is...well, my name isn't important, but I have important information regarding Anatoly Medlov for your ongoing investigation, if there is one."

Agosto looked around his office through the glass doors to make sure that no one could hear him speaking. Reaching his leg out, he caught the end of the door with his foot and closed it. Lowering his voice, he moved over to his seat and grabbed a pen and paper.

"Go head," he said, waiting for the woman to continue. Whoever was calling was doing so from a blocked number. *Dammit.*

"You may or may not already know this, but Anatoly Medlov is running a large amount of guns through your city. They are from a big deal that went down in Sochi, Russia during the Olympics earlier this year. And he's filtering all the money through art."

"What kind of drugs. What kind of guns? Who's the art dealer?" Agosto asked, trying to place the woman's accent. He wrote down on his pad. *Female. Race unknown. Accent questionable. Possibly east coast.*

"I'm not sure of what kind. But I think that quantity is important. He dropped off a shipment to a group of Jewish men in Istanbul a few months ago and since then he's been selling them in bulk to the largest bidder."

"Where is he housing the guns? Who's been some of the largest bidders?"

"Not sure," the woman huffed. "I don't know much, but I can tell you this. They are in the city of Memphis."

"Well, the city is pretty big. Do you have an idea of where he might be storing them?"

"No, but I'll try to find out."

"Any other information?"

"Not right now. He's pretty tight-lipped, but I'm telling you, he's the head of the Medlov family not Dmitry. And he's right under your nose."

Agosto looked up from his paper. His suspicions where correct. "How do you know all of this?"

"I can't give you that either. I'm not trying to be killed anytime soon."

"Well, why are you doing this?"

"The usual. The whole *woman scorned* bit," the woman said in a condescending voice. "The bastard has it coming to him."

"I hear ya," Agosto said with a grin. "So, what's your name? Maybe you can come and we can talk, or I can meet you. Some of the information you're giving me is out of my jurisdiction. So, I'll need to pass it on the FBI."

"No deal. I just want him to know what it's liked to be caged like an animal. I'll get you what I can when I can, as long as it doesn't come back to me."

"Maybe you can answer one more question for me then."

"Okay," she said, holding her breath.

"Is Royal Stone still alive?"

The woman laughed and hung up the phone.

Agosto put the phone down on the receiver and sat back in his seat. Biting his lip, he quickly wrote down more notes on the pad under his pen, scribbling quickly, then pulled the piece of paper off the sheath and put it in his pocket.

A million questions crossed his mind, but in his time on the force, he had learned to still them in order to move from a clue to an actual bust.

There was a knock at his door that interrupted his swirling thoughts. Looking up, he saw Cory. He waved him in and kicked his feet up on his desk.

Cory, a friend and subordinate of Agosto's and the former undercover for the first undercover Medlov investigation, came in and closed the door behind him. With a file in his hand from his current case, he pulled a seat out and sat down.

"Sup," Cory said, picking up on Agosto's far-off gaze. "You look like you just saw a ghost."

Agosto gave a devilish grin. "Not a ghost. I think I just finally got a lead on the Medlov's."

"What kind of lead?"

Agosto hesitated.

"Oh, come on man. I damned near got killed trying to bring Dmitry Medlov in. How are you going to sit there and hold out on me?" His clever eyes beam in anticipation.

"You were always close but no cigar, Cory. Not worth shit."

Cory scratched his freckled nose and squinted. "I got closer than anyone else...even you."

"What the hell," Agosto said, throwing his concern to the wind. "I just got a call from some woman. I want to say that she was black, who told me that Anatoly Medlov is in fact the new Czar and that he's housing a shit load of guns here for distribution. Now, we knew that he was the boss, but what we didn't know is that they were moving any product out of Memphis anymore. The word was that the product went with Dmitry, but this proves otherwise."

Cory's face was blank. Blinking his eyes, he finally swallowed and sat back in his seat. "You don't say. Well, do you have any idea who the woman is?"

"Nope. She called from a blocked number, but she said that she'd call back with more as soon as she could." Agosto reached down into his side drawer and pulled out the Medlov file. With a quick lick of his thumb, he flipped through the pages and pulled out a lead sheet. "I have to call Sorrello over at the Bureau and let him know."

Cory silently watched Agosto as he logged the conversation with the mystery woman. "Do you need me to go back under on this? I could."

Agosto smiled and closed the file. "Nope, I've already got someone."

"Who?"

"You know that I can't tell you that."

"But I could help."

"No, man. Look, you got pulled off this thing over three years ago. Now, my new UC has gone through a lot of training on this and he will get the job done. Trust me. He's a stand up guy."

Cory smiled. "So it's a dude."

Agosto shook his head. "That's about all I'll tell you. Now, get the fuck out of here, and go do some cop work, will ya."

Cory stood up. "Alright. Alright. I'm out of here. Just remember. I'm your man, whenever your UC fucks this up. And he will."

"He won't. Trust me," Agosto said, sitting back in his seat.

As Cory closed the door, he felt his heart finally start to beat again. He wasn't getting paid by Dmitry to be *the last to know*. Shit. He had to get out of the precinct now and get to his other cell phone to let the Medlov family know. Another UC. Another problem. At least, he could inform him that it was a guy. But there was no telling how long he had been under. Hopefully, whoever had been assigned hadn't been there long.

Foregoing the elevator, he pushed the door to the stairs open and zipped down the four flights to the back entrance of the police precinct. Within in minutes, he was out at his truck. He cranked it up quickly and pulled onto the streets. By the time that he was at the first light, he was on the phone to Prague.

"Hello," Dmitry answered his personal cell.

"You've got a UC back in the fray and a leak from inside."

"Start with the UC. Who?"

"Don't know."

"Find out. That's what I pay you for."

"I'm on it."

"How long have they been inside my organization?"

"I'm not sure that he's inside, but I do know that he's a guy. He's been trained well, so you won't recognize him as an outsider."

"Find out how long he's been under and find out who it is. Now, what of the leak?"

Cory could hear a child laughing in the background. He pulled over to the side of the street, hands shaking and calmed his voice. "It's a woman. A black woman. She called and gave information about the guns. She didn't give enough to be completely useful but she's looking for more."

"A black woman?

"Yes."

"Well, there's only three, and one of them, I am certain is not your person," Dmitry said, looking at his wife.

"Then it's possibly Renee or someone else."

"Very well." Dmitry didn't sound the least bit put off, which scared Cory more.

"I'll inform my son, myself. But you've got to find out who the UC is, I can find the leak."

"I'm on it."

"You had better be," Dmitry said as he hung up his cell.

Cory closed his phone and took a deep breath. He had been warned several times about late Intel from inside the department. Dmitry would only be so forgiving regardless of their past relationship. He had to find out who the UC was. The only thing he could think of was to start hanging out more at the restaurant and clothing store during his time off and when he was supposed to be working these other bullshit cases. Whatever it took, he'd do it.

***

When his father had originally assigned him to the kitchen when Anatoly first came to Memphis many years ago, he felt slighted. What did working in Mother Russia have to do with learning his duties as a Vor? He had never been a cook, never appreciated the fine art of cooking, never wanted to learn. But over the years, he figured out that his father didn't want him to work with him in the kitchen to teach him lessons of the Vor. He had him work there, because it gave them time to do something together as father and son away from their responsibilities to the men and to the organization.

Now with his father many thousands of miles away, when Anatoly really missed Dmitry, when he really needed to work things out in his head, or when he really wanted to get away, he found himself in the kitchen among his workers fixing the meals that he at first thought to be a punishment of some sort.

Today was like any other day for him. Work in his kitchen was going well. He had hand-made the Borscht and cabbage and was carefully preparing the salad and pelmeni. His other workers labored diligently beside him, making sure to move out of his way every time that he passed them.

He worked with his I-pod in his ears, listening to music and thinking about the other tasks before him that would take a great deal more effort than his meals.

Outside the kitchen, the staff put fresh flowers in all the vases and made sure the place was tidy for the lunch crowd.

Vasily sat in the corner, scanning the newspaper and watching the exits for anyone who might enter.

As he turned the page of the *New York Times*, Destiny came in through the front door with a bundle of magazines in her hand.

They made eye contact and he stood. Walking over to her, it crossed his mind that with her hair in a ponytail pulled to the back of her head, she looked like a cop.

"Can I help you?" Vasily asked.

"I'm here to see Anatoly," Destiny explained with a bright smile.

"I'll see if he's available. You can have a seat, if you'd like." Vasily pointed at the table near the back of the restaurant.

"Oh, I can wait here for him," she said, looking towards the kitchen.

"I insist," Vasily said sternly. "If he's available, I'll let you know." His voice was gruff and thick with his Russian accent. Glaring at her under menacing green eyes, he motioned once more towards the back of the room.

As she turned, a hostess was there to guide her to the back. "Follow me," the woman said with a smile, looking back at Vasily with worried eyes.

Destiny followed quietly. This wasn't exactly what she had in mind, but she'd allow it. Based upon her short interaction with his bodyguard, she wasn't sure that she had a choice. *Sit or get out.*

Several minutes later, Anatoly emerged from the kitchen in a dark pair of jeans and black t-shirt.

Curly blonde locks danced about his head and his boyish face was unshaven. With a half-smirk, he came to the table, pulled a seat out and sat down.

"Are you looking for a free meal?" he asked, running his hand over the tablecloth.

Destiny smiled. "No, I came to see you."

"Really?"

"Yes, I wanted to see if you liked my story."

"It was pretty good. You're a decent reporter."

"Wow, is that a compliment?"

"The best one I can give," he said, looking behind him. "Bring us over some borscht, bread and vodka, Amelia," he ordered the woman standing only a few feet from them.

The woman bowed and turned to go and get their food.

"Oh, I can't stay long," Destiny said, setting the magazines down. "I just thought that you'd like a few copies for the restaurant."

"You can stay long enough to have lunch with me. You did after all, interrupt me from cooking. It's the least that you can do." Reaching into his pocket, he pulled out his cigarettes.

"Are you going to smoke that in here?" she asked.

"Yes, I don't plan on going out back."

"But what about your customers?"

Anatoly flicked his lighter and lit his cigarette. With his blue eyes squinted, he blew a puff of smoke in the air and grinned. "Fuck'em."

Destiny tried to repress her smile but could not. She let out a loud laugh and reached across to him. With her palm up, she raised her brow. "I'll have one too then."

He passed her a cigarette and watched her light it.

"I never guessed you smoked," he said.

She lit the cigarette quickly and sat back in her seat. "There's a lot you don't know about me."

Anatoly liked her playful manner. As the waitresses came and carefully placed their food in front of them, he took the bottle of vodka and poured them both a shot.

"Let's get shit faced and find out a little more about each other, shall we?"

She grinned. "Okay, why not. If I get fired from work, I'm sure I'll be able to find another job as a food writer in this city."

"Don't be so sure," Anatoly said, passing her the shot. "Drink up."

"Aren't we supposed to toast to something?" she asked, holding up her shot glass.

"Go for it."

She bit her lip and looked up at the ceiling. "To...to dinner tonight at my place."

Anatoly lifted his shot glass and toasted her. "And to breakfast."

As he downed his vodka, his cell phone rang. Holding up his finger, he nodded. "Give me minute," he said, turning from her. When he saw it was his father, he quickly got up from the chair and stepped away.

"*Da*," he said quietly.

"You have a leak and an undercover. The undercover will be taken care of, but the leak is a problem...your problem."

Anatoly didn't answer immediately. He turned and looked back at Destiny, who was sitting at the table talking to the waitresses about the dishes.

"Who?" he asked, moving toward the kitchen.

"My source says it's a black woman. Either Victoria or Renee."

"Not Renee," Anatoly said quickly.

"Are you sure about that?" Dmitry snapped.

"No," Anatoly answered gravely. "But she wouldn't be my first guess."

"Don't *guess*, boy. It's a black woman. So, you only have two choices."

"Three now," Anatoly corrected. He stared at Destiny.

"You're fucking up, Anatoly. I don't really mind when it's just with your love life, but you can't be so careless with the family. Find out who it is. Flush her out. Get rid of whoever this *number three* is and do it now. Then find out if it's Renee or Victoria."

"Then what?" Antoly asked irritated.

"You damned well know what."

The phone went dead.

Anatoly looked at it and thought about throwing it across the room, but instead stuffed it back down in his jeans. *Was there never a minute when he could just have a normal life?* Now, his father wanted him to just get rid of everyone while he enjoyed his wife and kid, his retirement and worked the shit out of him? *Wasn't he the boss now? Didn't that carry some weight?*

Walking back over to his table, he quickly pulled the seat out and sat down.

He smiled. "Now, where was I? Oh, yeah, we were going to get shit faced. And then later tonight, I'm going to have dinner with you at your place."

"That's right," she said smiling.

Chapter Eight

The door chimes rang as Renee came into the restaurant. Nodding at Nadiya, the head hostess, she made her way to the bar, where she lazily plopped down on the leather stool, laid her purse on the bar and ordered a drink.

Vasily eyed her quietly, knowing that her presence would be the very water in the oil of the moment that wouldn't mix well for Anatoly. Making his way across the room to her, he stepped in her view of the back table where his boss sat with Destiny.

"I see you take early lunch today," Vasily said, raising his finger for the bartender to come over.

"Hey Vasily." Renee barely looked up. "I just needed a break. We've been busy all day," she said with a huff. "What about you? Anatoly isn't running you around like crazy today?" She looked over at him.

"He's cooking and around the restaurant," he explained. "Why don't I get you seat in comfortable spot."

"I'm fine here. I'm waiting on someone," she explained. She nodded her head. Anatoly couldn't be far if Vasily was nearby.

"You have girlfriend to meet today?" Vasily asked.

Renee looked at him curiously. "No," she said tilting her head. "Why?"

"No reason." Taking his eyes off her, he looked in the mirror behind the bar and eyed his boss. He was still laughing and talking. It was going to be hard to get the word to him that Renee was here without her seeing Destiny.

Renee covertly followed his gaze. Plus, she could smell the distinct, rancid odor of cigarette smoke clouding the restaurant. Tennessee law prohibited smoking in public restaurants. The only person brazen enough to do it had to be Anatoly.

Moving back away from the bar and out of Vasily's way, she looked over and saw him smiling and laughing with the reporter from the magazine. His broad back faced her.

"Figures," she said, sitting back up. She looked over at Vasily and crooked her full lips. "I don't know why you're hiding him, Vasily. We aren't dating, you know."

Vasily did not respond.

"I don't care what he does," she said aloud.

Vasily cocked his brow. Moving out of her way, he uttered something in Russian and walked over to his boss.

Anatoly leaned back from the table to listen to his bodyguard, then nodded.

Destiny put down her shot glass and swallowed hard. The man's entire exterior changed instantly.

He was suddenly guarded. Pushing his seat back, he stood up and put out his cigarette.

"I'll be back," he said with a joker-like grin.

"I'll be here," she said flirting.

Renee was thumbing through a magazine and drinking a glass of tea when he came up behind her. He knew that she felt him close to her back, but she didn't look up or move.

"Ana, what do you want?" she finally asked, closing the magazine. "Don't you have enough to do with little Miss Muppet over there?" she asked, trailing her eyes over his chest before she locked in on his gleaming blue prisms.

"You never like anyone, Renee. I'm not surprised. You try to be my mother," he said, sitting down beside her. "Just because she's dead, doesn't mean you have to move right into the position."

The bartender quickly put a glass of water in front of him. Without acknowledging the worker, he picked up the glass and gulped down the water, chasing the vodka he had just drunk.

Renee watched him swallow then continued, "I'm not trying to be your mother," she said unreadable. "I just know trouble when I see it." Her eyebrow raised and to add insult to injury, she turned and looked over the woman who eyed them both. "Anyway, I didn't come here to see you."

"Oh, well then who?"

"I came over here to meet Cory. He called just a little while ago and asked me over here to catch up."

"Cory?"

"Yeah, you remember, the once gay, undercover cop who used to be my friend," she said sarcastically.

"What does he want?"

"I don't know. That's what I'm here to find out. Maybe he just wants to see me. Did you ever think of that?"

Heat formed at the base of his neck. "He's married, you know," Anatoly said, forgetting all about the woman waiting on him. "And he's a pig."

"There is nothing wrong with cops," Renee admonished. "Well, maybe for me, there's not," she retracted. She rolled her eyes. "Look, if it's a problem, I can't meet him somewhere else. He was the one who wanted to have lunch here. I didn't see -"

Anatoly cut her off. "Here is fine. Better here than away where he can try to be a fucking snake."

Renee whirled her long straw around in her glass. "Are you still uptight about your sister's letter?"

Her question disarmed him. He looked away, trying not to be as transparent as he felt at that very moment. "Why don't you try staying out of my business for one damned day," he snapped.

Renee rolled her eyes. "I'll take that as a yes."

He huffed and stood up. "I have someone waiting on me. Enjoy your lunch."

"Yeah, whatever," Renee said, pushing the glass away from her. She didn't look over at him. She knew it would give him too much satisfaction.

Hearing his footsteps move away from her, she glanced up at the television mounted on the wall.

Anatoly went back to Destiny, who sat obediently waiting. His mind was on the woman at the bar, but his hunger was for the woman in front of him. Why was he surrounding himself with black women? He was getting more and more like his father by the day. The thought crossed his mind out of the blue and a frown suddenly colored his dark features.

"Something wrong?" Destiny asked.

Anatoly's eye twitched. "No." He gave a clever smile. "So, I've got a lot to do here before tonight."

"And you want to wrap up our lunch, right?" She interrupted him before he could finish his sentence.

"Right," he said, raising his brow. "But we'll pick up where we left off tonight."

"I don't want you to get the wrong idea about me. I want to have dinner with you, but breakfast is..."

"Negotiable," he said with a stern face. "I'm not a regular guy. If you want regular guy, you should go somewhere else. If you want good time, no string attached, you come see me."

"And where are the regular guys in this city?" she smiled.

"I don't know one," he laughed.

"You may be a no-strings attached type of guy," she licked her lips. "And I'm okay with that. But we go at my speed."

"I can deal with that," he said in a low, seductive tone. "But trust me when I say, you'll want to accelerate things along."

"Really," she smirked as she grabbed her purse and stood up.

"Really," Anatoly replied. He didn't bother to get up. Instead, he watched her as she walked off.

"See you tonight," Destiny said, looking over at Renee as she passed.

Cory eyed Destiny from the corner as she walked out the front door. Shortly after Anatoly had walked away from Renee, he had walked in and got them a more private place to talk.

Now Renee sat visibly sulking.

"You look amazing," he said, noting her weight loss.

"Thanks," Renee looked up from her empty plate. "This diet sucks, but the doctor says that I'll get used to it."

"Lifestyle changes are never easy," he said, grabbing the menu.

"So what did you want to talk to me about?"

Cory sighed. "Well, I wanted to apologize to you after all of these years for deceiving you and gaining your trust just to disappear." He put the menu back down.

"You're a cop. You don't owe me an explanation. I don't see why after three years, you'd call me out of the blue to apologize at the very restaurant that started all of this."

Renee was quicker than he expected. He imagined that the Medlov's had kept her around because of her knowledge of their inner workings and because of her relationship with Royal. He had been told that she didn't know that the woman was alive. Without asking, he was certain that she was still grieving for her. Renee was that type of person.

"Well, you've been on my mind for three years," he said with a smile.

Renee didn't smile back. She picked up the menu to order and as she was about to ask another question, she smelled Anatoly's cologne. Looking back, she saw him only feet away.

"Cory, you remember Anatoly, don't you?" she asked as she turned back in her seat.

"How could I forget?" Cory said, eyeing his old adversary.

"You have a lot of balls to come here," Anatoly said with his arms folded.

A couple sitting across from the unfolding event stopped talking and watched the confrontation.

"Well, I just wanted to see Renee and apologize," Cory said with a stern glare. "I was hoping to catch up."

Anatoly's face reddened. "Renee is now the shop manager. She's lost about thirty pounds and she's single, but you're married, so there'll be no fucking around."

"Ana!" Renee admonished.

"So now you're caught up. So take a hike," Anatoly said, ignoring Renee.

Renee rolled her eyes and grabbed her purse. Standing up, she turned to see Vasily standing behind Anatoly awaiting her. With a nod, he extended his arm, indicating that it was time to take her away. Without bothering to excuse herself properly, she stormed past Anatoly and followed Vasily out of the restaurant.

Anatoly walked over to Renee's chair and sat down.

"It was the only way that I could see you quickly," Cory said under his breath.

"I have a leak."

"You have a leak," Cory nodded. "And the woman who just walked out of here is a cop."

Anatoly almost laughed. "Destiny?"

"Yes." Cory looked around the restaurant to observe anyone who might see them talking.

"Fucking figures." Anatoly shook his head. "Okay."

Cory stood up. "Okay." He tapped the table with his knuckles. "So, I've done my part?"

"*Da*, we're good."

Cory nodded and walked away.

As Cory left Mother Russia, a grave feeling overcame him. He thought that he'd gotten away from all of this, yet here he was. When he had first committed to the Vory, specifically to Dmitry, he thought that after the Medlov's went to Prague, he would be free. However, there had been a constant stream of requests by the family. Little pieces of information on both cops and convicts were always needed. And if the FBI special agent Sorrello didn't provide it, he had to. It seemed like he would always be in debt to them. A part of him wished for nothing more than the entire family to be caught, but he knew he wasn't the man to bring them down.

***

Anatoly felt like screaming, but he sat at the table alone digesting his disgusting situation. He had mole in his organization, and while he bet that it was Victoria, it could very well be Renee. He had a cop posing as a reporter to get close to him. He had a cousin who dropped out of the sky and was now trying to get in with his father and get a piece of his money. His council felt he was too young for the job. And his father probably felt like he was incompetent.

How did Dmitry do it for so long? How did he deal with the constant backstabbing and the utter betrayal of it all?

Vasily walked over and sat across the table from him. He knew that whatever Cory said to Anatoly was serious. Awaiting an order, he pushed back in the chair.

"That bitch is a cop," Anatoly said blankly.

"The reporter?"

"*Da.*"

"What do you want to do about it?"

"I'm supposed to meet her tonight."

"A set up?"

"How? I haven't told her anything. Since she wants an inside track, I'll give her one," he smiled. "Vasily, do you ever get the taste for blood in your mouth, in your spirit?"

"Often enough."

"Well, I have it now. I'm so angry, I could kill the whole world. There's a mole inside the organization. My father seems to think that it's a black woman."

"Not Renee," Vasily said disgusted.

"I hope not. But if I find out that it is, I don't know if I can do it."

"I'll do it," Vasily nodded.

"Let's not get too ahead of ourselves. There's a little cunt in Italy who may be up to her old tricks again," Anatoly said, pulling his phone from his pocket. "Call Agent Sorrello's fat ass. Tell him you need everything you can get on Destiny Palmer before tonight."

"Yes, boss," Vasily said, excusing himself.

Chapter Nine

Renee was furious. Slamming the back door behind her, she went up to her apartment and left the store to Miriam's care. *What did she care about sales today?* Anatoly was messing everything up for her. One minute, he was just supposed to be her best friend and the next minute, he made her feel like they had something going on between them. He was jealous as hell. But he never was without a woman hanging on him. He was caring in one action, then a complete jerk about the smallest things. Overall, his mind games were too much for her. She wasn't the man. She wasn't supposed to be chasing his ass. And she wasn't supposed to this wrapped up in someone that she'd never even kissed!

The confusion of the moment made her dizzy. She kicked her shoes off at the front door and went straight to the kitchen. *The world doesn't revolve around that asshole*, she thought to herself as she snatched open the refrigerator. What she needed to do at the very moment was cook. Cooking always made her feel better.

Grabbing a pot roast from the back of the top shelf, she threw it on the countertop and went to the pantry for potatoes and vegetables. Then it hit her. She couldn't fix a pot roast without a pie. She needed to make something from scratch. Opening the refrigerator again, she filled her arms with butter, eggs, nutmeg and milk.

"Just look at what you've made me do," she said under her breath of Anatoly. "Why did I even lose all of this weight if I can never hold your attention more than five damned minutes?" Tears formed at the side of her eyes. "Today it is the bimbo news reporter. Tomorrow it will be the Asian stripper. Day after that it'll be an Australian model." She threw the food down on the counter. "I'm just sick of this shit."

Leaning against the counter, she wiped her face and sighed. A *Weight Watcher's* commercial came on the television across the room and Jennifer Hudson sang out in happy joy.

"Ugh!" Renee said, grabbing the remote. She quickly turned off the television. What was she doing? It had taken forever to get the weight off, and she was about to work towards putting it all back on for a man who barely noticed her if he wasn't hungry or checking the numbers from his shop.

More and more, she was beginning to sympathize with what Royal had gone through with Dmitry. Her life must have been a living hell, trying to keep it together in a world like this. "I'm sorry, girl," she said aloud to her dead friend. "I'm sorry that I wasn't there for you more. Lord knows that you must have needed it."

"It freaks me out when you talk to yourself," Anatoly said, leaning against the doorway watching her. He gave her a penetrating look.

Renee jumped. Turning around, she rolled her eyes. "Who told you to just come into my damned house?"

Anatoly's hands were fisted inside of his pants pockets. He gave a clever grin. "You do it to me all the time. I never make a fuss."

"Well, I don't spy on you," she said, wiping her face.

"You sure about that?" he asked, narrowing his eyes at her.

"What is that supposed to mean?"

Anatoly walked over the table and grabbed a napkin from the porcelain holder. He passed it to her and raised his brow. He had only ever seen her cry over Royal, but he knew that today there was something else. He worried that it was guilt – possibly the guilt of being a snitch. The thought pained him. Still, he continued, "You know that I don't like beating around the bush."

"Yeah, so?" she said, trying to pull herself together.

"So, have you been talking to the police about me, about my family?"

Renee shook her head in sheer disbelief. "You better be kidding, Ana." Her nose flared in anger.

"I'm not." He walked up to her. Face-to-face they stood. He looked down at her and clenched his jaw. "I need to see your face when you say it. Have you spoken to police about me at all?" he asked calmly. His gaze was cold and lethal.

She put her hand on her hip. "Yes," she said as her full mouth twitched. "Right after Royal's death, I was interrogated by five different government agencies. Then I was audited by the IRS. I've been followed on countless occasions. Since then, I'm pretty sure my phones have been tapped, too. Today, I was asked to lunch by a cop who used to be my *good gay* friend. You remember all this don't you? I sure as hell hope you do considering it was your family's fault." She didn't blink. Fury clouded her eyes. "But if I recall, and I would, I haven't gone to the police with anything," she said with a frown. "Probably because I don't *know* anything."

Anatoly could see in her face that she wasn't lying, and the knowledge of that fact gave him complete relief. He tried to explain. "Someone's talking. I had to be sure it wasn't you."

"How can you see me every damned day – no-how can I come to your house, fix your dinner, console you, confide in you and then turn you in for shit I don't even know about? I can't believe you. I thought you knew me well enough to not have to ask." Tears fell down her cheeks. Her eyes reddened.

He tried to wipe the tears away, but she pushed away his hand.

"I didn't mean to hurt you," he said reluctantly.

"Bullshit." She moved out of his way. Pointing her finger at him, she shook her head again. Her long black hair fell over her shoulders. "Bullshit, Ana. You've gotten so lost in this, you don't know which way is up anymore."

"And you're so much better?" he protested with a frown. "Look where you work. Look where you live. Look at your friends. You're just a hypocritical as the rest of world."

"Maybe you're right," she said, shaking her head. "But I know when to stop." She looked down at the ground, praying for strength. Finally, when she had her bearing and she was sure of her decision, she straightened up and spoke. "I quit."

Anatoly looked over at her quickly. "Now, you're just overreacting."

She walked up to him and pulled his beautiful face into her hands. Quietly, she nodded. "I. Quit. I'm giving you my two-week notice now." She tried to stop the tears, but they gushed freely from her eyes. "I'm tired of being...not enough."

"*Enough* for what?" he asked in a near whisper. He searched her face, realizing in that moment, just how beautiful she really was.

"Enough for you," she said, letting his face go. She shivered. "I'm done playing this game. I'm too good for this shit. So, I quit. I'm going back to Atlanta. I'll find a job there."

"Give yourself sometime to think about this," he said, reaching out for her.

She stepped back. "There is nothing to think about. What happens if one day, I can't convince you that I'm not the bad guy? Huh? What happens then?"

"I would never hurt you." His eyes did not meet hers.

She laughed. "I know. You'd send Vasily to do it."

There was a long silence.

"Most of the people around you are here because there is nowhere else to go. They won't really tell you when you're fucking up. They won't tell you when you're not being a real man. They won't question your authority, because of who you are *supposed* to be. But I was here for *you*. And up until this very moment, I could rationalize why."

"Then why give up on me so easily?" His voice was grave.

"It wasn't easy, baby," she said, looking away. She turned her back to him.

"At least wait until I get back from Prague," he pleaded, looking at her back. "Let's talk about it then."

She shook her head. "No, Ana. I'm done waiting for you." Walking out the room, she left him alone in the kitchen.

***

Agosto had a bad feeling in his gut. He sat in his office on the phone talking to Destiny and something just didn't sit well with him. She had just informed him that Anatoly would be coming over to her apartment for drinks and to *talk*, and while that normally would have been good for a seasoned UC, he wasn't sure that Destiny was smart enough to handle the Medlov men, especially the cold-hearted, young one, Anatoly.

The MPD had a hundred unsolved cases surrounding the young boss, and yet, he constantly remained untouchable. Nothing was ever traceable back to Anatoly. While he was always near or at the scene of a crime or a horrible catastrophe, not once were they ever able to prove that he was guilty of more than just bad luck.

"Make sure that you wear a wire?" he reminded.

"I can't wear a wire," Destiny said quickly. "I'll have the surveillance equipment in the apartment. You can watch the entire thing. I just want him to feel safe around me. You know. He's going to open up. I can feel it."

"He's not a regular guy. This isn't a regular date. These aren't normal people. If he's sees one chink in your chain, he'll hang you with it."

"I wish that you would trust me," she said as she held a dress up to her in the mirror.

"*I wish that you* would listen to me," Agosto replied. "Just remember that you can't sleep with him."

"I'm not a whore, and I'm not hard up. You forget that I'm dating Harrison in homicide. We've been together for a year. We plan to get married soon. "

Agosto knew Harrison. He was nothing to brag about. "Be careful. Ask the questions that we've gone over. Make the date short."

"How can I get in his head if the date is short?"

"If it's too long, he might get in your pants; he might figure you out. He might just reach over and snap your neck or rape you."

"Then you'll have it on tape and you can prosecute."

Agosto shook his head. He should have chosen someone else for the job, but it was too late now. "Fine. We'll be watching. If you need help, if you need to blow your cover and pull your fire arm, if you need to arrest the guy for assault or attempted rape, do it. Just be safe. Remember, there will always be other cases."

"I know," she said, looking at her watch. "I better go. He'll be here in an hour."

***

Anatoly sat outside of Destiny's apartment in his Maserati and drank out of his flask. Brooding over Renee, he continued to relive the moment in her kitchen over and over again. He'd lost her in one stupid move. The funny part of it all was that he'd never known that he had her. Her confession, while light, had made his heart heavy. She looked him in his face with tears in her eyes and confessed something that from any other woman would have been meaningless but from her was priceless. However, there was one thing that confused him more than anything else. Did he feel the loss of her as his friend or as his...dare he say it...soul mate? He laughed at the thought and looked over at the light coming from Destiny's apartment.

And this bitch was trying to set him up.

He thought of walking in, grabbing her by her hair, leading her out to the balcony and putting one in her head right in front of the unmarked squad car a few blocks down. That would be a great way to say fuck them all, but then he'd have to deal with his father. The thought sent chills down his spine. His old man had gone soft for his wife, but he was still a brutal *sonofabitch* to everyone else, including him when he screwed things up.

Throwing the flask down on his passenger seat, he got out of the car and made his way to her place. With every step, he dreaded what he had to do. And it was not because he had lost the taste for this life; it was because he knew he should have been off trying to get Renee back.

Destiny opened the door as quickly as he rang the bell. With a smile, she greeted him.

"Wasn't hard to find, I hope," she said, gesturing towards the sofa.

"No," Anatoly said with a deceiving smile. "You have a nice place." He looked around. *This was a hole-in-the-wall, unworthy of his dogs.*

"Thank you," she said, going to the kitchen to fix them a drink. "Like scotch?"

"No," he said, sitting down. "Got any Russian vodka?"

"Sure," she said, peeking her head around the corner. "Make yourself comfortable. I'll be out in just a minute."

You want to make me comfortable, you dirty bitch. Then come and let me ride your face, he thought to himself as he moved the pillow from behind him. "So, do you like Memphis so far?" he asked, looking around her apartment. He wondered if this was really her place. If not, the MPD was entirely too cheap. It was barely 1,000 square feet and poorly built. He felt as though he was in a shabby box.

"It's okay. It's not better than Alabama," she answered.

"What *is* better than Alabama," he said sarcastically under his breath.

"Did you say something?" she asked, rounding the corner with two drinks.

He took the glass from her and sighed. "No. You...you look great." He swept her body with a sensual gaze. That part was real.

"Thank you." She smoothed her red dress down over her wide hips. Sitting down beside him on the sofa, she smiled, revealing perfect, white teeth. "You alright? You look different."

"It's just been a long day," he explained. "I don't get out much, because I work so hard."

"At the restaurant?"

"Yes, at the restaurant," he said, shaking his head. Taking a sip of the drink, he sat back. "It's really good be out with a beautiful woman and just relaxing for a change." He watched her carefully.

"Same here. I mean, I'm always looking for the next big story, and I never get a chance to just hang out." She shrugged her shoulders.

"What's the next big story in food, anyway?"

"Well, a hot, new restaurant is opening not far from yours. It's a Mexican place."

"I don't like Mexican food."

"Really?"

"Well, I like Cuban food. I enjoy....," he moved over a little closer to her. "I enjoy going to Little Havana and having a real meal. I fly down there all the time."

"That sounds exciting." Her eyes sparkled.

He reached over and touched the lobe of her ear. She closed her eyes and smiled. "Not as exciting as sitting here with you," he said, taking her drink out of her hands. "I don't want you to get too drunk. Let's talk for a while. Tell me something about you that I don't know. I'm always interested in meeting new people. With what I do, I don't get a chance to socialize much."

"As a restaurant and boutique owner, I would think that's all you get a chance to do," she said curiously.

"Well, that's not *all* I do." He winked at her.

Destiny could barely contain herself. She told Agosto! This guy was already breaking. Looking at him while he placed her glass on the table, she titled her head. "Well, I'm originally from Mobile, Alabama. Then I moved to Birmingham after college."

Anatoly listened to her as she went on and on about her childhood, teenage life and college life at an HBCU. He entertained her, asking questions every once in awhile to ensure that his interest was not waning. A few hours into the conversation and after he's let her drink more than her share, he made his move.

"We've been here for hours, and I haven't even asked if you hungry," he said, standing up.

She looked up at him. "I actually had something in the oven. I totally forgot about it."

"Well, I'm sure that it's cold now, and you've been such a great host. Why don't you let me take you to get something to eat?"

She stood up beside him. "Sure, where would you like to go?"

He smiled. "I fell like having a little Cuban. You up for it?"

"But there isn't a Cuban restaurant in Memphis."

He looked at his Rolex. "I know. I was hoping we could go down to Miami."

Destiny chuckled in disbelief. "Miami? Tonight?"

Anatoly put his hands in his pockets. "Yeah. I do it all the time. My jet's fueled up and ready. The pilot's on call 24-hours a day. It'll only take a couple of hours to get there, and on the way we can continue this awesome conversation." He smiled at her.

"Well, I have to be at work tomorrow at eight."

"I'll have you back here in no time. You won't miss work, and you won't be late. Promise." He crossed his heart.

There was a pregnant pause before Destiny grabbed her purse. "Sure, why not."

Chapter Ten

Miami, FL

The truth of the matter was that Anatoly had business in Miami that couldn't wait. Vasily had informed him after his *run-in* with Renee that one of his transporters was in fact cutting into the Medlov money by not delivering all of their product to trusted clients. It didn't take a genius to know that this was a problem.

As soon as it had been confirmed, Anatoly had Vasily send word to the guy that he wanted a meeting this evening. Finding out about Destiny was just a way to kill two birds with one stone.

After they were loaded on the plane, Anatoly took it upon himself to entertain her. At first, she had been apprehensive about loading the jet with his entourage, but he had calmly explained them away. Plus, he knew that she wanted to go *deep* undercover. This was his way of helping her do that.

As soon as they reached Miami, they were escorted off the private airstrip into the back of a Mercedes and zipped away. Anatoly could tell that she hadn't been many places. Her eyes were glued to the window, much like he remembered Royal's when his father had taken her to New York. Only, his intentions were not so well-placed.

Three motorcycles led their small motorcade - one Land Rover traveled in front of them, one behind them. Quietly, he checked his Blackberry while they stylishly made their way through the city.

Destiny tried to keep her bearing, watching every move that he made with a pasted-on smile.

He finally sighed and looked up from his work.

"Are you enjoying yourself?" he asked, putting his phone away. There had not been one text from Renee, even though he had texted her twice.

"I'm speechless," she said, crossing her legs. "And you can do all of this as a small business owner?"

He looked at her and smiled. "*Da*."

"I need to start cooking Russian food then," she smirked. Playing with the tendrils of her hair in front of her face, she looked over at him and bit her lip. "What else do you do, Anatoly?"

"What else do you want me to do?" he asked back, running his hand over her exposed knee. "I can be just about anything you want me to be."

Destiny raised her brows and ran her hand over the console to open the windows. She needed some air. This man was suffocating her.

Anatoly stopped her. "Are you hot?" he asked adjusting his vents towards her.

"Sort of?"

"Turn up the air," he ordered to the driver as his voice rose. He turned to her and smiled. "Better to leave the windows up, *eh*."

Nodding, she took her hand off the console. "So where are we going again?"

"A fellow restaurant owner of mine owns the best place in Little Havana for good Cuban food. We're going to pay him a visit, and I'm going to set the bar for you in Cuban cuisine, just in case a Cuban restaurant ever did open in Memphis or you relocate."

The car stopped abruptly on Calle Ocho.

In front of a small restaurant hidden under huge yellow awnings and decorated with bright colors and palm trees, the mystery of Cuban cuisine awaited. Instantly, the doors were opened by Vasily and his men as they waited for the couple to get out.

"Here we are, *La Pequeña Habana,*" Anatoly said, stepping out and offering his hand to Destiny.

She looked up at him with greedy need. His blue eyes sparkled under the street light. He looked heavenly with his bold blonde locks and startling blue eyes. He smelled richer than any man she'd ever known and his firm hand felt masculine and safe with the softness of his fingers tickling her and the worn-down calluses of his strong grip bracing her.

Destiny could not deny herself the utter lavishness of the man's clandestine lifestyle. As she followed him inside the closed restaurant, she realized what it might have been like to really be his woman. Suddenly, being a cop didn't seem so exciting.

The white shuttered doors opened for them and they were greeted by two beautiful Cuban women in sundresses, who offered Anatoly several cigars on a platter.

Destiny took in the marvelous interior. The building was airy and exotic. Large ceiling fans rotated above up in the beams of vaulted ceilings. In corners were mini palm trees rooted in large, elaborate pots. Cuban music played on the stereo system, pictures of Cuba hung on the walls along with famous Cuban-Americans like Desi Arnaz, Nona Gaye, Andy Garcia, Cachao López and Oscar Hijuelos. In a nutshell, she felt as though she had stepped into a different world.

Dimmed receding lights cast a glow over the space and made the marble floors gleam, indicating their recent mopping. Each table was covered in white, crisp cloths and decorated with beautiful candle-lit lamps. Modern and vintage woodwork on the walls and bar gave it a truly Latin feel.

They were quickly escorted to a large booth covered with small appetizers and drinks. "After you," Anatoly said, allowing her to sit.

He sat across from her and took off his suit jacket to reveal rippled muscles under a soft, cotton t-shirt. Tattoos colored both of his arms and hands.

"Care if I smoke?" he asked as he thought of Victoria.

"No," Destiny said, looking around. "Is the placed closed on a Thursday night or something?"

Anatoly looked around. "Well, it's closed to the public for tonight." He winked at her. "But there is another party right over there." He motioned to the back, where a large, balding man in a white suit sat with three women surrounding him and bodyguards standing guard behind him.

"He looks *unsavory*," Destiny said, turning back around to Anatoly. "You know him?"

"No, but I know that he knows my father. I should probably go and say hello, *eh*?" He lit his cigar and took a puff. "In a minute." Looking at the fine tobacco, he shook his head. "There is nothing better than a good Cuban cigar."

She laughed. "Is that a real Cuban or is it made here at one of the local shops by a native Cuban?"

"It's straight from Old Havana," a man answered as he strode over.

Anatoly smiled. "Good to see you," he said with a grin. "This is my dear friend, Diego. The coolest Cuban Jew I know." He stood up and they embraced each other.

Diego was a short, stocky man who wore black dress pants and white button down. Deep tanned with a bright smile and pure white hair, he looked over at Destiny and gently smiled.

"How are you?" he asked, bowing. "I am Diego. And you are?"

"Destiny Palmer," she replied intrigued.

"Well, I hope that you enjoy my restaurant, Ms. Palmer. Are you here visiting Miami?"

"No, we're just here for dinner," Anatoly interjected.

Diego nodded and looked oddly at Anatoly. "Well, enjoy. I'm going to step out for just awhile, and I'll be back later. However, I did tell the cooking staff that you'd be back there to make up a special meal for your guests."

Anatoly smiled. "It's always good to have someone you can count on. Thank you, Diego."

"You're very welcome." He put his hand on the young man's shoulder before he departed. "Make sure to tell you father hello for me."

"I will," Anatoly said, sitting back down. "Now, where were we?" he asked Destiny, sticking his cigar back in his mouth. "Okay. I want you to taste a little bit of everything. Just sample it all, but not too much, because I don't want you too full before the main course."

Destiny laughed as she looked at all the food. "I'm supposed to *not* get full?"

"Exactly," he said as Vasily leaned into his ear to whisper something to him. He looked over at the fat man again and nodded. "Now, if you'd excuse me," he said, standing back up. "I'm going to the kitchen and do what I do best, and I'll be back in just a bit."

"Okay," she said, picking up her spoon to taste the *Moors and Christian* in the blue, porcelain bowl in front of her.

***

Within minutes, Anatoly appeared from the kitchen in a white apron carrying a platter of food. He stopped at the table in the back with the mystery man first.

The man looked up at Anatoly with surprise in his face. "It's good to see," the man said, waving away the women and bodyguards, who quickly dismissed themselves.

"It's good to see you too, *brat*." Anatoly set the platter down on the table and took a seat across from him. Sighing, he wiped his tired eyes. "So, how are you after the surgery?"

"Doing better. Thank you. The doctor said I had three bleeding ulcers. Plus, the heart isn't doing too well. I guess that I should consider losing a little weight, *eh*?" The man chuckled. Sweat poured down his shiny head.

Anatoly smirked. "I'm glad that you're doing better and that you're out of the house." Anatoly yawned. "So, after all of that, you're here with three young women drinking vodka and smoking cigars?"

The fat man laughed. "It is okay. I am stronger than the doctors know." He tapped his chest. "I am Vor, after all."

Anatoly nodded. "That you are." He looked at the platter. "Where are my manners? I fixed this for you." He took the silver tongs and placed the food on the man's plate. "My very own version of the Cuban tamale just for you."

Anatoly narrowed his eyes on him.

"Just for me?" the man asked, looking at the food strangely.

Anatoly smiled. "Funny story. We've been looking over the numbers for our good Anti-Castro friends who purchase a great deal of product from us for their cause. And one thing that we have noticed is that since we put you in charge, while the inventory has gone up, the revenue hasn't. Plus, a few of the shipments were light."

The man swallowed hard. But Anatoly continued in a light voice with a pleasant smile.

"I had a few people look into your purchases and income over the last year. It's seems that everyone is in a recession accept you."

"Now, wait just a minute, Anatoly. This is not what it seems."

Anatoly raised his hand. "Please, let me finish. From what we have discovered, you bought a beautiful new place in South Beach, two new Bentleys and a few new mistresses on our dime. Then there is the matter of your three children in private school and one away at boarding school."

"I'm sure that you'll also see that I have created new revenue streams in the last year to be able to do those things." He wiped the sweat from his brow.

"Well, the last shipment that we set up to transport with you was a fake. We paid you to send our product to us, and we painstakingly counted each piece of inventory to make sure that we were not

accusing a fellow brother of something that was not
true. And you know what? It was short."

The man tried to interrupt, but Anatoly put his
finger over his lip and motioned for him to be silent.
He continued in a low vice. "Obviously, we must
respect you, *brat*. Otherwise, I wouldn't be here.
And you know who I am. Don't you?"

"*Da*, you are Boss Medlov."

Anatoly smiled. "But who am I?"

"You are Czar."

Anatoly smiled sheepishly. In a whisper, he said
words with reverence. "I am Czar, which means that
I don't move a finger. But I have moved it for you.
And I am here with my date to dine with you even
though you have failed me."

The man sat up in his seat, dragging his chair as
he did so. "Tell me what I must do, and I will do it."

Anatoly pointed at his food. Then he placed a
tamale in front of the man. "I'll have just a few bites
here before I take them over to my date. Now, I just
want you to eat with me." Anatoly waved the smoke
rising from the food. "Smell that. It's amazing."

The man picked up his fork.

Anatoly watched. "I made yours very special."
He smiled. "It has specially bred, super hot, killer
Habanera with my three-alarm chili sauce."

Shaking the man put the fork back down.

Anatoly shook his head. "Do not offend me again
by denying a simple request to dine with me. Please
continue."

The man felt his food nearly leap to his throat. With the fork to his mouth, he eyed the young man, who sat back in his chair with his legs crossed. "I do not wish to go this way," he said solemnly.

"Well, you love to eat." Anatoly pointed at the man's heavy size. "You love to drink." Anatoly pointed at the large bottle of vodka. "You love to smoke." Anatoly pointed at the cigar. "It's only right that you go in style and reminded of the family that you tried to fuck and the people that you *surely* fucked with their shorted product. Look at it this way. You can die with or without a knife stuck in your abdomen. You can die rest assured that your family is still safe, and that you had one last meal. Or you can run home, and I can come for you later tonight with family sleeping."

The man put the fork to his mouth. The heat singed his lips.

Anatoly smiled. "You'll want to do that in big portions. Otherwise, I'm afraid it will be more tortuous than it has to be."

The man could barely swallow the hot tamale. He cringed. His eyes watered and steamed from the pepper. But bravely, he took another large bite. The pain consumed him. His own tongue boiled and blistered. Dropping the fork, he grabbed the side of the table coughed. Dark blood ran from the burned sides of his mouth.

"It doesn't pay to be greedy does it, *brat*? It's the very greed that has brought you down," he said with a smile.

Anatoly looked back to see Destiny obliviously sampling the appetizers with her back turned to them. He turned back quickly to the man and smiled. "One more bite for the road. I don't have all night."

The fat man gasped suddenly and grabbed his left side. Leaning back in the chair, eyes averted to the ceiling fan high in the rafters, he moaned, unable to talk due to his mouth burning on fire, then dropped his fork.

Anatoly moved his napkin and screamed. "Shit! Vasily, call 911. Igor is having heart attack!"

Destiny quickly turned from her food to see the man staring up in the air and holding his heart.

"Oh my goodness," she said, scooting from her chair. She quickly ran over to him, but Anatoly knew that Igor was already dead.

"Why is he bleeding?" Destiny asked, signaling for Vasily to help her get him on the ground.

"Ulcers," Anatoly answered. "He said that he could handle them. He eats this food all the time."

"Help me lay him down. Is someone on the phone with the 911?" Destiny screamed out.

"*Da*, the hostess is calling now," Vasily said, struggling to get the fat man on the ground. He looked up at his boss, who stood watching the entire event play out.

"What are you doing?" Anatoly asked, standing beside the body.

"Checking his heart." She placed her head on his chest. She could hear nothing. As she went to open his mouth, she saw the blood and winced away. The guy could have HIV. "He doesn't have a pulse."

"The ambulance is on the way," the hostess screamed, running from her podium. The other hostess stood petrified in place, staring at the dead man.

"I need to administer CPR," Destiny said, adjusting his head to clear his air waves. She put her finger to his neck to check once more for a pulse.

Anatoly smirked at how her mouth would burn, but he allowed her to try. She did so, mouth burning, lips on fire from the transfer of the pepper, until the paramedic arrived.

They announced Igor dead on site.

After he was bagged and loaded on to the ambulance, Anatoly walked back inside the restaurant and sat down at the booth across from Destiny.

"I just don't understand why a man would eat such deadly, hot peppers knowing that he had a heart condition," she said, applying cool, wet paper towels to her singed mouth.

"People just don't take their health seriously these days," Anatoly said, tasting the cold appetizers. He shook his head. "You did all that you could do, Destiny. And it was a lot more than we could have done. I don't even know CPR." He re-lit his cigar and had Vasily bring over his plate of tamales. Carefully, he stuck his knife into his and tasted it.

Savoring the taste, he continued, "You were my witness for goodness sake. You saw that the man just keeled over after eating his tamales. I'm sure that the autopsy will show that he must have been very ill to have a heart attack just like that." He snapped his fingers together. "Life is short."

Destiny looked up at him in disgust. "I want to leave," she said, grabbing her purse.

Anatoly nodded and tasted one more bite of his food. "Okay. I take you one more place, and then we're on the plane out of here before it gets too late."

"I want to go home now," she insisted.

Anatoly stood up and touched her bare shoulder. "Please, give me change. This is not my fault. Allow me to take you one more place, and then we can go. And if you never want to go on another date with me, I will understand." He looked over at his bodyguard. "Vasily, make sure that the car is out front. We're leaving." He turned to Destiny. "Do you want to take any of this to go?"

"No," she said emphatically. "I don't see how you can eat after a scene like that. The man had blood coming from his rectum."

"I have very strong stomach."

Chapter Eleven

South Beach, FL

Destiny had never been to South Beach, but she had seen countless shows on its upscale neighborhoods. Half an hour after trying to revive a dead gangster on a Cuban restaurant floor, she was being escorted through the private mansions of a South Beach community and silently asking herself why she had volunteered for this job.

She was sure that Agosto would be insane with anger when she returned, but she only hoped that he would also see that she was capable of going further than anyone had before her.

Hands clasped together, she looked out of the window as she debated how far she was willing to go. Harrison, her boyfriend, had been furious when she took the assignment, but in a way, this was his fault. He had gone undercover several times, and each time, he had been rewarded with promotion after promotion for a job well done. But because she was a woman, her department hardly ever put too much faith in what she could accomplish. She wanted more than anything to prove them wrong.

Anatoly looked over at her and smiled. "I'm taking you to party," he said smiling. "Something to cheer you up."

She looked over at him and tried to smile. "It's that apparent, huh?"

"Oh, yeah," he laughed. "But trust me. Where we're going, you're going to have fun—just you and me." He slipped his hand in hers.

When they arrived at the gated mansion on Michigan Avenue, luxury cars lined the street. Their car was parked in the garage, and they were escorted through the back of the house.

Beautiful women and attractive men danced, laughed and talked all around them. Each of them knew Anatoly. They hugged and kissed him, shook Destiny's hand and raised their drinks to salute them.

Anatoly kept his hand tightly around Destiny's in the crowd, shielding her from too much attention and letting everyone know that they were together. She actually felt safe with him, allowing herself to get closer, to move into his hard, muscular body.

"I feel underdressed," she whispered into his ear as they stood by the piano talking to a blonde couple from Australia.

"You look great," Anatoly said, touching her face. "Do you want something to drink?"

"Sure, what do they have?"

"What do *I* have?" he asked, correcting her.

"Is this your party?" she asked, looking around in shock.

"*Da*, this is my house," he said with a grin. "Come on. I'll take you upstairs on my private deck, and you and I can have drink."

He led her without Vasily up the long, white stairwell to his master bedroom.

Opening the door for her, he allowed her to walk in front of him. Then he flicked on the lights, illuminating the swank space as he closed the door behind him.

"Wow, impressive," she said, smiling. Turning towards him, she clasped her hands in front of her. "Is this where you try to take advantage of me?"

Anatoly walked over to his dresser drawer and pulled out a pack of cigarettes. Pulling the plastic from its rim top, he hit the bottom and wielded out a single cigarette. After he slipped one in his mouth, he extended his arm. "Want one?"

"No," she said, putting down her purse. I'll pass this time. Too much can kill you, you know."

"A lot of things in this world can kill you."

"Like..." she said, urging him to elaborate.

Anatoly shrugged his shoulders. "Hot Cuban food for one."

She laughed.

Going to the balcony, he slid the glass door open and stepped out into the night air. The gusts of strong wind blew through his locks. He turned to her and motioned for her to join him. Turning back to the view, he looked over the waterway and smelled the hint of rain lacing the air.

"It's so beautiful out here," she said, leaning against the rail.

"*Da*," Anatoly answered absently. It was hard for him to focus with his every thought returning to Renee.

Destiny turned to him. She could see the frown lines in his prefect face. He was somewhat of an enigma to her. Even though he was a cold-hearted killer and a guns dealer, he was also very kind and thoughtful. It was his duality that vexed her, than warmed and warned her at the same time.

"Is there something you want to talk about?" she asked softly.

"No," Anatoly said, putting his wall up. He put his hand in her hair and felt the soft, cotton tendrils in his hand. "I just want to have a good time. What about you? You up for it?"

"Umm," she said, closing her eyes as he massaged her head. "I could use a good time."

Reaching into his pocket with his other hand, he pulled out his phone and called someone.

"Vasily, bring up some absinthe for us," Anatoly said, winking at Destiny. He closed the phone and shoved it back into his dark jeans.

"Absinthe?" Destiny asked.

"You don't like the green fairy? My father owns a bottling plant of the shit right outside of Prague."

"It's illegal here," she said apprehensive.

There was a hard knock on the door – Vasily. Anatoly turned to her and gave a clever smirk.

"What are you, a cop? Name one piss test at your job that would test for the stuff? It's legal in half the UK. American's are slow, though you claim to be progressive. This is just one example of how you continue to fall behind the eight ball."

"Well, if we're so far behind, why are you here?" she asked offended.

"A patriot." Anatoly smirked.

Vasily brought in a beautiful, crystal reservoir filled half way with green liquid and a silver, absinthe spoon. Setting it on the table, he nodded towards his boss and left.

"Is he your bodyguard or your personal butler?" Destiny asked, following Anatoly back inside the room.

"He's Vasily," Anatoly said, offering her a seat across from his bed.

"So this liquor is supposed to do what?" she asked.

"Technically, it's not liquor. It's a spirit," he said, putting the absinthe spoon on the rim of a very elaborate glass. She watched as he put a cube of sugar on the spoon, then grabbed a pitcher of ice-cold water and slowly poured in on the cube and down into the glass.

Bending down, she watched the green liquid slowly *louche*. She looked up at him and smiled in wonderment. She'd never seen it up close.

When he finished, he tasted it first then passed the glass to her before he made himself a glass.

Common sense told Destiny to put the glass down, but the excited curiosity building in her stomach would not allow her. Sitting on the edge of the bed, she put her lips to the glass and slowly tilted it. The liquid numbed her lips, tingling the bottom one especially. Finally, she opened her mouth and allowed it to flood in.

Anatoly sat beside her. He fixed a much bigger glass and sipped it at first then tilted it up and swallowed it all in one big gulp.

She looked over at him and laughed, shrugging her shoulders at him.

"I feel funny," she said, moving her hair from her face.

"Let's have another, *eh*?" he said, going back to the table.

"I don't know if I should," Destiny protested.

"You only live once." He winked at her. "You really feel the effects after three. So, we'll drink three together, and then we'll go downstairs with the others."

Destiny pursed her lips together. A warm wave washed over her. Nodding, she took a deep breath. "Okay, but for everyone that I drink, you have to drink."

"Sounds good to me."

Chapter Twelve

Memphis, TN

The alarm blasted, bolting Destiny awake. Jumping up, she looked around and realized that she was in her own bed, back in Memphis. Fully dressed, she stood up and looked around. Her vision doubled, head pounded. Leaning against the wall, she put her hands on her face and wiped the make-up from her skin.

Ugh, she hated when she went to bed without washing her face. It always felt grimy the next day.

Flashes of the night before flickered in the back of her mind. The swimming pool. The people. The drinking. The sex...

"Oh my God!" she exclaimed, grabbing her heart. She had sex with Anatoly last night.

She made her way to the bathroom and turned on the faucet. Water flooded into her cupped hands. She splashed her face and suddenly remembered his hands on her breasts. His mouth on her vagina. His fingers inside her.

Swallowing hard, she turned off the water and looked at herself in the mirror. More flashes came. Waves of sex. Sex. Sex. Sex.

She could still smell him on her. He was deep down inside her. He was in her hair. He was under her nails. He was on her neck and her lips. She reeked of expensive cologne. Her body ached in the most intimate of places.

She couldn't bear to stare at herself a moment longer. Turning on the shower, she ripped off her clothes and put them in the garbage. It hadn't been rape. She remembered kissing him. She remembered pulling her dress off and walking into the pool. He had watched her and then joined her.

The music was blaring. Lights flashed out from the bare windows. People danced about, screamed and laughed. But his presence had drowned them out. In the water, naked and rock hard, he had kissed her, told her that he was lonely, told her that she was beautiful, told her that he was the boss. And that was when she had given in to him.

It was the heady combination of truth and lies, of power and seduction that had made her do it. And while the absinthe had numbed her from guilt, it had not numbed her from want. And she did want him.

They made love in the infinity pool, below a perfect sky, in the warm water illuminated by blue and white lights with the crowds of people inside, only kept at bay by the bodyguards, who turned their backs to give them privacy.

It had been the first time that she had made love in public, but he had made it perfect. She remembered floating in the warm water, nipples exposed and erect. Her legs were wrapped around his waist, his penis prodding against her. She remember curiously looking up to see the people on the second floor looking out of the window, watching in amusement.

She remembered realizing that she had gone too far, but with ever pump of her body, with ever lick of breasts, with every kiss, she found it harder to ask Anatoly to stop. Somewhere in between the heated sex and the absinthe, she forgot about the real world. The green fairy had made her forget about reality. She was in a dream.

With waves crashing against her body, and his strong arms gripping her, he had made her climax in the pool. By the end of their interlude, she was pushed against the side, crying in torment of the pleasure that he provided. She screamed aloud into his mouth as he kissed her, holding her hair in the tight grip of his hand. His blue eyes seemed a thousand miles away. He had finished himself, inside her. Hot seed pushed into her body and stopped at his latex guard. He had whispered naughty things to her. "I want to come inside of you without this damned thing," he had said. "If you stay, I will," he had promised. Her eyes were heavy, drowning in the very spirits that he had served her. So, he held her head up and spoke into her ear. "Destiny, did you come here to fulfill your name?"

Afterwards, he had carried her out of the pool in his strong arms, dressed her in a white robe and escorted her upstairs with the bodyguards pushing people out of their way as they went. They all looked on, sharing the knowledge of what had just happened. Suddenly, she had felt ashamed, and wished more than anything to be far away from them all. But he had assured her, "As long as you're honest with me, I'll protect you."

In the bedroom, he had rested beside her on the bed, holding her close with his rippling chest to her back. In a growl, he had reminded her of his promise.

"I have to get you home," he said, rubbing through her hair. "Unless you want to stay here forever. Miami's a nice place. You can start over here. Walk away from Memphis for good."

"And what am I supposed to do here?" she had asked, looking across the room at the patio door.

"You could write. You wrote all those stories in the magazine, didn't you?"

"Yeah," she smirked.

"Well, maybe, you could get a job working for a paper here. I could help you do that."

She had turned to him, looked him in his eyes and knew that *he knew* who she was.

Cover blown, she lamented. "I can't," she said, voice aching. "I have to go back. Face the music."

"You sure you want to do that? It won't be a pretty tune."

"Yeah, I'm sure."

He had nodded his head and got up from the bed. He was still naked. She looked at his tattoos, his stocky, taut frame. Her tired body shivered from the absinthe. He had pulled the covers over her to keep her warm.

He looked down at the carpet, shoulders slumped over, feeling rejected. "Well, thank you. I'm sure it won't seem like it by morning, but I enjoyed your company." With those words, he had disappeared into his bathroom, and she had fallen asleep.

The next thing she remembered, she woke up here.

The hot water from the showerhead ran over her face and wiped the invisible sin away. She soaped her body and pondered *what had he meant by his last statement*?

After a long shower, after the hot water had turned cold, she stepped out and dried her body off. Her cell phone had eight missed calls. Some were from her fiancé, some from Agosto. She dreaded both.

How would she hide what had happened? Maybe no one knew. *It will all make more sense once I've eaten,* she thought.

Once she was dressed, she dragged herself into the kitchen to fix breakfast. Her place seemed like a box now after spending a night with a mob boss.

Boom! Boom! Boom! A police knock on her door. She went to it reluctantly. Peering out of the peephole, she saw Agosto.

She opened the door slowly and moved out of the way to let him inside.

He walked briskly past her, his cologne lingering behind. "I've tried to call you a hundred damned times," he said gruffly.

"I know. I was sleep."

"Late night in Miami, huh?"

She looked up at him. "Yeah." Closing the door, she turned and folded her arms in front of her.

"You're off this case," he said, face red. He clenched his wide jaw and pulled his hands out of his pockets.

"If you could just let me explain..." she said, unable to look up at him.

"Explain how a video of you being fucked by a Russian mob boss is posted all over the internet? Explain how you've made a mockery of this department, of Harrison and of yourself. Explain that?"

Her mouth fell. "What?"

"Don't *what* me? There is a video of you at a party at Anatoly's house in South Beach being fucked by him in his pool. You appear lucid. You appear willing. And you appear to *enjoy* it."

Tears formed in her eyes.

Agosto shook his head. "I'm here to collect your badge and gun. You're on suspension. And investigation into your *entire life* is underway, though, you have to know that."

She shook her head, then walked into her bedroom and grabbed her badge and gun from the lock box under her bed.

With her knees planted on the floor, she began to cry. Now, she knew what Anatoly had meant by his last statement. He had set her up. He had ruined her life.

Agosto walked into the bedroom and leaned against the door. His tough exterior dropped. He shook his head, hating to see a woman cry. "Why'd you fuck up so bad?" he asked. In truth, he liked her. And he would have like to see a young woman like her take the Medlov men down.

"I don't know," she said, pulling her head up off her mattress. She looked at him. "I really don't know."

"Your career as a cop is over. I can't officially confirm it for you. The board will decide that, but I can tell you that I've *never* heard of anyone coming back from something like this."

"What should I do?"

Agosto took a stick of gum from his pocket and slipped into his mouth. "Quit," he said finally. "Focus on saving your relationship with your fiancé. Leave the city. Start over. Change your name, explain this to your parents before someone else does. I could go on."

"You're not the first one to tell me that," she said, wiping the tears from her face.

"Yeah, well, you probably should have taken *his* advice." He walked over and took the gun and badge from her. "Don't do anything stupid," he said, putting the badge in his pocket. "Don't go see Anatoly; don't kill yourself; don't fuck up anymore than you already have. Your next move will come to you. But you've got to wait for it. Plus, there is still Harrison to deal with. The boys say he's really taking it hard. Not that I could blame him. I had a fiancé once." He reached out and touched her face. "It isn't the end of the world, just the end of your career."

"Easy for you to say," she stood up. "You're still Agosto."

"Always will be. Now, I gotta get out of here. So, take care of yourself. I'll see you at the review board." With that, he rubbed her shoulder and left. The front door slammed behind him.

***

Destiny's video had already received over 200,000 hits. The guy he had paid to record it from the upstairs balcony got some really great shots. There was nothing traceable back to him. The entire thing had played out in a semi-public place. She was willing; he was able. Plus, he'd offered her a new start. It was her fault for not accepting it.

Anatoly clicked his computer off and turned around his chair. His father was on the phone cursing him out. He sat quietly and listened as the old man berated him for his stunt last night.

"I bet you think this was smart, eh?" Dmitry asked, looking at his own computer in disgust.

"I got her out of way, like I told you I would."

"You were seen screwing a cop. This family has no contact with cops."

"Papa, you have a hundred cops on your payroll," Anatoly defended.

"Name the last time you saw me fucking one."

There was silence on the phone.

"Well, she's out of the way," Anatoly said, running his thumb and index finger over the sides of his mouth. "Now, I just have to find the leak. And I already know who it is."

"Victoria," Dmitry said as more of an answer than a question.

"Yeah," Anatoly sighed. "I should have handled her when I first had a chance.

"Victoria is my problem. I should have handled her that night here in my house. I was weak. I'll fix it," Dmitry growled.

"I want to be there."

"Fine. You and your cousin will meet me in Italy in three days at my winery. We'll leave there and come back here to finish the rest of our business."

"I don't trust Gabriel. Something about him isn't right."

"Well, that is our purpose for inviting him to Italy. If he's not who he says he is, he'll be very shaken up after his visit. It will be apparent."

"I'm sorry that I fucked up, papa."

"You are young. I'm sure in that head of yours, you thought that you were doing something exemplary, but I can assure you that such brazen contact with police will only land you in more confusion. Let this be lesson to you to trust no one who is not Vor. And then trust only certain Vor. Keep the code, Anatoly. Keep the lines clear. Stay on your side *always*. No more screwing police women, *da*."

"*Da*," Anatoly answered.

"By the way, you fuck like school boy. Put more thrust into your hips for *her* pleasure next time. It is not *always* about you." His voice was lighter.

Anatoly smiled. He knew his father had already forgiven him. Maybe he was even a little jealous that he had never thought of something so clever.

"I'll remember that, papa."

Hanging up the phone, Anatoly looked over at Vasily. He clasped his fingers together and cleared his throat. "We go to Italy in three days. Arrange it. Have you found out any more on Gabriel Medlov?"

"Information is being collected. So far, everything checks out."

"Keep looking. I want something before I arrive in Italy."

***

Anatoly couldn't help himself. He had to see her. Pulling up to *Dmitry's Closet*, he turned off his motorcycle and went inside. Renee was behind the counter ringing someone up. She looked over at him and rolled her eyes.

He knew that look. She was still pissed. Pointing towards the back office, he motioned for her to meet him.

She did so quickly.

"What do you want?" she asked, closing the door behind her.

He loved when she wore her hair down. Walking up to her, he tried to touch her face, but she pulled away.

"Have you given any thought to staying longer?" he asked.

"Ana, I already told you," she said sighing. "I gotta get out of here."

"Give me some time, please. I need you." He pulled her face in his hands. "How can you deny your Ana?"

She smirked. "One-month notice. Then I'm gone."

He sighed. "Thank you." Wrapping his arms around her, he hugged her tight.

"What's wrong with you today? You're all touchy," she said, tapping his back. She pulled away. Her heart began to beat fast, but she tried hard to conceal it.

"Nothing is wrong," he said shortly.

"Don't lie to me."

"Something *is* wrong, but I don't want to talk about it. I was hoping we could go to lunch."

"Okay." She grabbed her purse. Her hair fell over her shoulder as she leaned into the desk.

Anatoly's gaze trailed up her short legs to her wide hips. He had just been with Destiny, but the entire time, he had been thinking of Renee.

She caught him looking and rolled her eyes. "Stop looking at me like that," she said, standing back up.

"Stopping bending over like that," he said, walking to the back door. "We can walk over, unless you want to ride on my bike."

"You know I don't like bikes," she answered, walking past him.

The sun was bright and warmed their skin as they walked side-by-side through the busy streets of downtown Memphis over to *Mother Russia*. Anatoly felt at ease once more. Just to be near her was all the relaxation he needed to get on with his day.

As usual, Renee had tons to talk about, but nothing to do with illegal transactions or hits. She talked about the eccentric customers, how her baby sister was doing at Clarke University and where she wanted to vacation next year.

He looked over at her in awe. Her life was so simple, yet so perfect. He often thought of what it would be like to be with someone like her. She was grounded, loving, caring...or as she often put it, "I'm real."

"Are you listening to me?" she asked as they made it to the front of Mother Russia.

"*Da, da*," he said, opening the door for her.

"Then what did I just say?"

"You want to go to Jamaica."

She smirked. He *had* been listening.

"I have a small place in Jamaica," he said proudly.

"You have a small place everywhere." As usual, she was not impressed. "And I want to go with my sisters and cousins. They're renting a place."

"Why would you want to spend money..."

As he was about to step inside behind Renee, he heard a familiar voice scream his name. He turned to see Destiny coming towards him. In a pair of jeans and a red tank top, no bra, breasts swinging, she called out to him, nearly running down the street.

"Who in the hell is that?" Renee asked, turning around to look out of the door.

He put his hand on the small of her back, "Go inside," he said, motioning towards Vasily. "I'll be right there."

Anatoly turned around and walked towards Destiny once he was sure Renee was out of sight. Slowly, he felt for his gun. He had to expect the worst considering what he had done to her.

"How could you?" she asked with tears in her eyes.

"I told you to stay in Miami. I offered you a new life. You didn't take it. That's not my fault."

She reached back to slap him in his face, but he instinctively caught her hand and pushed her against the brick wall of the neighboring building. People walked by quickly, trying to avoid the two. He pushed up against her and stared her in her eyes.

"You fucking bastard! I'll get you, if it's the last thing I do." Tears ran down her face.

"Sure you want to do that?" he asked, brow raised. "I could have killed you, fed you to my dogs. I could have cut your throat. I could have had your family killed. I could have served you up and fed you to your boyfriend, Harrison. I could have sold you to some drug dealer in Cuba. He could have turned you into a whore on the streets of Old Havana."

Her breath caught in her chest.

Anatoly's eyes were cold and empty. "I could have done a thousand things to you that would have left you none existent, except in memory - and not even in my own because I don't care to think of you. *But instead*, I screwed you. If you ask me, you got off easy. And you did get off," he said, trailing his hand down her breast. "Didn't you? It's so sweet, too."

She pushed away from him, rubbing her head that had been banged against the hard wall. "I hate you. I hate everything that you stand for!"

"Hate me?" Anatoly smirked. "I was honest with you. You knew who I was before you ever bothered. You came into my life. You knocked on my door." He pointed at her. "You asked for it. And you got what you deserved." His voice was low and menacing.

Vasily walked up behind them. "Is there a problem boss?" he asked, looking at Destiny.

"Destiny was just leaving," Anatoly said, never taking his gaze from her. "But if she ever comes back, kill her on sight. Wipe it under the rug. I don't even what to know about it." He wiped his face and smiled at her. "Fuck you, cop."

Chapter Thirteen

Memphis, TN

The alarm blasted, bolting Destiny awake. Jumping up, she looked around and realized that she was in her own bed, back in Memphis. Fully dressed, she stood up and looked around. Her vision doubled, head pounded. Leaning against the wall, she put her hands on her face and wiped the make-up from her skin.

Ugh, she hated when she went to bed without washing her face. It always felt grimy the next day.

Flashes of the night before flickered in the back of her mind. The swimming pool. The people. The drinking. The sex...

"Oh my God!" she exclaimed, grabbing her heart. She had sex with Anatoly last night.

She made her way to the bathroom and turned on the faucet. Water flooded into her cupped hands. She splashed her face and suddenly remembered his hands on her breasts. His mouth on her vagina. His fingers inside her.

Swallowing hard, she turned off the water and looked at herself in the mirror. More flashes came. Waves of sex. Sex. Sex. Sex.

She could still smell him on her. He was deep down inside her. He was in her hair. He was under her nails. He was on her neck and her lips. She reeked of expensive cologne. Her body ached in the most intimate of places.

She couldn't bear to stare at herself a moment longer. Turning on the shower, she ripped off her clothes and put them in the garbage. It hadn't been rape. She remembered kissing him. She remembered pulling her dress off and walking into the pool. He had watched her and then joined her.

The music was blaring. Lights flashed out from the bare windows. People danced about, screamed and laughed. But his presence had drowned them out. In the water, naked and rock hard, he had kissed her, told her that he was lonely, told her that she was beautiful, told her that he was the boss. And that was when she had given in to him.

It was the heady combination of truth and lies, of power and seduction that had made her do it. And while the absinthe had numbed her from guilt, it had not numbed her from want. And she did want him.

They made love in the infinity pool, below a perfect sky, in the warm water illuminated by blue and white lights with the crowds of people inside, only kept at bay by the bodyguards, who turned their backs to give them privacy.

It had been the first time that she had made love in public, but he had made it perfect. She remembered floating in the warm water, nipples exposed and erect. Her legs were wrapped around his waist, his penis prodding against her. She remember curiously looking up to see the people on the second floor looking out of the window, watching in amusement.

She remembered realizing that she had gone too far, but with ever pump of her body, with ever lick of breasts, with every kiss, she found it harder to ask Anatoly to stop. Somewhere in between the heated sex and the absinthe, she forgot about the real world. The green fairy had made her forget about reality. She was in a dream.

With waves crashing against her body, and his strong arms gripping her, he had made her climax in the pool. By the end of their interlude, she was pushed against the side, crying in torment of the pleasure that he provided. She screamed aloud into his mouth as he kissed her, holding her hair in the tight grip of his hand. His blue eyes seemed a thousand miles away. He had finished himself, inside her. Hot seed pushed into her body and stopped at his latex guard. He had whispered naughty things to her. "I want to come inside of you without this damned thing," he had said. "If you stay, I will," he had promised. Her eyes were heavy, drowning in the very spirits that he had served her. So, he held her head up and spoke into her ear. "Destiny, did you come here to fulfill your name?"

Afterwards, he had carried her out of the pool in his strong arms, dressed her in a white robe and escorted her upstairs with the bodyguards pushing people out of their way as they went. They all looked on, sharing the knowledge of what had just happened. Suddenly, she had felt ashamed, and wished more than anything to be far away from them all. But he had assured her, "As long as you're honest with me, I'll protect you."

In the bedroom, he had rested beside her on the bed, holding her close with his rippling chest to her back. In a growl, he had reminded her of his promise.

"I have to get you home," he said, rubbing through her hair. "Unless you want to stay here forever. Miami's a nice place. You can start over here. Walk away from Memphis for good."

"And what am I supposed to do here?" she had asked, looking across the room at the patio door.

"You could write. You wrote all those stories in the magazine, didn't you?"

"Yeah," she smirked.

"Well, maybe, you could get a job working for a paper here. I could help you do that."

She had turned to him, looked him in his eyes and knew that *he knew* who she was.

Cover blown, she lamented. "I can't," she said, voice aching. "I have to go back. Face the music."

"You sure you want to do that? It won't be a pretty tune."

"Yeah, I'm sure."

He had nodded his head and got up from the bed. He was still naked. She looked at his tattoos, his stocky, taut frame. Her tired body shivered from the absinthe. He had pulled the covers over her to keep her warm.

He looked down at the carpet, shoulders slumped over, feeling rejected. "Well, thank you. I'm sure it won't seem like it by morning, but I enjoyed your company." With those words, he had disappeared into his bathroom, and she had fallen asleep.

The next thing she remembered, she woke up here.

The hot water from the showerhead ran over her face and wiped the invisible sin away. She soaped her body and pondered *what had he meant by his last statement?*

After a long shower, after the hot water had turned cold, she stepped out and dried her body off. Her cell phone had eight missed calls. Some were from her fiancé, some from Agosto. She dreaded both.

How would she hide what had happened? Maybe no one knew. *It will all make more sense once I've eaten,* she thought.

Once she was dressed, she dragged herself into the kitchen to fix breakfast. Her place seemed like a box now after spending a night with a mob boss.

Boom! Boom! Boom! A police knock on her door. She went to it reluctantly. Peering out of the peephole, she saw Agosto.

She opened the door slowly and moved out of the way to let him inside.

He walked briskly past her, his cologne lingering behind. "I've tried to call you a hundred damned times," he said gruffly.

"I know. I was sleep."

"Late night in Miami, huh?"

She looked up at him. "Yeah." Closing the door, she turned and folded her arms in front of her.

"You're off this case," he said, face red. He clenched his wide jaw and pulled his hands out of his pockets.

"If you could just let me explain..." she said, unable to look up at him.

"Explain how a video of you being fucked by a Russian mob boss is posted all over the internet? Explain how you've made a mockery of this department, of Harrison and of yourself. Explain that?"

Her mouth fell. "What?"

"Don't *what* me? There is a video of you at a party at Anatoly's house in South Beach being fucked by him in his pool. You appear lucid. You appear willing. And you appear to *enjoy* it."

Tears formed in her eyes.

Agosto shook his head. "I'm here to collect your badge and gun. You're on suspension. And investigation into your *entire life* is underway, though, you have to know that."

She shook her head, then walked into her bedroom and grabbed her badge and gun from the lock box under her bed.

With her knees planted on the floor, she began to cry. Now, she knew what Anatoly had meant by his last statement. He had set her up. He had ruined her life.

Agosto walked into the bedroom and leaned against the door. His tough exterior dropped. He shook his head, hating to see a woman cry. "Why'd you fuck up so bad?" he asked. In truth, he liked her. And he would have like to see a young woman like her take the Medlov men down.

"I don't know," she said, pulling her head up off her mattress. She looked at him. "I really don't know."

"Your career as a cop is over. I can't officially confirm it for you. The board will decide that, but I can tell you that I've *never* heard of anyone coming back from something like this."

"What should I do?"

Agosto took a stick of gum from his pocket and slipped into his mouth. "Quit," he said finally. "Focus on saving your relationship with your fiancé. Leave the city. Start over. Change your name, explain this to your parents before someone else does. I could go on."

"You're not the first one to tell me that," she said, wiping the tears from her face.

"Yeah, well, you probably should have taken *his* advice." He walked over and took the gun and badge from her. "Don't do anything stupid," he said, putting the badge in his pocket. "Don't go see Anatoly; don't kill yourself; don't fuck up anymore than you already have. Your next move will come to you. But you've got to wait for it. Plus, there is still Harrison to deal with. The boys say he's really taking it hard. Not that I could blame him. I had a fiancé once." He reached out and touched her face. "It isn't the end of the world, just the end of your career."

"Easy for you to say," she stood up. "You're still Agosto."

"Always will be. Now, I gotta get out of here. So, take care of yourself. I'll see you at the review board." With that, he rubbed her shoulder and left. The front door slammed behind him.

***

Destiny's video had already received over 200,000 hits. The guy he had paid to record it from the upstairs balcony got some really great shots. There was nothing traceable back to him. The entire thing had played out in a semi-public place. She was willing; he was able. Plus, he'd offered her a new start. It was her fault for not accepting it.

Anatoly clicked his computer off and turned around his chair. His father was on the phone cursing him out. He sat quietly and listened as the old man berated him for his stunt last night.

"I bet you think this was smart, eh?" Dmitry asked, looking at his own computer in disgust.

"I got her out of way, like I told you I would."

"You were seen screwing a cop. This family has no contact with cops."

"Papa, you have a hundred cops on your payroll," Anatoly defended.

"Name the last time you saw me fucking one."

There was silence on the phone.

"Well, she's out of the way," Anatoly said, running his thumb and index finger over the sides of his mouth. "Now, I just have to find the leak. And I already know who it is."

"Victoria," Dmitry said as more of an answer than a question.

"Yeah," Anatoly sighed. "I should have handled her when I first had a chance.

"Victoria is my problem. I should have handled her that night here in my house. I was weak. I'll fix it," Dmitry growled.

"I want to be there."

"Fine. You and your cousin will meet me in Italy in three days at my winery. We'll leave there and come back here to finish the rest of our business."

"I don't trust Gabriel. Something about him isn't right."

"Well, that is our purpose for inviting him to Italy. If he's not who he says he is, he'll be very shaken up after his visit. It will be apparent."

"I'm sorry that I fucked up, papa."

"You are young. I'm sure in that head of yours, you thought that you were doing something exemplary, but I can assure you that such brazen contact with police will only land you in more confusion. Let this be lesson to you to trust no one who is not Vor. And then trust only certain Vor. Keep the code, Anatoly. Keep the lines clear. Stay on your side *always*. No more screwing police women, *da*."

"*Da*," Anatoly answered.

"By the way, you fuck like school boy. Put more thrust into your hips for *her* pleasure next time. It is not *always* about you." His voice was lighter.

Anatoly smiled. He knew his father had already forgiven him. Maybe he was even a little jealous that he had never thought of something so clever.

"I'll remember that, papa."

Hanging up the phone, Anatoly looked over at Vasily. He clasped his fingers together and cleared his throat. "We go to Italy in three days. Arrange it. Have you found out any more on Gabriel Mcdlov?"

"Information is being collected. So far, everything checks out."

"Keep looking. I want something before I arrive in Italy."

***

Anatoly couldn't help himself. He had to see her. Pulling up to *Dmitry's Closet*, he turned off his motorcycle and went inside. Renee was behind the counter ringing someone up. She looked over at him and rolled her eyes.

He knew that look. She was still pissed. Pointing towards the back office, he motioned for her to meet him.

She did so quickly.

"What do you want?" she asked, closing the door behind her.

He loved when she wore her hair down. Walking up to her, he tried to touch her face, but she pulled away.

"Have you given any thought to staying longer?" he asked.

"Ana, I already told you," she said sighing. "I gotta get out of here."

"Give me some time, please. I need you." He pulled her face in his hands. "How can you deny your Ana?"

She smirked. "One-month notice. Then I'm gone."

He sighed. "Thank you." Wrapping his arms around her, he hugged her tight.

"What's wrong with you today? You're all touchy," she said, tapping his back. She pulled away. Her heart began to beat fast, but she tried hard to conceal it.

"Nothing is wrong," he said shortly.

"Don't lie to me."

"Something *is* wrong, but I don't want to talk about it. I was hoping we could go to lunch."

"Okay." She grabbed her purse. Her hair fell over her shoulder as she leaned into the desk.

Anatoly's gaze trailed up her short legs to her wide hips. He had just been with Destiny, but the entire time, he had been thinking of Renee.

She caught him looking and rolled her eyes. "Stop looking at me like that," she said, standing back up.

"Stopping bending over like that," he said, walking to the back door. "We can walk over, unless you want to ride on my bike."

"You know I don't like bikes," she answered, walking past him.

The sun was bright and warmed their skin as they walked side-by-side through the busy streets of downtown Memphis over to *Mother Russia*. Anatoly felt at ease once more. Just to be near her was all the relaxation he needed to get on with his day.

As usual, Renee had tons to talk about, but nothing to do with illegal transactions or hits. She talked about the eccentric customers, how her baby sister was doing at Clarke University and where she wanted to vacation next year.

He looked over at her in awe. Her life was so simple, yet so perfect. He often thought of what it would be like to be with someone like her. She was grounded, loving, caring...or as she often put it, "I'm real."

"Are you listening to me?" she asked as they made it to the front of Mother Russia.

"*Da, da*," he said, opening the door for her.

"Then what did I just say?"

"You want to go to Jamaica."

She smirked. He *had* been listening.

"I have a small place in Jamaica," he said proudly.

"You have a small place everywhere." As usual, she was not impressed. "And I want to go with my sisters and cousins. They're renting a place."

"Why would you want to spend money..."

As he was about to step inside behind Renee, he heard a familiar voice scream his name. He turned to see Destiny coming towards him. In a pair of jeans and a red tank top, no bra, breasts swinging, she called out to him, nearly running down the street.

"Who in the hell is that?" Renee asked, turning around to look out of the door.

He put his hand on the small of her back, "Go inside," he said, motioning towards Vasily. "I'll be right there."

Anatoly turned around and walked towards Destiny once he was sure Renee was out of sight. Slowly, he felt for his gun. He had to expect the worst considering what he had done to her.

"How could you?" she asked with tears in her eyes.

"I told you to stay in Miami. I offered you a new life. You didn't take it. That's not my fault."

She reached back to slap him in his face, but he instinctively caught her hand and pushed her against the brick wall of the neighboring building. People walked by quickly, trying to avoid the two. He pushed up against her and stared her in her eyes.

"You fucking bastard! I'll get you, if it's the last thing I do." Tears ran down her face.

"Sure you want to do that?" he asked, brow raised. "I could have killed you, fed you to my dogs. I could have cut your throat. I could have had your family killed. I could have served you up and fed you to your boyfriend, Harrison. I could have sold you to some drug dealer in Cuba. He could have turned you into a whore on the streets of Old Havana."

Her breath caught in her chest.

Anatoly's eyes were cold and empty. "I could have done a thousand things to you that would have left you none existent, except in memory - and not even in my own because I don't care to think of you. *But instead*, I screwed you. If you ask me, you got off easy. And you did get off," he said, trailing his hand down her breast. "Didn't you? It's so sweet, too."

She pushed away from him, rubbing her head that had been banged against the hard wall. "I hate you. I hate everything that you stand for!"

"Hate me?" Anatoly smirked. "I was honest with you. You knew who I was before you ever bothered. You came into my life. You knocked on my door." He pointed at her. "You asked for it. And you got what you deserved." His voice was low and menacing.

Vasily walked up behind them. "Is there a problem boss?" he asked, looking at Destiny.

"Destiny was just leaving," Anatoly said, never taking his gaze from her. "But if she ever comes back, kill her on sight. Wipe it under the rug. I don't even what to know about it." He wiped his face and smiled at her. "Fuck you, cop."

Chapter Fourteen

Tuscany, Italy

The hills of Italy reminded Gabriel of the paintings he'd seen in expensive hotel rooms. He tried not to outwardly gawk at God's beauty as he was escorted from the private airstrip to Dmitry's wine estate, but it was hard to resist. With the sun slowly setting against the beautiful slopes of preserved land, the green and blue hues dancing right below the yellow-gold haze, he felt amazingly relaxed.

It was quite the contrary to what he had felt when he first got off the jet. He had been summons alone. His men were forbidden to attend, and he had the distinct feeling that this was a set up. Still, he had come. Things had gone much too far now, he was in too deep.

Word had traveled through the grapevine that Anatoly had uncovered an undercover last week. Her fate had been the destruction of her career and her name, still he had seen worse. In fact, he knew that the Medlov men would do a great deal worse to him, if they found out who he really was.

But Gabriel had to do this. He had to know from the inside why everything in his life had happened the way that it had. It wasn't just his father who had hated Dmitry. It had also been his mother, a militant woman whom had been cut out of her family estate because of his uncle Dmitry only a couple of years after he had been born. His entire life was a puzzle. The only way that he could make any sense of it was to finish this.

***

Anatoly pulled into the Medlov wine estate on his bike. He had arrived the day before and decided to do a little sightseeing. *In actuality, he had tried to stay as far away from Victoria as possible.*

When he got Italy the night before, his father had not arrived yet. The wicked side of him told him to go and get one last screw out of *her* before she was ended, but his father's voice in the back of his head forbade him from such a thing. Instead, he had ordered Vasily to make sure he had no visitors and stayed on the left-upper wing of the castle.

Now, the men were getting ready to convene. Only this was not a Medlov Organized Crime Family meeting, this was a Medlov family meeting. There was a distinct difference, and in his opinion, these were normally more dangerous.

The butler opened the door for him as he climbed the steps to his father's place. Taking off his helmet and leather coat, he passed them to the butler dismissively and headed up to his room to shower. He knew that on the right-lower wing, his cousin was getting ready. On the right-upper wing *that bitch*

Victoria was getting ready. And on the left-lower wing, his father was already ready for all of them.

The oak door closed behind him as he stormed into his room. Thoughts of Renee were consuming him. Since his arrival in Italy, the only thing that he could focus on was love. He questioned if he really was *in love* or if he was in lust. He questioned if she truly loved him or if she was simply enamored. Still, there were many things about Renee that he knew he would never find in any other woman.

Her honesty amazed him. Her cleverness consumed him. Her sexiness ignited him. Yet, he pondered why now? She had been in his life very intimately since his family had relocated. Considering that he was not exactly a holy man, she was his conscience. When he felt that he was truly in mental peril, she was there. When he was starving, she would cook him a hot meal. When he was hurting, she lovingly gave him a massage. When...when...when.

Throwing himself in the middle of the bed, he kicked off his shoes and comfortably rested his head back on the pillow. As he looked up at the ceiling, his mind drifted off to Memphis. He couldn't believe that she was actually leaving after all of the time that they spent together. What the hell would she do in Atlanta without him? Who would pay her like he would? Who would be there to need her like he did? And if she did find someone to console, to love, how long did she actually expect him to allow the *sonofa-bitch* to stay alive?

His new affinity for black women confused him tremendously. He had always been attracted to beautiful blondes, brunettes – not so much redheads. But he had never realized in the past that he had a thing for black women.

Then it hit him. He sat up in bed as the epiphany clanged about in his brain. Maybe the thing with Victoria and Destiny had nothing to do with their color. Maybe he was trying to find someone to *be* Renee. Both women were darker skinned. Both were outspoken. But neither had a thing on the southern belle who clouded his thoughts with fried chicken and long laughs.

"I can't believe I'm in Italy with a million beautiful women, and I'm thinking about you," he said aloud of Renee. He growled. *Great, now he was talking to himself too.*

He got out of bed and made his way to the shower. Stripping out of each layer of clothes, he jumped in the shower. It was a slow countdown before he had to see *her* again.

***

Dmitry was in a sour mood. He sat in his bed chambers looking over Victoria's phone records and reading his newspaper under his gold wire-rimmed glasses while classical music played in the background.

He didn't desire to be here tonight. He should have been at home with his wife. Royal was moving along with the pregnancy, and he had promised that he'd be there every step of the way this time. Yet, here he was, dealing with something that he should have taken care of many moons ago.

The maid knocked on the door and brought in a tray of food. Setting it on the table by his chair, she nodded his way.

"Would you like for me to close the windows?" she asked softly.

Dmitry barely looked up from his paper. "No," he said, turning the page. "I like the fresh air."

"The Tuscan winds in the spring can be quite powerful, sir. They tend to blow through and disrupt things."

Dmitry glanced up at her and uncrossed his long legs. "Thank you for your kind observation. Tell me, Sophia, how many are on staff tonight?"

"Ten of us," she said, glancing away from his beautiful gaze. He always made her nervous.

Dmitry pulled off his glasses and put them to his lips. "After we have dinner, please let everyone know that they are off until tomorrow after I have left. I'd like to be alone."

"Of course, Mr. Medlov," she said, bowing and departing quickly.

When she had gone, he quickly resumed reading the paper and waiting for his son to come and collect him. He knew that everyone had already arrived.

Anatoly. Gabriel. His special guest was in the adjoining bedroom, but he would not unveil her until much later.

Smirking a little, he glanced over to the door. He really wished his son would move into his role completely of boss. He was growing tired of having to be one step ahead of everyone.   There was another knock at the main door. He put down his glasses and newspaper, and then ordered it open. *Revolving*, he thought to himself.

"Come in," he said, reaching to pull his small leather satchel closer to him.

Victoria eased the door open. Wide-eyed, she came in with a faint smile. Dmitry still made her terribly uncomfortable. He was always direct now, with harsh judging looks and calculating eyes.

"Sir, you told me to come to see you before dinner."

"Yes. Please, close the door," he said, motioning for her to come and sit across from him.

She sat down, smoothing her pants out as she rested back in the leather chair. Her gaze was locked on his blue prisms.

"I need you to do something," Dmitry explained, pulling the leather satchel to his lap. "My nephew, Gabriel, will be dining with us tonight. I need you to help me test him."

"Alright," she said, sitting up straighter.

Dmitry pulled a gun from his bag. Smiling, he pulled the empty magazine from its bottom. "It's my trusted Glock," he said in a low, soothing voice. "It's empty. See." He pulled back the chamber, showing nothing was inside.

"Okay," she said, heaving out a deep breath.

"I want you to smuggle this into dinner for me. And my reason for this is that I want you to know the entire time that it's empty. When I signal you, I want you to pass me the gun. So, you'll need to sit beside me."

"Won't that be awkward with Anatoly?" she asked.

Dmitry nodded. "I need you to put aside your issues for a minute, and do as I ask. Can you?"

"Of course," she said, nodding her head.

"Good." Dmitry's voice boomed. "Now, I'm going to place the gun on the table and ask him to shoot you. I want to test his obedience to this family. And the reason that I'm giving you the gun is to ensure your safety during this test. You'll be com-pletely confident that it's empty if you have it the entire time."

"And if he doesn't shoot me?" she asked con-fused.

"Then he is *not* obedient," Dmitry answered. "And I will be very disappointed in him." He lo-wered his eyes at her.

She swallowed hard. "Okay. Then what?"

"Nothing. If he does as he is asked, then he will be rewarded later. I just need to know if I can trust this man. Obviously, you know that we are a very close-knit family. And considering what we do, we need to make sure that the people within our circle can be trusted. If not, we must root them out like weeds in a garden." His glare was icy.

"I understand," she said, taking the gun. "I'll do it." Smiling, she stood up.

"Keep it hidden for me, Victoria. Don't let anyone know that you have it."

"I won't," she assured.

When she had gone, Dmitry sat back in his chair and looked over at the fireplace. His eyes were fixed on the embers.

"Hell hath no fury like a woman scorned," he said aloud.

***

Dinner outside under the Tuscan sun was as close to God as Gabriel had ever been. He sat at the four-party table covered in Italian foods, wind blowing through the clean, fresh air and enjoyed a candle-lit dinner with his family.

Everyone laughed and drank the wine that Dmitry's estate was currently harvesting while Dmitry told an interesting story from his youth.

Looking around, he caught Anatoly staring at him. His gaze had not changed. It was full of angry malevolence, and he appeared to be continuously grinding his teeth, although his uncle had told him before dinner that there were matters excluding him that had created Anatoly's angst. "The woman," Dmitry had whispered in his ear. "The woman is

Anatoly's first brush with love. He's still bitter from it."

So Gabriel hoped that this was the case, because to be at the receiving end of the young man's scowl was to be truly unlucky this evening.

Dmitry, in his normal elegant style, carried a glass of wine in one hand and a conversation on with the other. Relaxed back in his chair with his legs crossed and his wire-rimmed glasses low on his nose, he talked and talked, making merriment with everyone.

"Which brings me to this point," Dmitry said, setting down his glass. "Young men such as you must learn blind obedience." He looked around the table, pointing at both Anatoly and Gabriel.

They both looked on wondering what new lesson they would be responsible for learning tonight.

"Blind obedience," Dmitry said again. This time he lifted a chrome-plated Glock from his side and placed it on the table.

Gabriel's heart nearly stopped. He looked down at the gun, then back up at his uncle, unsure if his cover had already been blown. If that were the case, then he was truly unfortunate. He didn't even get a chance to further his investigation for the agency or for himself.

Anatoly smirked. His eyes were now focused on the woman across from him. Victoria. The beautiful black woman whom Gabriel had read a great deal about in the many files the agency had on her. She looked back at Anatoly with daggers in her own eyes.

There was not one flinch in her demeanor towards the young Czar. It was as if she outwardly challenged him.

Dmitry raised his brow. His smile was uncanny and sent a shiver down Gabriel's spine. The man was like liquid sin, and in that he reminded him immensely of his dead father.

"What do you know of this?" Dmitry asked Gabriel.

"Excuse me?" Gabriel asked, sitting back as far as he could in his seat.

"What do you know of blind obedience?" Dmitry asked again.

"Obedience is a necessity. It is the thing that allows men to build empires," Gabriel answered.

"But what of that special brand of obedience. What do you know of *that*? Better yet," Dmitry said, putting his index finger to his lips. "When have you given such a thing to another man?"

"I don't recall ever doing such a thing," Gabriel answered.

"Not even your father?" Anatoly asked amused.

"No," Gabriel answered, turning his gaze from his uncle to his cousin.

Dmitry smiled. "Interesting. And would you give it to me? To make it to the next level of your life, would you blindly abide by my will?"

"I understand that my little New York organization is small."

"Moot," Anatoly corrected. "Miniscule."

"Both," Gabriel said, holding back his growing irritation. He looked at Dmitry. "But if you were willing to take me under your wing and teach me what I needed to know to grow to be a man like yourself, then yes, I would pledge you my blind obedience."

Dmitry shook his head. His look was grave. "Prove it to me then, nephew." He pushed the gun over to Gabriel's plate.

"How?" Gabriel asked, picking up the gun.

"Kill her," Dmitry said, pointing at Victoria.

Victoria looked over at the gun. Her breaths were even, her eyes still narrowed.

"Why would I kill her?" Gabriel asked, shaking his head. "She has done nothing to me."

"It is not about what she has done to *you*. It does not matter if she is the mother of your children. I have asked you one simple thing. To prove your allegiance to this organization, all I have asked is that you shoot her with the gun that I have placed in your hands."

"But I'm not auditioning to be one of your hit men," Gabriel countered. "I have men to do this type of thing for me."

"But what happens when those men aren't there? What happens when it's a personal matter? What happens when the point has to be made by you and you alone?"

"Then, I'll do it," Gabriel answered in a low voice.

"Now is one of those times," Dmitry answered. "She knows what she has done. Now, I have asked you to complete my wishes." He tilted his head. "Is this too much to ask for a man who claims to have murdered five people? Regardless of what people say, it does get easier with each kill. Trust me," he grunted. "I know." He touched his chest. "But I question your commitment. In fact, I question every part of you, so until you prove to me that you are worthy, there is nothing more to say."

Gabriel held the gun in his hand. He tried not to shake, to hold it steady with authority. The woman still had not flinched. That is when it hit him that this must be a test. It was her demeanor that gave them away. Shaking his head, he took a deep breath and pointed the gun at her.

"It's such a pity. She's a beautiful woman," Gabriel said, pulling the trigger.

The gun clicked, indicating that it was out of ammunition. He held his relief. Instead, he pulled the magazine out and checked it.

"I need ammo to kill her," Gabriel said wickedly. "You took my weapons. So, I don't have a gun myself."

"Here use mine," Anatoly said, reaching behind him.

Dmitry raised his hand. With a smile, he waved off Anatoly. "No, no. He did what I asked him to do. And that is all that mattered to me. I just wanted to see if he would do it. I wanted to see if he would risk the possibility that one was still in the chamber."

"You told him to *kill* her, but she still looks alive to me," Anatoly said, rolling his eyes.

Victoria shot him a deadly look then picked up her plate. "I'll be inside if you need me."

"No," Dmitry said, touching her arm. "You have done well. Thank you. Don't pay attention to Anatoly. He just has indigestion. It makes him irritable."

Gabriel sat back in his seat, ready to throw up but hid his shaky disposition.

"I wanted to take you out before it gets too late to see my latest creation. It's called Lilith – the family's newest brand of Merlot. There are special grapes on the other side of the estate. Victoria has been working very hard on the project. I'm very proud of her." He looked up at Victoria and smiled.

"Are you sure it's not too late," she asked, setting her plate down.

"No, dear. Tonight, you have our undivided attention. The men need to see something other than guns and the like. Let's take them out to see Lilith," Dmitry said standing. "Are we all finished here?"

"*Da*," Anatoly said standing.

"Sure," Gabriel said following.

Chapter Fifteen

The sun had nearly set by the time that everyone made it out to the other side of the farm. Walking through the rich soil with their pants rolled up past their ankles, they talked about what a great investment the winery had been and how marvelous Victoria's work had been.

Anatoly was silent. With a growl, he followed his father and Victoria and watched Gabriel carefully. He had told his father, but he didn't know if it had registered. He did not trust the man. What was blind obedience if a man questioned authority down to the very minute? When his father had ordered him to kill someone, he had done it without hesitation or reason. Plus, he had hoped the damned gun was loaded. He would have liked nothing more than to see Victoria's brains splattered against the concrete.

A small smile tugged at the side of his lip as he looked at the back of her head. She went on talking and pointing, like the queen of the Nile, showing them all what the farmers had done, taking credit for their work. All she had done was what she was supposed to do. *What was great in that?*

"What are you brooding over?" Dmitry asked, falling back from the crowd. He motioned for his and Anatoly's bodyguards to walk in front of them.

"I don't see why I have to stomach her much longer," Anatoly answered his father under his breath. "She irritates me."

Dmitry shook his head. "It's hard to whisper when I'm this tall." He looked over the vines of the vast farm and breathed in the fresh air. "We'll talk about this later, *da*. I'm sure you'll feel better then."

"I don't see how," Anatoly said, feeling his phone vibrate. He checked it. *It wasn't Renee*.

When they arrived at the vine patch named Lilith, Dmitry stepped up to the grapes and pulled one from the vine. Tasting it, he shook his head in approval.

"This is Lilith?" Gabriel asked, pulling a grape from the vine as well. "What's the meaning?"

"I was waiting for that question," Dmitry said with a smile. "I'm not Jewish, obliviously, but a man I met in Moscow a while back told me an interesting story from the Midrash, which is a collection of books that hold their ancient folklore. Now according to the Midrash, Lilith was the first wife of Adam. She was made from the same dirt as he was and considered herself his equal." Dmitry kneeled down and grabbed a handful of dirt in his hands. "Legend has it that she was very beautiful with fiery red hair. Now, Lilith didn't want to lay with Adam. So she called out God's name, was damned for her disobedience, sprouted wings and flew away."

Anatoly looked up at Dmitry with a *what-in-the-hell* expression on his face. He shifted from one foot to the other and looked around. All eyes were on his father. The bodyguards stood behind them, bewildered by the man's intriguing tale.

Dmitry continued, noting his son's confusion. "Anyway, she was turned into a demon that supposedly ate children. And she enticed men in their dreams to lure them away even though in reality she was a frigid, cold-hearted spawn."

Gabriel shook his head. "And you want to name a bottle of wine out of a child-eating demon? You might not want to tell them what the real meaning behind it is. It's not very marketable."

"I am naming the line of wine after her because of what she stands for. She is an enticer. She cannot be trusted not around men, not around their children." Dmitry looked at Victoria.

"You never told me why you gave the wine that name," Victoria said quietly.

"I named it for you," Dmitry said, pulling another grape from the vine. "You are after all an enticer. You cannot be trusted. And for all purposes of this conversation, you have always bitten every hand that has ever fed you." Dmitry sucked his teeth.

"We know about the call you made to Agosto," Anatoly said, happy to have finally arrived at the moment when he could get to his real purpose for being there. "We know that you told him about me."

She turned slowly to Anatoly. Her eyes spoke volumes, full of fire, shooting daggers. Clenching her jaw, she narrowed her eyes at him.

"Lilith," Anatoly said, lifting his palms to the air.

"Care to sprout your wings one last time for us?" Dmitry asked, pulling his gun into sight.

Gabriel was slow to grasp what was happening. He went from trying to understand the story to witnessing a murder.

Dmitry was less theatrical than his story. Ready to get the entire situation past him, he looked at his watch before he continued. Gun pointed, he sighed. "Do you need a moment to ask God for forgiveness? Need to make any last requests?"

"You're a monster," Victoria said with tears in her eyes. "And I hope that you burn in hell, but first I hope that you live long enough to see your entire legacy die before you." She spat at Anatoly's feet.

The rest was in slow motion for her. She glanced down the path toward the fleeting sun and took a deep breath. The dirt crunched under her feet as she pushed down against it, running as hard as she could, as far away as she could. She ran towards the sunset, towards the beauty she had found in Tuscany, towards the end.

Dmitry always hated harming women, but he couldn't bring himself to have his men do it. This had been his mistake. He had brought her here. He had introduced her to his son. He had put his son, his wife, his daughter in danger. In truth, this was his problem to fix.

It only took one bullet. Her graceful run had halted as the bullet hit her in the back of her head. Blood shot from the wound. Her long arms extended

up and out as she fell forward into the dirt.   The
wind blew through Dmitry's hair as he turned, ignoring Gabriel's telling eyes. He turned his gun on her
bodyguard.

"You were responsible for watching her every
move, *da*?"

The man stepped back into the bushes.

Dmitry's restraint was less resistant for men.
With the pull of his trigger, he shot him twice in the
chest. The muscular man fell backwards into the
vines.

Anatoly looked over at the dead man curiously.

"He was sleeping with her," Dmitry answered his
son's gaze. "He got so wrapped up in his own will,
he forgot mine. I told him to watch her phone
records, listen to her calls, watch her every move to
ensure that she didn't get out of hand. If he had only
done his job, he wouldn't be joining her." He turned
to Vasily. "Get rid of this," he said, giving the gun to
Anatoly's bodyguard.

Gabriel could not believe what he had just witnessed. A woman and her bodyguard had been
brutally murdered in front of him, and he was incapable of doing anything about it. Swallowing his fear,
he fought hard to keep his control. Dmitry walked up
to him, looked into his eyes and spoke softly into his
ear.

"Are you sure that you're ready for this?" Dmitry
asked as he walked past Gabriel.

"What about the body? Are you just going to leave her...it here?" Gabriel asked, watching the men walk off.

"I'm not an undertaker," Dmitry said, rolling his eyes.

Anatoly smirked as he looked up at him. He was happy, truly, genuinely euphoric. The bitch who had stood in his way was finally gone. He felt better than the moment he had found out that she was still alive many months ago. He felt better than the first time that he had held her in his arms. Without giving her a second thought, he followed his father back towards the house with Vasily in tow.

Gabriel stood in the path as the sun set behind him. The wind blew past his body taking with it the soul of a woman he'd barely known. Defeated, he finally followed. If he turned to her now, he might just meet her end. *I'll get you all*, he thought to himself, *for her, for my father, for my mother...*

Chapter Sixteen

Prague, Czech Republic

As they arrived at the Medlov Chateau amid the blue skies and warm sun, Anatoly finally felt the ease of life. Home. He looked out of the window and sighed, anxious to smell the fresh air and the smell of the house that brought him certain peace.

As the doors opened to the truck, Anatoly stepped out and felt his feet crunch the rocks below. He looked up at the sun and smiled. Finally in a place where he was accepted just as he was, he reveled in his existence. This is where the Medlov's resided, away from everyone in the country side of Prague.

The doors to the chateau flung open, and Anya came running in her pink lace dress, baby doll in hand. Her eyes were focused on the men whom she had dearly missed. Daddy. Brother. Screaming their names and grinning from ear to ear, she headed down the steps with her arms wide open.

Instinctively, she ran to her father first. He grabbed her up in his embrace, kissing her rosy cheeks with grateful enthusiasm. He whispered words into her ear, brushing her long, black hair with his large hands, while her brother waited for his turn to cuddle the angel whom he affectionately referred to as *the princess*.

Dmitry could feel the pull from his son, the desire to hold her. Handing her off to Anatoly, he headed up the stairs to see the other woman in his life, Royal, who stood at the door with her hands cupping her growing bump.

But Anatoly stood still, hugging his Anya with all his might. She smelled of candy and roses, her own unique fragrance of purity and promise. Bright blue eyes flashed at him, nonjudgmental and delighted by his presence.

"I missed you so much, Anatoly," she said with a tinkle in her voice. "What took you so long to come home?"

"I was busy," Anatoly explained. "But I missed you too." He walked with her in his arms as Vasily followed with his luggage.

"Did you bring me presents?" she asked, holding on to him tightly.

"Don't I always," Anatoly answered as he climbed the steps.

"You brought the stranger," Anya said, looking behind her brother.

Gabriel looked on with a smile. Still intrigued by the complex relationship between the girl and the men, he suddenly wanted dearly to be a part of their priceless transaction.

"We did," Anatoly said, arriving at the door. He didn't bother to look back and be irritated again by

Gabriel's presence. He found it revolting that the man had been invited into their home. It should have been omen enough with the extermination of Victoria that strangers should never be allowed into the most intimate place of their lives.

"How are you?" Gabriel asked, lifting his finger to touch her out-stretched hand.

"I'm well. And you?" Anya asked politely.

"I'm doing great," he answered.

Royal unwrapped her arms from her husband long enough to greet her stepson with an endearing kiss on the cheek. With a curious and untrusting smile, she also greeted Gabriel.

"We meet again," Royal said, extending her hand. "Welcome to our home."

"Thank you for having me," Gabriel said, taking her hand gratefully. He wasn't sure how in the least she would receive him this time, considering the last time that they met, she made it painfully clear that he was a threat.

Royal made Gabriel dreadfully nervous. It wasn't anything that he had read in the file. It was her knowing glare, and the knowledge that they both shared of who his father was. In truth, he carried guilt for what had been done to her. *Raped. Beaten. Nearly murdered.* It had all been done at the hand of his father, yet she welcomed him in her home as a guest. *Truly a noble woman,* he thought to himself as he entered their luxurious home.

Anatoly had to get some room in between him and Gabriel. After setting Anya down, he excused himself up to his room to prepare for dinner. The one thing that he could count on at home was dinner by six. Certain that a hot shower and quick drink would at least ground him for the evening, he jetted up the long, red-carpeted steps and headed straight for his bedroom.

Royal and Dmitry watched him disappear quietly and gave each other a glance. Then in their normal gentle manner they turned their attention to Gabriel.

"Gabriel will be here with us for a few days to a week," Dmitry explained to his wife as they all walked. "There is a great deal to discuss."

"Well, I hope that you make yourself at home," Royal said, looking back to make sure that the staff carried off the luggage. "Dinner will be at six. I've arranged for Briggy to show you to your quarters and make sure that you have everything that you need. And there is more than enough transportation just in case you'd like to visit the city."

"I can't thank you enough," Gabriel said, walking beside Dmitry.

Just then, Briggy, the maid for the family quarters on the second floor, emerged from one of the closed doors. She looked up at Gabriel and smiled.

"Briggy, we were just talking about you," Royal said, touching her shoulder as she walked up. "This is Gabriel, Dmitry's nephew."

"Very nice to meet you, sir," she said with a nod.

"Why don't you show him up to his room," Dmitry said, picking up on the instant vibe. He turned to Gabriel. "I'll call for you later, and all three of us can have a chat, *eh*. For now, there are a couple of people that I need to reacquaint myself with." He put his large hand on his wife's arm and bent to kiss the top of her head.

"Yes, sir," Gabriel said, following Briggy as she led him away.

***

Gabriel tried to stay focused. He walked slowly behind her, watching her hips sway in her dark denim jeans. *Whoever decided the maid should dress casually deserved a raise.*

Briggy was beautiful. It felt like a stab in his heart when he first saw her. A burst of adrenaline pumped through his body, stinging the very tips of his fingers. Her smile muted any clever words that might have saved him.

With the turn of a key in the lock to the guest bedroom, she pushed the door open and stepped aside for him to enter. He went inside, hoping that she would follow. If she would just stay, just a moment, maybe he could pull himself together enough to say something that might convey his mounting attraction.

"I'll be responsible for your needs while you are here," she said, stepping inside the room. She left the door open. He followed.

"Your bathroom is through that door." She pointed to the left. "Your closet area through that door." She pointed to the right. "I'll bring you breakfast in the morning. And if you need anything, you can ring me. My number is by the phone."

Gabriel turned and looked at the room. *Nice.* Although lately, he was growing used to the lavish lifestyle of the Medlov clan. Normally, he would have taken time to observe more. His eyes, however, quickly found their way back to her. He hated himself for still not saying anything, but he knew that she could read his face. He was enamored.

"So, you're Anatoly's cousin," she said nodding.

"Yes. Our fathers were brothers."

"I know." She blinked, her long lashes fluttered like wings. Blushing, she grabbed the door handle to leave. "If you need anything at all, call that number," she said, bowing out of the room.

"Anything?" he asked in one last ditch effort to keep her there.

She stopped for a moment. "Anything," she answered. Her eyes locked on his as she closed the door.

***

With all the trouble that his son had found himself in lately, Dmitry only grew more grateful for the relationship he had with his wife. Young men were nothing if they were not fickle. He had been young once, and he sympathized with his Anatoly for what he was surely going through. The woman whom he had bedded, albeit against his wishes, was just murdered. The woman whom he had chosen as a lover once was now being courted by his first cousin upstairs. And then there was Renee. He wasn't sure where she fit into the puzzle, but he was certain that she was a part of it – a very large part based on his most recent behavior. However, he'd wait for the boy to come to him to broach the subject. Even though Anatoly was his son, he was still a man. He still needed time to come to grips with things himself.

"Did you have an exhausting trip?" Royal asked as she helped him pull off his shirt.

He sat on the end of the bed with her standing in between his legs and yawned. "It was eventful," he answered, helping her with his clothes.

"What happened?" she asked.

Dmitry smirked. "You do better not to ask." He trailed his long finger down the side of her arm. "How's the baby?"

"Great," she said, touching her stomach. "Growing fast. I feel like a big ole goose."

"Hen," he corrected. "Not goose."

"Well that just makes me feel so much better," she said playfully.

"What of Gabriel. Do you trust him yet?"

"I trust no man, my love. You know that. Do I think he's up to something?" He shrugged his shoulders. "I don't know yet. I've got everyone in the northern hemisphere checking on his background. But one thing is for sure. He does look like his family."

"Like you and Ivan?" Royal shook her head. "I can see it, but it's the height that makes him look more like a Medlov, not his face."

"He looks like a Hutton also." Dmitry's voice was low.

"Who are the Hutton's? Do you know his family?"

"Very well. I knew his mother, his grandmother, his uncle. It's a shame that they've all past away. They were activists – the whole lot of them. And they were English royalty."

Royal was flabbergasted. "Are you serious?"

Dmitry nodded. "He's from what some people would call *good stock*. His grandmother was Lady Catherine Hutton and his mother Lady Emma Hutton."

"How do you know this, Dmitry?" she asked bemused.

Dmitry looked at her, calculating her exact response. "Because his grandmother was my first wife."

Royal stopped in her tracks. Dmitry had confided in her many years ago that he had been married once *on paper* to a woman for the purpose of defecting from the USSR and to acquire a considerable amount of money, but he had never spoken any more of it. She had accepted that fact like many others as a part of his sordid past. From that day until this, she had never really thought of it again.

Now, like so many other parts of his life that had done the same, his past had come full circle to his present. And like so many other parts of his past, she worried about what the ramifications would be for everyone around him.

"You had better start explaining," she said with her hands on her hips. "And start from the beginning, Dmitry. Don't leave anything out that might affect this family."

Dmitry pulled her onto his lap. He knew that he should have waited to tell his nosy little wife until after he had bedded her. But he owed his Royal an explanation. In fact, he owed them all at least that. It was the reason that he had brought the boy here. Gabriel was as much a part of this family as his own son or daughter.

"From the beginning is a long story, Royal," Dmitry said, touching her face lovingly.

"I've got time," she said, staring into his eyes.

***

At six on the dot, the family moved from their rooms on the second floor and went downstairs to the main hall for dinner. Gabriel had never seen such a grand layout before. The long dinner table was dressed in fine silver, covered in Russian foods, manned by two servants and served a party of the most feared criminal elements in modern organized crime.

Such a fact confused Gabriel immensely. These people were supposed to be blood-sucking monsters, yet their behavior was no different from others. In fact, they were more family oriented than his own family or any families that he knew. They respected each other on a level that he only envied.

When Gabriel was escorted into the dining room, Anatoly was already sitting at the table with Anya, talking. He looked up from his conversation to see the giant make his way into the room.

"Am I early?" Gabriel asked, sitting down in the chair across from Anatoly.

"No. It's not like Royal and Papa to be late." Anatoly looked at his watch. "But they're probably still doing whatever it is that they do."

"Making love," Anya answered.

Anatoly looked at his sister. "What?"

"I heard them making funny noises once, and I asked Mommy what they were doing. And she said that they were making love."

"What do you think that means?" Anatoly asked with a smile.

"They are kissing and hugging. That is what momma does when she loves someone. She hugs them."

Anatoly smirked. "That's right. They are hugging."

"Who is hugging?" Royal asked, walking into the room with Dmitry behind her. Dmitry pulled her chair at one end of the table out for her.

"Your daughter was just saying that the reason you were late for dinner is because you were *making love*," Anatoly answered, raising his brow at his father.

"Out of the mouth of babes," Dmitry said, pushing Royal up to the table. "Sweetheart, we do not discuss what goes on in an adult's bedchambers. It's rude."

"Sorry, daddy," Anya said, ducking her head.

"And we were not making love," Royal answered her daughter, seeing that she was now sad. "We were talking." She looked up at her husband as he made his way down to the other side of the table.

Shortly after, Briggy and Davyd came into the dining room and sat down as well. It had become a custom of the family to have both of them dine with the rest of the family considering their status in the house and in their lives. Plus, Dmitry liked having a table full of people.

"Before we get started, I have a gift for you," Gabriel said, standing up. He pulled a small file that was rolled up in this back pocket out and walked it down to Royal. She looked up at him as he did, curious to see what the man was giving her. She was accustomed to diamonds, pearls, chocolates, etc. but not files.

"I hope that it's okay. I didn't know when a better time would be than during dinner. I'm sure that it's been discussed that I have a gift for finding people and for identities," Gabriel said, smirking at Dmitry. "So, after learning more about you, I took it upon myself to find this. It took some digging, but I'm getting better and better at breaking codes."

Now Royal was very curious. The bent up folder, lay curled in front of her. She smoothed it out and opened it to find a birth certificate, a photo and phone number."

Tears formed in the sides of her eyes.

Dmitry watched unsure if he should have Davyd break the boy's neck or place a crown on it. He shifted in his seat and motioned towards Briggy to go down to the other side of the table and collect it for him.

"Well, what is it?" Anatoly asked irritated.

"Royal's birth mother's contact information," Gabriel answered, looking to his uncle for approval. "I shouldn't be the only one to enjoy the family reunion," he shrugged.

Royal wiped her eyes and picked the picture up in her shaking hands. The diamond on her ring finger sparkled across the room against the candle in front of her.

"It's her. It's my mother." She looked up at her husband in disbelief.

"I didn't know mommy had a mother, daddy," Anya said, looking to her father for some understanding of what was taking place.

Dmitry knew then that it was best to go to his wife himself. He stood up and made his way down to Royal quietly. She sat at the head of the table, covered in tears. He kneeled down beside her, looking at the picture himself.

"Are you alright," he asked, wiping her face. "Do I need to take you back up to our room?"

"No." She turned to him with a smile. "Honey, this is wonderful. Look." She passed him the picture. "I look like her."

"She's...she's still alive. She lives in Dallas," Gabriel said, looking down at the table. "She never married or had children. She's a nurse."

"Do you realize what you have done?" Royal asked, looking down the table at him.

Gabriel shook his head. "I didn't mean to offend you. I just thought..."

"You didn't offend me." She shook her head. "You..." She cried. "I have wondered for my entire life if even one person from my family was still alive." She wiped her face. "You've given me a gift, Gabriel."

Standing up from the table, she walked down to him. He stood unsure of himself but was moved by her warmness. She reached out, and he bent to her. Her warm hands grabbed his face and his kissed him on both cheeks and hugged him. He could feel her trembling body, the warmth that it gave off. She felt like a mother. Hesitantly, he hugged her back. She smelled of jasmine and peace. Closing his eyes, he held her.

"Well, I'll be damned," Davyd said finally. "Looks like the boy is some good to us."

Everyone laughed.

Briggy sat in the chair beside Davyd wiping tears and smiling as well.

However, Anatoly watched with a grimmer look. He didn't bother to smile or to share any kind words. Instead he saw red. If Gabriel thought that he would win the family over by wooing his stepmother, he had another thing coming. And if he hurt Royal, considering who he was to her, he would kill him himself with his bare hands.

Royal released Gabriel and took his hand. "I want you to come and sit down by me." She smiled. "Tell me all about yourself."

Dmitry stood by her chair, pleased. Whatever had moved the boy to do such a good deed made him have more respect for him. It was an incredible gift, and if even only for tonight, he would indulge his entire family in good cheer. However, tomorrow, he would pay more men to do more investigating. There was something about the boy that was off. Perhaps, it was just the mere fact that Gabriel was Ivan's son, and such a spawn should naturally be more evil.

He caught a glimpse of Anatoly, holding on to Anya, restricting her from joining her cousin down at the other side of the table. He knew what his son was thinking. He was still untrusting of the entire thing. Dmitry nodded cleverly at him, quietly encouraging him to relax.

"Tonight, we will enjoy a great dinner and after-wards, I'm going to play for everyone."

Joyfully, Royal looked up and clapped her hands together. Dmitry hardly ever played the violin anymore, except for special occasions, and she couldn't think of a more special one than this.

Chapter Seventeen

Briggy looked great. Anatoly couldn't help but noticed her the entire time at dinner, and she could not help but notice Gabriel. Throughout the entire dinner, they had continuously glanced across the table at each other, smiling, flirting. For once, she had ignored him completely.

She seemed to be happier now, since her mother passed a month ago. Evidently, she had started to sleep full nights again. The dark circles under her eyes had finally started to disappear.

In a way, he was relieved that she had set her sights on someone other than him. But just in a way.

Lately, he was starting to fully understand the full measure of what it meant to be lonely. It was not such a big deal before his mother died, but now with Renee leaving, he questioned more and more what the benefits of the role he had chosen to take on actually were.

Halfway through his father's violin performance in the great room, where the family always gathered, Anatoly quieted excused himself. With a kiss to Anya's head, he picked her up off his lap and stepped out of the room. As soon as the doors closed behind him, he felt like a huge weight had been lifted off of his shoulders.

The walls in there with his family were beginning to close in on him. Everyone seemed too happy, yet he was miserable inside.

Vasily soon followed. "Boss," he called out in a low whisper. "Are you alright?"

Anatoly had nearly made it down the hallway. He turned and nodded. "*Da, da*. I'm fine. Go back in and relax, Vasily. I'm just going to step out and get some fresh air, take a drive. You know," he shrugged. "I need some time alone."

Vasily nodded. "Alright boss, be carefully, *eh*."

"Not too long ago, I was you, Vasily. I'll be fine."

A night drive was just what Anatoly needed to clear his head. He jumped into his father's black Maserati and headed down the drive, allowing the wind to blow through his hair. With the music blaring, he lit a cigarette and headed down the dark, quiet road towards Prague.

A full moon shone down on him. Luxury surrounded him. And in that moment, the woman that he wanted sitting across from him was Renee. She had given him only a month more of her time, and he was here. It didn't make much sense. This meeting was very important, but he was certain that it could have been done over the phone or at least in the states. However, his father was committed to being as close as possible to his own family. *At least he had his priorities together.*

Prague was always most beautiful at night. He liked the fact that it had such a rich history and beautiful and diverse culture. There were always people walking, talking, gathering at coffee shops, shopping. It reminded him mildly of St. Petersburg with its glorious statues and ancient buildings. He like everyone else was enamored by Prague Castle. The way that it lit up on clear nights over the city was something from fairytales that he often told Anya. He laughed at the thought. She would often beg their father to *buy* it, so that they could live in a castle in the city. However, he would have liked to bring Renee here one day and take her out on Golden Lake. While that was as much of a fairytale as Anya living in the castle, he too wished.

Tonight he headed straight for Wenceslas Square. As he passed the mounted statue of Saint Wenceslas, he felt the tension in his back begin to ease. For the many tourists of this city, it was just a place on the map to visit. For him, it was one of the only places in the city where he could relax.   By day, the Dup-lex Club was for business lunches and coffee breaks. However, by night, the swank spot situated at the top of a high building in the centre of Wencelas Square was one of the most elite clubs in the city. And they always had a VIP booth just for him, where he could sit alone or *not*.

Music blaring, he pulled right in front of the building and parked his car. Lines of people looked on, assuming correctly that he must be someone important. A man in a red shirt ran out to him and offered to park his car for him.

"Just leave it," Anatoly said, waving him off. "I don't know how long I'm going to be tonight."

"Yes, sir," the man said, opening the door for Anatoly.

He stepped out of the car and looked up at the building to the club that resembled a glass cube, then checked his watch.

As he stepped towards the front door of the building, the bodyguards opened it for him. The women stopped talking and gawked at him.

In a pair of dark distressed jeans that fit his muscular wide legs, a white cotton t-shirt that clung to his taunt defined muscles and did nothing to hide his many tattoos, he breezed past the well-dressed, suited men and stylishly dressed women into the building.

He exuded confidence that they surely lacked. And where most men liked to travel in packs, he preferred the solitude of his own company when he wanted a drink and blend into the backdrops of society without a label, without a title.

The club was packed when he arrived at the top floor. Stepping out, he felt a woman brush his arm and kiss his ear. He looked over at her and gave a quick grin, but his thoughts sated any desire that he might have had normally.

Moving through the thick crowd and the strobe lights to his booth in the back of the bar, he didn't have anyone to push the people away for him or to see to his needs. Instead, he was on his own like years ago before he was boss. It felt good to be independent again. With a drink in his hand, he slipped into the booth, and watched the people dancing and talking, kissing and moving in the synchronic motion of the DJ's music.

He wasn't even on his second drink before he was approached. A tall, blonde woman in a short silver dress slipped into his booth and smiled.

"Hi," she said, winking at him under hooded, smoky eyes.

"Hello," Anatoly said, putting his drink down.

"I saw that you were over here alone, and thought I'd join you. Do you mind?" She put her small silver purse on the table and scooted closer to him.

"Well, I was actually just grabbing a drink and relaxing for a little bit before I headed back home."

"Where's home?" she asked, raising her perfectly-arched eyebrow suggestively at him.

* * *

After dinner and the family gathering in the great room, Gabriel retired to his bedroom. With so much on his mind, it was impossible to sleep, but he knew better than to actually sit and write anything down or use the computer. The room could be bugged, the phones tapped. It was best to just rest. However, there was something more curious on his brain than the investigation at the moment. The little blonde

French woman with the beautiful accent down the hall had him vexed. *Briggy.*

He laid back in the bed and looked up at the ceiling. His heart was heavier than when he arrived. These people, who were supposed to be monsters, who were supposed to make this easy to do, were not monsters, were welcoming and warm.

Having spent most of his life alone or with his mother as a youth, it was hard to grasp that all of these people were his family. How he wanted this to be under different circumstances.

There was a soft knock on the door that tore him out of his thoughts. He sat up on the end of the bed.

"Yeah," he said curiously.

The door opened and Briggy appeared. With a smile, she stopped just beyond his threshold.

"Do you need anything before your evening is completely over?" she asked with a blush.

Gabriel popped up. He looked around the room and shoved his large hands in his pocket. "Don't think so."

"Alright, well breakfast will be brought in the morning around seven," she said, bowing back out.

Gabriel reached out to her. "Before you go..."

"Yes?" Briggy said bright eyed.

"What are you doing for dinner tomorrow night?" He walked up to her.

She looked up at him and swallowed hard. "Serving the family and washing my hair."

He laughed. "After you serve the family and wash your hair?"

"Gabriel, I like you, but you obviously don't know."

"Don't know what?" He stepped back. *What was wrong with her?*

"I was once Anatoly's *friend*." She didn't blink, and she did not make her confession with pride. Instead, she stood waiting for his approval.

He quickly gave it. "Do you guys have any kids together or something?" he asked with a frown.

"No." She laughed. "No. It was over as quickly as it began. It was just a fling, at least for him."

Gabriel nodded. "Let me guess. He dumped you."

She nodded. "*Oui*, he is such a gentleman," she said sarcastically.

Gabriel laughed and bent down lower to her. "I don't care about that or about my cousin. I like you. And I think it would be really cool if we got together for dinner tomorrow night. You could show me the city, and I could be around someone who isn't either my family member or someone's bodyguard."

She laughed. "Okay."

"Okay." He moved her blonde tendrils from her face. "I have to confess that I want to kiss you right now." His voice was low, sexy.

She bit her lip. "Maybe I'll let you tomorrow. Maybe. Now, *bonsoir*."

"Goodnight," he said, standing back up. "I can't wait until tomorrow...to get that kiss."

She closed the door behind her and left him in his room.

***

Anatoly looked at his watch and asked for his tab. The waitress came over quickly to him and shook her head. "No charge, Mr. Medlov," she said smiling. "It was a pleasure to serve you."

Anatoly smiled and past her a wad of money. "A tip for you, love," he said, standing up.

The blonde sitting beside him stood up also. She licked her lips and pulled her short dress down over her slender hips. She was at least a few inches taller than he, but Anatoly knew that it wouldn't matter back at the condo.

"Let's get out of here," he said, motioning towards the door.

"Sure. Let me just let my friend know that I won't be coming back," she screamed above the crowd.

Anatoly waited as she headed towards a booth on the other side of the bar. *Wouldn't be coming back* was a stretch. He didn't want her to spend the night with him. In fact, they could have really handled this in the bathroom as far as he was concerned.

Sitting against the table, he yawned and noticed that his supermodel was approaching with a man following behind her.

"Hi honey." She waved as she came back to him. "This is my friend, Yarveene. He's sort of like my bodyguard. I told him that you would be taking me out tonight."

Yarveene, a tall, stout brunette raised his hand to shake Anatoly's, but he didn't offer it. Instead, Anatoly stood up and smirked.

"You want to go home with me, cool. But I'm not fucking paying for it," he said, ignoring Yarveene.

"No, no. I think you have the wrong idea," the woman explained.

"Do I?" Anatoly finally looked at Yarveene, who had stuck his chest out a little further. "How much does she cost?"

"5000 Kč for all night," Yarveene answered.

Anatoly could barely hold his laughter. He moved closer into the man, invading his space. "I'm not paying for her—period." He looked at the woman. "Do you want to go or what? I don't have all night."

Her eyes said yes, but he could tell that she was very much afraid of her pimp. She stepped back out of the way.

Anatoly sized the man up and smiled.

Chapter Eighteen

Morning came early at the Medlov chateau. Pulling the warm comforter from his legs, Gabriel checked his watch. 6:30 a.m. He had just enough time to do his morning calisthenics and jump in the shower before *she* came.

He tossed and turned the entire night with thoughts of her drowning him. A grown man wasn't supposed to think of a kiss like this, but all that clouded his mind were her lips. He wanted so badly to kiss her the night before, to taste the sweet nectar of her warm mouth. Oddly enough, he hadn't even thought about making love to her, as he normally would have. Instead, he just wanted to kiss her. That would be enough.

Getting down on the hardwood floor in front of the fireplace, he planted his hands shoulder-width apart and pushed his body up and down against his own weight. One push up after another, he stretched his bulging muscles to the brink and his mind continued to race.

He was supposed to be here to find out where the drugs were. That was why he taken this case. . A confidential informant had contacted the DEA regarding large shipments of cocaine that was being transported into the states from the south by the

Medlov family. The leak had reported that it was being smuggled by Anatoly Medlov under instruction of his father. Yet, everything that he had heard was about guns. No drugs. And he wasn't the ATF. So far, not one mention had been made about the shipments. Had all of this been done for nothing? Was he destroying this family for nothing at all?

Then thoughts of Victoria crossed his mind. She had been an innocent. What about her? Wasn't he supposed to give a damn about her murder?

Rolling over on his back, he pushed through his sit ups. The sweat began to pour down his body. The muscles tensed up and burned. Breathing through the pain, he crunched his abdomen tightly, exhaling out of his mouth.

What about his father? His father had been the one who had taught him the Medlov way before any of them. Then, Ivan had found out what he was. A leak in his own organization had tipped his father off and told him that his son was a federal agent. When he had gone to training, when he had been accepted into the DEA, he had told his father that he was going off a few months to get some things clear in his head. He had lied to him and told him that if he didn't hear from him, it was because he just needed some time. And that excuse had been enough. But when he had arrived back, a few months into being undercover, his father had found out.

The news had nearly killed Ivan. He came to him one night, snuck into his small one-room apartment and put a gun to his head. With every intention to kill him—to murder his only child. But the murderer, the psychopath could not do it. He sat on the side of his bed weeping. When Gabriel had awakened, his father had stopped crying and disowned him, told him that he was leaving for Memphis and his fate was his own. That had broken his heart a great deal more than his father wanting to kill him. He had never heard from him again. Word had traveled shortly after that Ivan had been killed by his brother's son.

To this day, he still didn't know why he had chosen one side instead of the other. He was after all a Medlov. It would have been easier to go the easier path, to be his father's pupil. But his mother's teachings had been the fuel for the fire deep inside of him. She had preached righteousness and justice to him his entire life. And in the background, his father had preached the opposite. He could still hear his voice even now. "Gabriel, this world functions on greed and power. If you think any differently, if you function any differently, it will consume you. And you will be forgotten," Ivan would say to him, even as a child.

He rested his head back as he panted, thinking of his dilemma. No, it was more than a dilemma. It was it an all-consuming situation that would end either with him overcoming it or dying. He had to face that fact. He had to know deep inside that he was more than likely headed to his own early death, if he continued. Because the Medlov's had proven so far that they were larger than anything he was a part of. They traveled the world like he traveled the subway. They owned banks. He barely had a checking account. They lived by the Vory v Zakone's code. He worked for the very government that they swore to hate. How could he not be headed toward his death? And in truth, he was ashamed of it, ashamed of the side that he had chosen.

There was a knock on the door. He looked at his watch quickly and realized that all of his thinking had pushed him past getting at shower. It was 7:00.

The door opened and Briggy came in with a bright smile. She looked down at him on the ground and stopped. "Are you alright?" she asked pushing the tray in front of her.

He sat up and pushed his back against the bed. "Yeah, I was working out."

"I can see that," she said, closing the door. "It's the look in your eyes. You look as though you've seen a ghost."

***

Royal sat in the middle of the bed still looking at the picture of the woman who was her mother. She had stared at the picture all night. In her mind, she had thought about what she would say to her when she found her.

Dmitry came out of the bathroom dripping wet with a towel wrapped around his waist. He stopped at the door and leaned against it.

"You're still looking at the photo?" he asked.

She looked up at him and smiled. "I just can't believe it, Dmitry. How did he get it? You've been trying to track her down for years."

Dmitry hid his jealously quickly. "Maybe it was just meant for him to find."

"Did you see him last night? He was like a boy who had just found his home. He fits in perfectly here."

"So, you like him now?" Dmitry asked, pulling his towel off. "Don't want me to kill him?"

"Something about him is right...I can't explain it. He's a good boy." She ignored his constant reminder of her growing harshness of others.

Dmitry nodded. "There is one thing that I'm certain of and that is that he is *not* like his father."

"Thank God," she said with a sigh.

Dmitry walked over to the bed and crawled in with her. Naked, he pulled her body up in between his legs still damp with shower water and kissed the top of her head. She ran her hands down his hairy thighs and shook her head.

"I'm so happy, baby," she said with tears in her eyes.

"It's the hormones," he explained, massaging her small shoulders. He had become extremely accustomed to outbursts of both happiness and sadness from his pregnant wife.

"No, it's more than that. Everything around me seems right. Last night seemed so peaceful with the entire family here. Waking up this morning with a full house of people seemed so right. Having this baby... Even Gabriel." Suddenly, she was over-whelmed again.

Dmitry chuckled. "Sounds to me like you have a lot of joy bundled up inside of there." He rubbed her stomach. "Having a boy will do that do you."

"I do feel happy...even though it's a girl." She felt his strong hand slip over hers. "I love you," she confessed in a state of pure euphoria.

Dmitry carefully turned her around to face him, straddling her body over his long legs. "Let me look at you," he said gruffly. His sparkling eyes flitted over her, instantly causing her blood to boil.

Running his hands over her half-buttoned pajama top up to her neck, he pulled her precious face to his and kissed her full mouth slowly. "I love you, too," he said softly. His deep voice vibrated in her chest. "I love you with all of me." He said this with his eyes open, staring right into her soul.

She raked her nails over his chest, on top of his tattooed pec muscle, feeling his lion-like heart beat hard and strong. He was all man, every inch of him.

As she drifted into his kiss, she felt him slowly adjusting her legs, moving her over his erection. His large hands cupped her bottom and squeezed tightly the extra pounds she had lovingly put on.

He had said *I love you* to her a million times, but each time it sent warm butterflies down to the core of her. There was something so dramatically spectacular about him. The knowledge of being adored by a man like him was mind blowing. And yet each day, she tried to understand it, to comprehend him. And each day, he did something else even more outstanding.

The flame of her hot body against his own immediately began to ignite his insatiable passion. Pulling her clothes from her body, he ran his hands over her bare skin and moaned. His thumbs brushed against her pebbled nipples, and he rested them there while he spoke.

"I want you again," he said with a grin. The long dimples in his cheek emerged. "And again," he said, undressing her. "And again." With a strong grip, he curled his fingers around the sides of her underwear and tore them off. *His signature move.* He licked his lips and pulled the lace from between her legs as if her undergarments were a diaper.

"Why do you always do that?" she asked, looking at her panties. "I loved those underwear."

"Umm. I love them, too," he said, dropping them on the floor beside the bed.

The wet silk from her sex slid down his inner thighs and made Dmitry forget all about her playful banter. Raising her up in the air as if she were a feather, he planted her on the tip of his erection.

"Ease down on it," he commanded, resting his head back on the headboard. Closing his eyes, he felt her body stretch around his own. "No more talk of nephews, *Malen☐ kaya zhenshchina* All I want to hear now is my wife in pleasure." His accent made the act sound even more erotic.

"How can you even call me a *little woman* now, as big as I'm getting?" she asked with her eyes closed shut.

"You are perfect size." His hips pulled back and drove inside of her. The words lingered on his lips. "Perfect."

***

When Anatoly's eyes popped open and he realized that he was in the same bed that he had once spent with Victoria, he jumped up. For a minute, he could smell her perfume. *Chanel.* He could see her perfect mahogany face smiling at him. He wiped his eyes and pulled the comforter from his legs.

"Stop fucking with me," he said to himself as he stood up.

"Did I do something wrong?" the blonde asked, peeking her head from under the cover. She blinked hard at him, trying to understand his sudden mood.

Anatoly didn't look back at her or respond. Instead, he bolted into the restroom and slammed the door behind himself.

What was wrong with him? He'd killed a hundred times for his father, for his organization, for his family. And to add insult to injury, he had not even killed her. His father had done the job for him. However since that day, he wondered if his father had done it because he knew that he could not. Was he getting soft or was he going crazy?

The cold water splashed against his face and over his stubby beard. He stared at himself in the mirror, judging himself harshly in his mind.

Nothing made sense anymore. He had beaten the shit out of the pimp at the club last night. However, it had done little to cool his red-hot temper. And he had taken the man's whore and brought her here with every intention of screwing her blind, but instead, they had talked all night. He couldn't bring himself to touch her. *Why?* The answer was ridiculous but true. *Renee.*

"Get a fucking grip, you pussy," he said to himself as he jumped in the shower.

The woman tapped her knuckles on the bathroom door. "Mr. Medlov, I'm going to leave now," she said, listening for him to say something...anything.

He ran his hand over his face and scowled. "*Da da*," he said gruffly. "Lock the door when you leave."

There was silence on the other side of the door as she waited. Evidently, even though he had gotten rid of her pimp, she still expected payment.

"And be a smart girl and don't take anything on your way out," he said, adjusting the shower jets. Dismissing the very thought of her, he grabbed the soap and washed the dried blood from under his nails.

The water was cold by the time that he pulled himself out of the shower. His mind had raced from

Prague to Memphis, and he had arrived at one conclusion. He had to call her.

After getting dressed, he headed downstairs in the lonely condo, down the quiet halls on his bare feet, missing his dogs and wishing for her voice. The kitchen was spotless. It was an aesthetic temple of expensive monochromic appliances and pewter-colored countertops, of abstract paintings and muted walls of absence. However, while it passed for expensive taste and fine living, it did not pass for the southern grace of his mansion in Memphis. This place was not warm, was not pleasant. It was a testament to modern living, a picture for an architectural digest. It made him lonely. It made him ache inside for the human touch, for laughter, for conversation.

With a bowl in front of him, he sat at the kitchen table with the phone in his right hand. Staring blankly into the milk and oats, he thought of her. Finally, he dialed her cell phone.

"Hello," she finally answered.

Anatoly looked up, focusing his eyes on the stainless steel refrigerator in front of him.

"Renee," he said softly.

"Hey, Ana." Her voice was rich and full of life.

"Renee, I miss you."

He couldn't believe that he had allowed himself to say it. But there was something hollow deep inside of him that needed to be filled, and he was certain now that she was the only person capable of doing so.

Renee was quiet on the other end of the line. Her breaths were short, like she was fighting for air. Looking across the counter at her customer, she quickly passed the patron her credit card back and bid her a good day.

"Miriam, can you watch the front for me?" she asked her assistant, making her way to the back office.

Anatoly waited. He wanted her to say something. *Anything would suffice.*

She closed the door quietly behind her and sat behind her desk. Holding the cell phone close to her ear, she calmed her beating heart.

"I...I miss you, too," she said unsure if this was real.

Anatoly pushed away his bowl. Slumping down in his chair, he felt the weight of the world on his shoulders. "I can't stop thinking about you, no matter what I do. Every time I breathe, it hurts."

Renee wiped the bolder-sized tears from her face quickly.

"What's happening to me?" he asked.

She laughed. "I don't know. But whatever it is, it's happening to me too. I stayed up all night last night. I almost called you ten different times."

"Me too," he said, feeling a little better that he was not alone. "I want to come home and see you.

There are some things that we need to talk about that shouldn't be discussed over the phone."

"Things like what?" she asked.

"Our feelings for each other," Anatoly said, rolling his eyes. He felt like an idiot. How did his father do this? Killing was a much easier form of self expression.

"Well, how do you feel about me, Ana?" Renee asked with a smile. She could not wait; had to hear him say it.

But Anatoly would not give her the pleasure. He balled up his feelings and tucked them away. Clearing his throat, he sat up a little straighter. "I have a meeting with my father and Gabriel this afternoon that cannot be postponed. Once I am done here, I'm flying straight to you. It will take me a couple of days to get home, but when I do, we need to talk, *da*."

Renee smirked. *Typical Ana.* He was nearly incapable showing true emotion. But she settled as she always did. Sating her emotions, she clicked her nails on the table and shook her head. "I only ask one thing of you before you get here."

"Anything," he said in a near whisper.

"Lose the wall before you get back home. If we're going to really talk, I need you to be capable of staying focused on your true emotions. It's just us talking, no one else. I want you to be honest with me. Anatoly Medlov will have to stop at the door. Ana's the only one allowed in."

Anatoly shook his head. He thought he *was* being honest. "Fine."

"Well, hurry," she said, swallowing hard. "It's my birthday in two days, you know."

He bit his lip. *Dammit*, he'd nearly forgotten. "I didn't forget. That is why I'm rushing."

She smiled. He was lying, but she knew he'd make up for it with some ostentatious gift from some exotic place that she'd never visited.

"Okay, well, see you then," she said, ending the conversation. She always hated to be the one that listened to the dial tone. Something about hearing him hang up always tore her up inside.

"*Do svidaniya*," Anatoly answered, waiting for her phone to click. Setting the phone down beside him, he waited for the pressure to lift off his chest, but nothing happened. He still felt the same stress, and it was apparent why. He hadn't told her the truth yet.

Chapter Nineteen

The real meeting was finally underway. Mid-afternoon over lunch, the men sat in Dmitry's private study behind locked doors with three bodyguards to discuss what Gabriel's official role in the family would be.

Dmitry sat behind his desk. Anatoly sat in a leather wing-backed chair by the fireplace, and Gabriel sat across from his uncle. Vasily stood in the corner with another one of Dmitry's bodyguards while Davyd sat in the corner, in the darkness watching them all with a careful eye and a loaded gun.

Gabriel had never seen such protection. This place was locked up better than Fort Knox. And inside, two men – both related - with more wealth than many small countries sat discussing the future of a family structure with enough power to last the ages over chicken salad, croissants and southern iced tea. It was an interesting site to behold.

"I don't see how he can be of any real use to us, papa. He's a drug dealer and an identity thief. Name the last time that we needed either," Anatoly said disgusted.

"I'm a drug *trafficker*," Gabriel corrected. "And you'd be surprised how I could be useful regarding changing your identity or getting you clearance into a particular place." He looked at Dmitry for support. "Whether it's for personal or business reasons, document and identities are always needed."

"He's right," Dmitry said to Anatoly. "Didn't you just get rid of Igor?" An idea hit him. He could use the boy there.

Gabriel's ears rose. He'd heard of Igor Zchensky during his many briefings on the Medlov Organized Crime family. And recently, his contact, Agent Lee, had informed him that the well-known Vor had a heart attack in Miami.

Supposedly, Igor was a major gun trafficker for Anatoly with freight ships and truck lines in five countries.

Anatoly nodded. "*Da da*, papa, but -" he raised his hands towards Gabriel. "*YA yemu ne doveryayu.*"

Gabriel sighed. "But you can *trust me,* Anatoly. What other reason would I be here other than to try to connect our families and be of some use?" He sat up in the seat. "I'm a trafficker. It doesn't really matter if it's guns or drugs."

"We don't traffic drugs," Anatoly corrected. "We're not low level pushers."

"And we do not traffic people," Dmitry added for extra measure. "It's been the one thing that has always separated us from *them* since our beginning. We only deal in guns. Everything else is legit. All the businesses thrive on one another, and at the core is the true industry run by the brotherhood."

Gabriel listened to the lesson carefully. "So, you've never dealt in drugs? But my father..."

"Your father was a Vor. He was a business man, but he was not a part of the Medlov family for many years," Dmitry said, cutting Gabriel off. "We never approved of his extracurricular activities. In fact, it is what separated us in the beginning. But I am aware that he was heavily involved in drugs. Ivan always went against the grain. It proved more often than not to be a problem for him."

"So you never?" Gabriel frowned. His perception of the organization had been flawed from the beginning.

"Never," Dmitry said, clasping his hands together. He picked up the crystal tumbler and sipped his vodka. "You sound disappointed. The strength of our organization comes from our code and our own set of morals. We have helped a hundred small factions, fueled the underdog in a hundred wars. If anything, we are guilty of capitalism at its finest. We are doing the same things that governments have done for centuries. But we have never been involved in the trafficking of drugs or people, regardless of what the common misconception is about us. It counters the very core of what we stand for as men of the Vory v Zakone."

"But so many of us *do* deal in drugs and human trafficking. That is what our organization is most known for around the world. How can you sit here and say that The Medlov Crime Family has become as great as it has only through guns?" Gabriel countered. "You have to admit that it sound farfetched"

"That is what distinguishes us. There are so many of us that do not deal in rape of the poor and misfortunate. Many of us are brothers of the time before the great USSR was no more. Besides, there are entire industries that we control, entire governments that we have infiltrated. There is no need to seek profit in things that are so disorganized and corrupt. Women, children, drugs. These things are all off our radar for a reason." Dmitry looked Gabriel in the eyes. "There used to be a time, before you were old enough to walk, before you were born, when men were held down because they were not a part of the government. We were starving in hovels, down trodden by a system designed to monopolize on institutionalized and wide-spread fear while our government profited off the sweat of our brows. The men of the Vory reversed that by taking power in our own hands. The Medlov family used guns to balance the financial and political means to gain more control over our own lives." His stare was ice cold.

"You make it sound make so noble," Gabriel said with a smirk. "But how is anything that we do noble?"

"We never said that we were noble. We are not the round table of fairytale knights in shining armor here to save the world from itself. We simply have saved ourselves. Besides, what government is noble? Show me one. Just over one hundred years ago, slavery was still a systemic revenue base for the free world. Cocaine and meth are still the underlying main products of export for many third world countries. Caste systems and religion fuel the basis for continual oppression of whole peoples. War is a part of mankind, and if this is so, *and it is,* then so is weaponry. If anything, the Medlov family is simply an instrumental supplier of human nature and its desire to control, maintain or balance the ebb and flow of the power structure within any society."

Gabriel didn't know how to argue against it. This man sitting in front of him – his uncle – was obviously committed to his cause. It made him envious to see someone so certain of his path. He looked over at Anatoly and saw the same unwavering strength. These men had been bred on power and structure beyond what his mind could comprehend. Again the thought crept into the back of his mind. *You're in over your head,* he thought to himself. *You're going to get yourself killed.*

Anatoly picked up on his inferiority. Normally, he would have pounced on him, tore him apart. However, he was sympathetic in a way to how lost the man apparently was. He remembered being the same once.

"He can take over for Igor," Anatoly said, nodding at his father. "It will be on a test basis for now. Igor has a team that was assigned to him by my council. You will come to Memphis and meet them. Then, you will be instructed on how and when you are to transport the product." He stood up. "You are my cousin, and for that reason *only*, I will give you one chance to do things the right way. But if you start to show signs of being anything like your father, you will be ended." Anatoly clenched his jaw.

"Thank you for the opportunity," Gabriel said humbly.

"Just don't fuck up," Anatoly said, walking over to his father's desk. "I have to go, papa," he mumbled under his voice.

"Where?" Dmitry asked, cutting his eyes at Gabriel. "This is important, Anatoly."

"The larger decision has been made. I will send for him in a few days... a week maybe. Until then, maybe it is best that he stay here and get to know you better. Maybe you can talk to him. Find out where he mind is."

Dmitry nodded. "I can do that for you, if you tell me why you have to hurry off so quickly."

Anatoly ran his hand over the desk and lowered his voice more. "*Rech□ idet o zhenshchine*," he said smirking. He had told his father that it was about a *woman*, but he didn't say whom.

"Renee?" Dmitry asked, standing up.

Anatoly nodded.

"Walk with me out in the courtyard. Let's get a breath of fresh air, *eh*," Dmitry said, smiling. "Gabriel, we are finished here. Why don't you go and relax for a while. What are you doing for dinner?"

"I actually have a date," Gabriel said, standing up.

"A date?" Anatoly turned around. "With whom?"

"Briggy," Gabriel answered.

Davyd grumbled in the background. It was the first time that he had made a noise throughout the entire meeting.

Dmitry shook his head. "What is wrong with the Medlov men that we continue to share women in every generation?"

Anatoly rolled his eyes. "If you have ill intentions toward her, then cancel your date," he said fuming. "She's not the family whore."

Gabriel put his hands up. "*Whoa*, man. I would never treat her that way. I just wanted to take her out in the city for dinner."

"We'll talk about this later," Dmitry interjected. "Anatoly," he said, motioning towards the door. "Will you join me?"

They left Gabriel alone in the room with the bodyguards. He stood looking out of the window and contemplating his next move. By sheer luck, he was finally in on a job. By sheer grace, he'd gotten a date with Briggy. And it looked like he was finally getting a chance to prove himself to his family. But there was an interesting more human side to his situation. He was pleased with himself, pleased that he had been accepted, and it reached far beyond that of his job as an undercover agent. Something deep inside him felt comforted by Anatoly's approval.

***

Dmitry liked to walk around the large farm. Rolling hills, a beautiful lake, mountains in the nearby view and fresh air made for a truly serene environment. It cleared his mind and gave him time to put things into perspective. He only hoped that it would do the same for his son.

As they walked past the lake that oddly enough his unborn child had been conceived near, he stopped and looked out at the ducks basking in the sunlight.

"I always liked Renee," Dmitry said, slipping on his Aviator shades.

Anatoly stared out at the lake as well. Silently, he tried to formulate his thoughts for the woman into one complete thought, certain that his father would not stop probing until he received the answer that he was looking for.

"And I think that she'll truly make someone very happy." Dmitry turned and looked down at his stocky son. "But I have to question why a man in your position would even consider taking on the job when the one that you currently have as boss requires so much of you."

Anatoly smirked. "I didn't say that I wanted to marry her."

"No, you didn't. But here's the thing about women like Renee – unlike Victoria or Victoria's type- Renee is a real woman with die-hard values and priceless conviction."

"You make her sound like a saint."

"What I'm saying is that a woman like that requires one hundred percent of your devotion. And as the former boss of the Medlov family, I can tell you that you cannot give her the type of love or protection that she needs."

"How do you explain Royal then?" Anatoly argued. "Are you really going to stand here and tell me that a boss cannot have anyone in his life?"

"I'm telling you that having a woman like Renee makes you re-evaluate things. You find yourself questioning everything that you used to hold dear. And so early in your career...".

"Is that what you call this?" Anatoly interrupted. "My career? Please," he scoffed. "This position requires every solitary drop of my blood, every part of my soul. It consumes me."

"You always knew that it would," Dmitry said sighing. "It was what you wanted. Remember?"

"I know." Anatoly rolled his eyes and shook his head. The constant pain of being torn between his desire as a man and his obligations as boss were starting to exhaust him.

"You know, if you'd like to take some time off and make sure that this is what you want, that is what the council is there for. They are older, distinguished men who have been where you're going."

"They are a bunch of money-hungry demons who want just one opportunity to completely usurp my position. And I will not allow it." Anatoly rejected any notion of the pseudo-council he so dearly wanted to replace in its entirety. "I feel things for her that I've never felt for a woman," he confessed. "And I'm close to losing her."

"Will she be patient? Will she wait?" Dmitry asked. "There will be many, many years before you can even think of settling down with a family."

"I haven't even told her how I feel yet. For all I know, she has no intentions of being with me."

"Then maybe, as a man, you should make your intentions known," Dmitry suggested. "It's always easier to rule an empire than to love a woman." He smirked, thinking of his own wife. "So, you're going to Memphis to talk to her."

"Yes."

"And if she says that she wants to be with you, what then?"

"I have no clue."

"And if she says that she does not want to be with you," Dmitry asked.

Anatoly didn't answer. He knew that she would take him. He knew it the day that she told him that she was leaving. It was just amazing to him that he had been so blind before. And it was exactly why he had to get out of Prague and get back to her. The hourglass was still pouring the sands of their time, and the longer he was away, the closer he got to losing her completely.

Putting his large hand on his son's shoulder, Dmitry smiled and gazed up at the mountains. This was what he lived for, for moments that were not necessarily involved with the Vor but were all about his family. His son needed him and he knew it. This was what life was about for him. All of the struggles, all of the pain, all of mayhem over the years had been so that he could fulfill his role as a father. He had the chance to do for his son what no one ever did for him. He gave him an out, an option, a choice.

"Anatoly, I know that you're a young man, and everything seems to be confusing right now. I remember being in your shoes many years ago. Only, I was not as lucky as you to have even the inkling of love. So, whatever happens, remember that you only have one life. And so, you must live it to the fullest. While every decision has an opportunity cost, the point is that there is an *opportunity* involved."

Anatoly nodded. He needed to hear that.

Chapter Twenty

Royal couldn't wait any longer. After putting Anya down for her nap, she went into her office and closed the door quietly behind her. Sitting down behind her desk, she pulled the file from her top drawer and sat it in front of her on the table beside the fresh bouquet of roses and picture of her family.

The silence of the room only made the act more reverent. The birds chirping in the background, the panoramic view of a beautiful day outside and the vacuum humming down the hall reminded her that there was peace all around.

Trying to meld into the moment, she talked herself through the process. Even though it all seemed surreal to know what she was about to do, she knew that it had to be done. There was a chance to change her entire life right in front of her, right in her hands. All she had to do was have the courage to follow through.

Opening the bent file slowly, she pulled out the single page with her mother's number and picked up the phone. A million thoughts crossed her mind. And for once, she did not know if she should be happy or sad. Should she scream at the woman or cry out for her? What? What should she do? What should she say?

Sitting back in her chair, she wiped the tears and tried to still her shaking hands. A picture of her dead sister, Chloe, flashed through her mind. Chloe would have loved to be here now, to make the call with her, to hear their mother's voice. And here she was afraid, after all that she had been through in her life, to dial a number.

An abrupt knock on the door, caused her to sit up in the chair.

"Come in," she said, voice shaky.

Ducking into her office, Dmitry emerged with a bright smile.

Royal was glad to see him. She assumed with his meetings that he would be too busy today to deal with this. However, he had not forgotten and somehow God had sent him to her.

"Hey, love. What are you doing?" he asked, sitting down in the chair in front of her desk. The sun beaming in from the window behind her made his blonde locks glow like strands of spawn gold. His beauty calmed her. Her knight in shining armor had arrived.

"I'm calling my mother for the first time," she answered.

Dmitry bit his lip. "Are you nervous?"

"Do I look nervous?" she laughed. "Yeah, I'm shaking in my boots here." She wiped the sweat from her brow and rubbed it on her jeans.

"Well, considering that you're supposed to be dead," he said, squirming in the seat. "You may not want to disclose who you are over the phone. Just in case. I know it is very bad timing to bring this up right now, in the middle of something so *historic*."

Royal cut him off. "I thought about that," she said in a huff. "But I just want to hear her voice, you know. It's torture to wait." She searched his eyes for answers. "What...what would you suggest?" She shuffled the papers around on the table. Her wedding ring sparkled in the sunlight.

"Umm." He was lost for word. "I did this once, actually." He laughed.

"What?"

"*Da, da*. I did this once, when I had the opportunity, if you can call it that, to talk to my father. It was many, many years ago." He would have preferred to never bring up that horrid event, but he knew that sharing would help ease her anxiety.

"I never knew that you actually got a chance to talk to him. You've never talked about it." Her intrigue sparked.

He sighed. "Well, it was unremarkable." He nodded at her, unable to mask his pain. "But that doesn't mean that yours will be the same." It was best to keep the focus on her current situation instead of strolling down memory lane. He edged up to the end of his chair and placed his large elbows on her desk. His blue eyes focused on her. "Why don't you just make a general inquiry about what she does, and pose as a person looking for someone to care for their grandmother or something. She's a nurse, right?"

"That's what the file says." She opened the file back up again and looked at her photo. "What if this is a mistake, baby?" Doubt began to slip in and steal her courage.

"It's not," he assured. "Just relax and take a deep breath. I'm right here with you."

He reached his hand out. Grateful, she slipped her hand in his and smiled. "Thank you for being here." Her voice was trembling.

Dmitry nodded. "That's what I'm here for...the hard...stuff."

"Stuff? You never use that word."

"Well, the kids are rubbing off on me. I have young men all around me, and they never use proper English. It's their fault really."

She laughed. "Okay." Taking a deep breath, she picked up the phone. "Let's do this."

Dmitry paused. "It's midnight there."

She stopped. "Oh, shit. Well, maybe I should wait until later." She put the phone back down.

He saw the tear forming in the slits of her eyes and immediately wished he hadn't said anything. "No...go on. Call. There is no better time than the present. Just...act oblivious to the hour."

***

Royal had to take a nap after her conversation. On cloud nine, she crawled up into bed, and Dmitry tucked her in, kissing her on the forehead, then on the stomach. He was happy that she had a chance to hear her mother's voice, although the conversation had been short. The point was that she had spoken with her.

Because of the hour, Royal had ended the conversation reluctantly, acting as a niece traveling and looking for someone in the Dallas area to help her with her dying aunt.

The woman, even though oblivious to the real intent of the call, had been kind. It was a perfect beginning to a new beginning for his wife. However, he knew that it was up to him to iron out the kinks of how and when Royal would meet her. But he didn't mind. It was an honor really, considering how much he had taken from her in order to make her his wife.

Now, she was asleep in a state of euphoric bliss and dreaming of a reunion that would be surely coming.

With her content, he could focus on the young man upstairs.

After checking in on Anya, who was still napping, he headed up to Gabriel's room. They really had not had a chance to speak privately, and Dmitry could see no better time than now to face his own past.

Gabriel was watching television when he came into his room. He quickly grabbed the remote and turned it off. Standing by the chair, he waited like a child for the instruction from his father.

Dmitry smirked at himself. He seemed to be everyone's father figure these days.

"Mr. Medlov. I mean Uncle..." Gabriel stammered over his words.

Dmitry raised his hands. "Please call me Dmitry. Titles don't mean much here." He closed the door behind him and motioned for the chair in the corner. "Do you mind if I sit? My back aches a lot these days. I'm getting old."

"No, sir," he said, trying to maintain his character while still containing his wonderment of his uncle.

"And do me a favor, and don't call me sir," Dmitry said, noting his acknowledgement of authority. *That was odd.* "I wanted to speak with you very briefly before your dinner date."

Gabriel sat down as well. He clasped his large hands together and sat at the edge of his seat.

"Briggy is a family member. Though she is not blood, she is very dear to us," Dmitry said smiling.

"So I have gathered," Gabriel said nervously. "I assure you that I'd never hurt her. I know everyone is worried for me to be around anyone including the dog, but I'm not a deviant."

Dmitry smirked. "Well, that's good to know. I just want you to be mindful that everyone in this house has a history. Briggy, for example, had a short relationship with Anatoly. And I'm sure that I should leave this for her to discuss with you, but she doesn't have a father, and I want to make sure that you understand that because she does not, I feel the need to step into that capacity."

Gabriel was impressed. He cared not only for his son and daughter, for his wife and his code but also for his maid. Again, his perception of the man was altered.

Dmitry nodded. "So I have made myself clear."

"Treat her with respect," Gabriel answered.

"Exactly," Dmitry said, pointing at him. "Now, I'm not old fashioned in every way. I understand that young people have needs, but I would ask that if you two find yourselves fulfilling them under my roof that you keep it discrete and that you not at any point embarrass her, because after you've gone on, she still has to work and live here."

"Yes, I completely understand," Gabriel said seriously.

"Good. Now that we have that out of the way, I want to talk to you about something more important." Dmitry sighed. "I want you to know that you can talk to me. If you have questions, you can come to me. You see, I am acutely aware of who you are."

Gabriel's breath caught again. He felt himself shaking.

Dmitry raised his brow. "The Hutton's were a very powerful family in London during the time that I was there, and I'm sure that your mother discussed with you, before her passing, the very sensitive nature of my relationship with both her and your grandmother."

Gabriel exhaled. "Yes, she did."

Dmitry shook his head. "And I'm sure that there may even be some resentment or questions that at some point you'll need answered, some reasoning validated."

"Yes." Gabriel was at a complete loss for words.

"I just want you to know that while I am a man with a sordid past, I am still a man, and being that, I am willing as your uncle and as your step-grand father to talk to you frankly about the things that led up to and happened after your birth." Dmitry smirked. "I understand what you did. You gave Royal this opportunity to find her mother as a way of telling me that you were in search of your own identity's truth. And I respect you for it. And you deserve it. No one should ever be denied their history, especially by their family."

Dmitry had all but deflated Gabriel with his words. He was never sure how much his uncle knew about him, but evidently, he knew a great deal. And the fact that he had come to him and was open to the possibility of a discussion about the things that had left him scarred for his entire life made him even more torn about his dual identity.

"I appreciate that, Dmitry." Gabriel searched for the right words. "But to be honest, I didn't do what I did for Royal to get to my own identity."

"Maybe not consciously, but subconsciously I believe we arrived at this moment because of your own search. Don't be ashamed. Now that you've finally arrived here with your family, you never have to worry about being misunderstood or denied again.

We are very accepting here, because we are all that we have in this world."

Dmitry's words caused a strain in Gabriel's chest. He held down the pain as far in his gut as he could. Suddenly, he wished that he was not here as an undercover agent, but just as a man, as a Medlov.

"When the time is right, I will take you up on that," Gabriel said finally. His voice was low and solemn, matching his dimming soul.

"You look changed. Have I offended you?" Dmitry asked outright.

"No," Gabriel answered quickly. "It's just over-whelming."

"Such is the theme of the day, it seems," Dmitry said, running his hands over his jeans. "Well look, I just wanted to put that out there in the open. We may be a secretive family, but it's only with the outside world. Within the confines of this world, we are open and honest. Never hide anything from me."

Gabriel hesitated. His eyes could barely meet his uncle's.

Dmitry titled his head, processing the boy's sudden discomfort.

"Are you hiding something now?" Dmitry asked.

"No...no." Gabriel looked down. "I just wasn't prepared for this."

Although Dmitry did not know the man well, he didn't buy it. He cleared his throat. "I try to be a forgiving person, because of what I've done in the world and where I come from. But once I've made a decision, I never go back on it. You've been accepted as long as you are honest. But if you're hiding something, if there is something that we need to know, I would ask that before you leave my home to go back to the states, you tell me. If you do, whatever it is can be forgiven and taken care of. However," he said with a grim tone. "If you are hiding something, and you do not disclose to me this thing before you leave, you realize that you will have forever set yourself on a path that will pit you against this family."

Gabriel understood what his uncle was saying, but he also knew that if he actually told him that he was a special agent undercover in an investigation to put both he and his son in jail on drug trafficking charges, he would kill him. He reminded himself of that fact before he spilled his confession at his uncle's fcct.

"I'm not hiding anything. It's just that I've never had anyone to acknowledge me in such high regard or treat me like I was special just because of what runs through my veins. If anything, I've been treated as a leper my entire life." He looked at his uncle and tried to tell him the truth even though it was also a lie.

Dmitry nodded. He completely understood. "I am a billionaire, a business owner, a business man, a leader, and yet I know exactly what it means to not fit." He smiled and stood up. "I won't take up anymore of your time. However, my offer still stands."

Gabriel stood as well. "Thank you...for everything."

"You are a Medlov. This is your home. We are your family. The rest is now forgiven. I only hope that the same applies for both myself and my son. It can't be easy to carry around the knowledge of what we both are guilty for in your own life, regardless of how it came about."

Gabriel thought of his father. "No, it is not easy, but trust me, when I look at Royal and your beautiful child, I feel the same."

Dmitry reached out for the boy. Gabriel came to him and hugged him. In his arms for the first time, he felt as vulnerable as a small child. He had spent his entire adult life hating and studying this man only to find that he was nothing like he had been painted. It was a painful reality check.

Releasing Gabriel, Dmitry placed a set of keys in his hands. "It's to the Bentley. Take her out, spend as much time and money as you like, enjoy yourselves."

"*Spasiba*," Gabriel said, humbled and ashamed.

Chapter Twenty - One

Although having a private plane to jet around the world was great, there was nothing like planting his feet on solid ground. After several months of going from one place to the next, never having a meeting in the same place and constant situations to handle, Anatoly was actually glad to be back in Memphis.

The flight had been a tedious one. He didn't want to see another customs agent or flight attendant for at least a week. All he really wanted was to rest his head in his own bed and see his dogs. A lot of people traveled with their animals, but he had taken a page from his father and decided against it. However, the torture of leaving them to other people's care made him feel as though he was neglecting the only thing that was rightfully his in this world.

When he crossed the threshold of his front door, Vasily was behind him toting his luggage, and the maids were in the entrance way awaiting further instruction. In his normal fashion, he threw his backpack in the corner and waited for the sound of little feet tapping against the marble floor. It wasn't long before he heard them. His dogs came rushing, nearly knocking each other over to greet their master.

He knelt down to hug them, allowing them to kiss him on his mouth as he checked them over before he stood to observe his home. Everything appeared to be as it should have been.

Walking quietly with the mail in his hand, he made his way to his office and sat down in the chair behind the wooden credenza that his father had spent many hours behind during his time as boss.

Today was not like any other day, however. It was Renee's birthday. And while he did rush to get home, he had stopped to pick up a special gift for her in New York.

They hadn't spoken since the night before. He had told her to take the day off from the boutique and get dressed up for their date. But she had insisted that it was imperative that she only take a half-day to wrap up some end-of-month obligations.

They finally agreed to meet at six. He had offered to send a car to pick her up from her apartment, but she said that she would meet him here after she was finished.

He couldn't quite explain his excitement, but he felt it deep down inside of him. Tonight, he would finally tell her how he truly felt. It was odd that they had arrived at this point and ironic that he found himself finally understanding his father's position with Royal only after going through the violent rollercoaster of emotions that he was faced with after Victoria and Briggy. But he truly felt that now he was ready. If he was sincere enough with her, he hoped that she would consider staying on in Memphis as more than his shop girl.

Anatoly had never had a real girlfriend. In fact, the very title sounded utterly ridiculous to him, but he was attempting to try something normal, although he had never had much normalcy in his life before.

His father had given him advice once that he never had followed through on before now. Before buying Royal one of the most expensive diamond necklaces that Anatoly had every laid eyes on, Dmitry had explained to him one thing. "You cannot buy a real woman, he had said to him, but you woo her to the point of reason with fine things. And the one thing that all women respond to is jewelry. It's in their genetic code to be responsive to diamonds," Dmitry had said adamantly. "If you shower her with the best in life, she'll shower you with the best in love."

So, for once, he had tried his father's approach. He stopped at Tiffany's and bought Renee a diamond bracelet that was fit for a queen.

He dug into his pocket and pulled the blue box out. Setting it on the table, he opened it slowly, basking in the amazing brilliance of the perfect cut stones. He knew that she had never had anything as nice as this, and he couldn't wait to see her face when he gave it to her. Maybe if his words didn't quite convey his feelings, this would help him along.

***

Renee worked feverishly through the last of her tasks in the back office. Filing away paper and sending off the last of her emails, she jumped up from her desk and grabbed her purse. It was already noon. Time to go. There were still a hundred things to do before her date.

She smiled at the thought.

Anatoly hadn't let her down. He had come as he had promised to be with her, and she had the distinct feeling that tonight would change the rest of her life. Butterflies began to flutter inside of her stomach again. How she wished that Royal was here today to talk to. It was strange not to be able to confide in anyone about what was going on, but after all that had happened, she had learned that it was always best to keep her own council.

"Miriam, I'm getting ready to leave," she said, walking out of the back room with her purse in one hand and her dress for tonight in the other.

"Yes, ma'am. There's someone here to see you," her assistant said, moving towards her.

Renee looked up at the front to see the reporter, Destiny, standing by the counter flipping through a fashion magazine and waiting.

"What does she want?" Renee asked quietly.

"She didn't tell me. All she said is that she needed to speak with you personally."

Suddenly, Renee had a bad feeling in her stomach. It quickly took the place of the butterflies.

"Can I help you?" Renee asked, moving towards Destiny.

Destiny looked up from the magazine and smiled. Grabbing the black, unlabeled CD from the counter, she stuck her hand out.

"Hey, do you remember me?" Destiny asked.

"Of course. You're the reporter who did the great article on the restaurant," Renee said guarded.

Destiny nodded. "That's right." She passed Renee the CD. "You're a friend of Anatoly's right?"

"Yes." Renee took the CD and looked at it.

"Well, I made this for him, but I was hoping that you could take a look at it first. It's a surprise – my last gift to him before I get out of here."

"You're leaving Memphis?" Renee asked, stuffing the CD into her purse.

"Yes. I'm looking to change careers thanks to Anatoly, but I know that he cares so about what you think. So, I was hoping that you'd take a look at it and tell me what you thought of it before I gave it to him."

"What is it?" Renee asked.

"Just the book trailer for a new project. I've decided to sit down and write a *memoir* of sorts."

"Wow, well congratulations." Renee adjusted the strap of her purse on her shoulder. "I'm supposed to meet him tonight, so I can pass it to him, if you'd like."

"That would be awesome, but could you take a look at it first. It's really short and to the point. If you don't like it, then don't show it to him, but if you think it's got potential, would you give it to him with my regards?" Destiny asked with a bright, almost innocent smile.

"Of course."

Destiny looked at the dress. "What's the occasion?"

"It's my birthday," Renee said, remembering herself. She pulled the plastic cover from over the dress and showed her. "Versace."

"Oh, that's beautiful," Destiny said, touching the fabric. "I know you're going to look amazing in it."

"Thanks," Renee said, checking her watch. "Well, I better go and get ready, but I'll take a look at it tonight before I go over there. I have a hair appointment right now, and I don't want to be late."

Destiny nodded and turned towards the door. "Well, I don't want you to lose your spot. But it would mean the world to me if you would do that for me."

"No problem," Renee said, walking to the door.

"And happy birthday," Destiny said, finally as she walked out.

* * *

Vasily had never seen the mansion look as nice as it did tonight. Anatoly had ordered flowers and had them strategically placed along with candles all over the dining room, living room, foyer and especially the bedroom. Plus, he couldn't recall ever seeing his boss so dressed up.

Anatoly stood looking at himself in the mirror, checking to make sure that every stitch was in the proper place. He was normally a jeans and t-shirt guy, but tonight, he had decided on an all-black, tailor-made designer suit. The barber had been over to cut his hair. The butler had helped him dress, and the maids had ensured that entire the house looked like something out of a fairy tale.

In truth, Vasily was afraid for Anatoly. He'd never seen his boss put so much effort into anything outside of the business, and he knew that if everything didn't go perfect tonight for Anatoly, he might not ever do so again. Plus, this was just a first date. It was evident that his boss knew very little of such a thing, because he had the place set up like he was about to propose.

The sun had begun to set, casting a beautiful glow on the horizon. With the summer season slowly slipping away to fall, there was a hint of chill in the air. It was a perfect panoramic view. He had insisted that the maids open the windows and let the fresh air inside. He could hear the leaves on the trees rustling in the wind and feel the evening setting in. It was almost time. She would be here any moment and they could finally begin what they started on the phone two days ago in Prague.

Vasily stood in the corner watching his boss. When the text came over his Blackberry, he checked it quickly and cleared his throat. Anatoly looked back at him.

"Boss, she's here," Vasily said, opening the door to the bedroom for him. "They sent her to the solarium like you asked."

"Better not keep her waiting then," Anatoly said, feeling in his jacket pocket for the box.

"Good luck," Vasily muttered.

"Thanks." Anatoly hit Vasily on the shoulder as he passed. "Take the night off, *eh*. I'll be fine."

Chapter Twenty-Two

The solarium was already filled with beautiful exotic flowers, but tonight they were accented by white lights on dancing strings. A single bottle of champagne was on ice with two glasses beside it on a table in the middle of the floor.

Destiny stood looking out of the glass at the setting sun with her back to the door and her hands clasped together.

Anatoly walked into the room quietly. For a moment, he just wanted to observe her. She looked amazing from what he could see. Her very shapely, petite frame was put on display in a way he had never seen in the simple black knee-length dress.

He walked to the table and poured them both a glass of champagne. Certain that she could hear his footsteps, he walked up beside her and looked out at the sunset too. It was so peaceful and serene, a perfect start to their first evening together.

"Happy birthday," he said, turning to pass her the glass.

She looked up at him with fresh tears in her eyes. They had streamed down her cheeks and onto her dress.

"Renee, what's wrong?" Anatoly asked in a deep, gravelly voice.

Renee took a deep breath. She tried to smile to mask the pain radiating from her beautiful face, but her voice cracked in pain, giving her away. "I've been waiting for today for so long, Ana. And all day, I kept thinking that this all was going too perfect. Even when I got here and saw all that you had done, even after I had witnessed this..." she held the CD in her hand. "I still couldn't believe that you had done something so special."

Anatoly wiped her face. He tried to make sense of what she was saying, but he was hopelessly confused.

"Your friend, Destiny, stopped by the shop today." Renee looked away. "She asked me to take a look at this CD. It was supposedly a book trailer that she wanted to surprise you with. After I got dressed to come over, I remembered it and popped it into my computer."

Anatoly felt his heart breaking. He didn't have to ask what was on the CD. He already knew.

"Renee, if you could just let me explain," he begged.

Renee laughed. Her sobs clouded her eerie sarcasm. "If you can explain having sex with this woman in the pool while everyone watched, I'd really like to hear it."

"I found out that she was a cop, undercover and trying to set me up. So, this was my way of getting her off my back."

"I'm sure she was grateful for your counter measure." Renee turned away from him.

Anatoly realized that both of his hands were still filled with the glasses. He placed them on the windowsill and sighed. The beautiful sunset was officially ruined. "It was stupid. I wish that I had never done it."

She whipped her head around to face him. "That's just it, Ana. I know that there must be something wrong with me, because I know what you have done. I know what you are capable of even without seeing it with my own eyes, and I could take that. The killing. The guns. The mafia." Her voice drifted off. "But I quickly found that I can no longer take the idea of you being with another woman. And seeing that with my own eyes killed me."

"Don't do this, Renee."

"You did this, Ana."

"It was before I realized that I wanted to be with you." He allowed the words to clumsily fall from his lips.

"I've known for a while that I wanted to be with you, and it's my fault, really, for never telling you, but I'm old school. You know. I still think that a man should chase you, not the other way around."

"So because of some woman that I screwed who means nothing to me, you're just going to walk away?"

"Yes."

"I can't..." Anatoly felt his frustration boiling. Pulling at his tie, he opened his shirt to breathe. Sweat formed on his forehead again. Turning red, he clenched his jaw. "Why are you doing this to me?"

"Doing this to you? You're so fucking selfish, Ana. I didn't do this to you." She hit her chest. "I didn't set you up like this. The woman that you just finished..."

"That was weeks ago."

"Oh, forgive me! I guess that I'm bringing up old shit!" She grabbed her purse. "This was such a mistake."

"Why can't we focus on right now, on this very minute? Are you really going to hold me accountable for everything that happened before this point? Do you think that is fair?"

"Life isn't fair, Ana. You of all people know that. And yes, I am going to hold you responsible for your actions, because it takes a lot of balls to do something like this. It takes a monster. Do you realize how disgusting this is? Or can you justify it in that brain of yours because it protects your precious Vory."

Anatoly paused. He'd never heard her say that she knew exactly what he was.

Renee shook her head. "That's right. I know. And I took a really long look at myself today and asked myself what the hell I was doing, knowing who you really are. Boss Anatoly Medlov. The Medlov Organized Crime Fucked Up Family. I don't want to end up like Royal. I don't want to be just another dead woman buried because of your past. I don't want women showing up with sex tapes and men showing up with blood vendettas and..."

Anatoly was desperate. He felt her quickly slipping out of his hands again. The hour glass was pouring the last of their sand right in front of him.

"Royal's not dead."

Renee stopped her rant and frowned. "What? Okay, now you're just being cruel."

Anatoly walked over to her. The click of his shoes against the hardwood floors only magnified the silence. "I just left Prague. Royal is not dead. She's alive and so is her daughter. In fact, she's pregnant again."

Renee held her stomach. Stepping away from him, she let the tears fall from her face. The look in his eyes told her that he wasn't lying. Only the truth of his confession was more painful than the lie that he'd been hiding.

"The family thought it best to protect you and to keep you out of things that you might not understand. Royal wanted to tell you but..."

"Stop it!" Renee cried. "Just stop fucking talking!" She screamed louder, pointing at him. "What is wrong with you people? You can't just play everyone like pawns in a damn game!"

He'd never heard her curse so much. Reaching out to touch her, he tried to calm her. "Renee, you mean everything to me."

"Liar! You've watched me in pain for years," she cried. "And you could have told me. You know that I wouldn't have told a soul, but instead you watched me mourn that woman."

"It was to protect you." His voice was low, steady.

Renee put her hand up in protest. "It was to protect yourself." Turning away from him, she tried to leave, but he quickly grabbed her, wrapping his arms around her waist.

"Let go of me!" She fought, flaying her arms about, trying to hit him, but he picked her up off the ground. One high heel fell to the ground. "Let go of me, Ana!"

"No!" he growled. "No. Renee, please." He put his mouth to her ear. His breath burned her skin. "I love you."

Completely obliterated by his truth and his words, she crumbled over in his strong arms. With her back nuzzled into him, she cried out, still trying to fight, but he continued to restrain her.

Anatoly refused to let her go. He refused to see her just run out of his life. *Not without a fight*, he said to himself. His grip broke her iron will. They both collapsed onto the ground.

The golden sun had finally gone completely down, and a bright, vibrant moon had emerged. They were left alone in the darkness with only the white lights high above them in the rafters to illuminate the room. The hollowness of the airy space made their quiet movements echo.

Anatoly could feel her body trembling, but he knew that it was more than just pain. There was also want, both hers and his. The silence was thick with raw emotion, choking out any ability to lie. Vulnerable and bemused, he cradled her. His grip had become a blanket that shielded them both from the outside world. In that moment, they were alone with no present or past.

Carefully and ever so gently, he turned her face towards his. She shifted her body slightly and looked up at him, her big brown eyes full of rage and visceral passion.

Anatoly swallowed hard as he watched her. His thumb wiped her tears and slowly he pulled her mouth to his.

"I love you," he said again. Where only months ago when Victoria had confessed her love for him while they made love and he had denied her, he willingly said it to Renee. As he said the words, he knew that the reason he had not given them to Victoria was because the words, the act, the fact belonged to Renee. The only thing he wasn't sure of was how long he had loved her. As he held her, he felt as though it had been had a lifetime. There was no awkwardness, not need or desire to flee. He wanted to melt into her, to become one with her. He meant the words to the core.

The words rushed into her like a wave of intoxicating drugs. He clutched her tight to him. The heat from his body warmed her, igniting a hungry flame deep inside.

Renee cried. "I love you, Ana."

"I'm so sorry for what I've done. I know that you can't begin to forgive me for all of it." The tears formed in the sides of his crystal blue eyes. "But I need you to know." He smiled. "I'm so lonely for you, Renee. I've tried to fill the void in my life with other women, but I can't. I can't replace you. I can't..." He suddenly felt light headed. Having never been so honest about his own emotions, he suddenly felt afraid. He held her tighter. "What am I supposed to do without you? You've been there for me the entire time since my father left. There were so many days, so many situations that I only got through because I knew that when I came home, you'd be there."

"I don't know if I can continue to be, though. Ana, this is so hard." She buried her head in his chest. "This is so damned hard."

"Think about it. Give it some time. But don't tell me *no* tonight. Don't turn me away. Give me a chance to prove myself, first. I've never needed to prove myself so much to one person, not even my father."

"I'm going to need some time." She knew that her strength had left her, but she also knew that she had to be honest. "There is nothing left for you to prove. I just have to have some time to digest all of this. I know it sounds selfish, but it's the truth. What my heart feels is so overwhelming."

Morning would come with the daylight and so would their changed reality. She had to make sure that they would both be ready for what that would mean for them. But she also knew that tonight, she would give in to him.

Anatoly read her face. He felt her resolve.

This time as he leaned in to her, it was not to talk. Both of his hands moved to her soft face and he pulled her into his kiss.

She turned all the way around to receive him. Her lips parted, warm and full, fleshy and wet. Desire engulfed her. Their minty breath mingled and heaved into each other.

As their mouths touched, slow and sensual, a whimper escaped her. His taste was decadent, mixed with the fragrant sandalwood cologne on his skin and clothes. She wrapped her arms around him, tangling her fingers in his feathery, curly locks.

On his knees in front of her, holding her, caressing her face, he continued to search her mouth, sucking her bottom lip, tasting her velvety tongue, kissing her until she was weak. His nimble fingers ran down to her throat, stroking her skin as he slipped his tongue in and out of her mouth, tickling her senses with the least of his masculine sexuality.

She had thought about kissing his full, rose-colored lips a thousand times, but never had she imagined that it would be this good.

He focused intently on his deed, pouring himself into her. He became hungrier for her—all of her. Snatching his suit jacket off, he returned to her quickly.

"Let's go to my room, *da*?" he said, gazing into her eyes. "I want to make love to you there."

The verbalization of their action made Renee even wetter. Her thighs were slicked together under her clothing. Nodding, she reached out and grabbed his hand as he helped her up.

It seemed to take forever to get to his room tonight. They walked hand-in-hand through the quiet home, down the long halls, up the stairwell, down the corridor to the master bedroom.

When they got to the door, Anatoly slowly twisted the knob and pulled her inside.

For the first time in his life, he was genuinely nervous about sex. It was important to him to make this the best that Renee had ever experienced, but his desire had accelerated to a point of near madness. He ached to have her. The blood pumped through his veins and rushed to his already pounding heart as she stood in front of him.

Renee toyed with his desire. Seductively stripping her clothes off, she brushed her small hands over her skin as she undressed. He'd never known how sexual she could be. Her eyes were hooded.

Her lips wet and open. With a kinky grin, she dropped her dress at his feet, then proceeded to slowly take off her bra. Trailing her hands down her torso, she slipped her fingers into her panties, then pulled them down to her ankles.

He dropped to his knees to help her take them off. She still had on her fish net high-thighs. As she went to take them off, he stopped her.

"Leave them on," he growled. "And the heels."

Still on his knees in front of her, he breathed close to her slick thighs. She bit her lip as she watched.

"Is there anything else you want me to leave on?" she asked, looking down at him.

He grabbed his suit jacket and pulled out the blue Tiffany box. Opening it, he looked up while offering her the diamond bracelet. And with a devilish grin, he said, "Just this."

Shocked, she put her hands to her mouth, but he quickly pulled her wrist to him and placed the six-carat bracelet on her. It sparkled in the candlelight, reflecting around the room.

As she marveled at her $50,000 gift, he marveled at her clean-shaven vagina. In a swift movement and still on his knees, he cupped her curvy behind in his hands, pulling her close to him. His meaty tongue lapped at the top of her mound, licking her exposed, sex lips and titillating her meaty surface. The musky scent of her body transferred to his mouth, making him harder in his pants.

Moaning, she watched him dip lower, tilt his head to a perfect view and slip his tongue in between her labia. The tip of his tongue snaked up to find her clitoris. Sucking at it, he felt her tremble above him as he drank the wetness from her body, cleaning her dry.

Anatoly stood up, mouth wet and picked Renee up off the ground. Her short body cradled into his embrace as he carried her to the large bed covered in rose petals. He laid her down carefully, splaying her legs open.

She gazed up at him. He was still in his black dress shirt and black pants, looking powerful and magnetic. The sleeves were rolled up to his elbows, showing his many tattoos. His chrome watch glittered in the light. His eyes sparkled nearly as brightly as the bracelet on her right wrist. He looked amazing, dominating.

Unable to control herself, she reached out for him. Her hand caught the back of his neck. He came to her, kissing her again with a fierce passion. One hand stroked her neck and collarbone, the other made its way back down to her sex where he slipped a finger inside of her and rested his thumb on her clitoris. As he was massaging and kissing her, she began to whimper, squirming under him and completely pliable to his every demand.

Anatoly trailed a kiss from her cheek to her neck, then moved back to her hot, aching sex. He parted her lips with his fingers and blew against her exposed body. Arching her back, she felt him lap her sex again. She moaned. He licked. She moved, he adjusted. She clenched. He kissed her, sucked her, tongued her until she finally felt herself begin to shake. He bent to her, kissed her dry again. Finally, he stripped out of his clothes.

In all the time that they had been around each other, she'd never seen him naked. His taut muscles were carved into his sleek skin. His body was a temple of deep valleys of sinewy flesh with marble rock-hard definition and tanned golden-bronze skin embellished with intricate tattoos. And his erection silenced any question of his bloodline. Like a true Medlov, he left nothing to question. His width and length were testament to his manhood – to his dominance.

But Anatoly paid little attention to himself. He was too engulfed in finally seeing after many years what Renee actually looked like. This was odd for him, exhilarating. There was no question in his mind that he would dominate her, but he wanted her to enjoy it. Sex for him, for the most part of his life, had been a one-way pursuit. The woman had only been there to please him, but not Renee. He was only interested in her pleasure.

Renee's short stature made it easy for him to sweep her compact body in one gaze. Her baby soft skin was a deep, rich shade of mahogany that only darkened around her nipples, the dip between her legs and her delicate knees.

There was a perfect little beauty mole in her inner thigh and a birthmark on her hip. Her areolas were large and inviting, pebbled nipples ripe and perky. He longed to taste them, but he was saving them for last, for when he was completely inside her.

The wideness of her hips was just right for absorbing the raw shock he intended to transfer. He wanted nothing more than to pound his body into her, feel his sweat on her stomach, taste every inch of her until he had it committed to memory.

Erotic thoughts began to multiply in Anatoly's head. She had an inner belly button. He liked those most *for the finish*. He glanced into her eyes. She swallowed hard, realizing that he was actually strategizing his attack.

"Is there anything that you don't like?" Anatoly asked, kissing the inside of her leg and slipping on a condom. His eyes were hooded and dark. His breaths were deep and heavy, each exhale drawing attention to his carved abdomen.

Renee bit her lip, feeling his tongue against her ankle, snaking against her skin. "No. Is there anything that you don't like?" she asked.

He smiled deviously. "No."

Anatoly kept his possessive eyes on her as he dipped in to her lips. His stare was so carnal until it aroused Renee to near orgasm. Her burning legs opened to fit him comfortably between. Though she was mildly embarrassed that she was already soaking wet again, there was no way to hide it. He was slowly sliding his erection through the wetness as he kissed her mouth. Still, he had not penetrated her.

The wait was driving Renee crazy. She longed for him to be inside of her. Lifting her hips, she moaned and palmed her breast.

Anatoly slipped his hand behind her and helped elevate her hips. Without a word, he guided himself into her.

"God, you're so tight," he whispered.

Renee whimpered at the feel of his body. Liquid heat united them in a locked position. Stretching her body to the brink, he finally went for needy her breasts, begging for his sincere attention. His breaths made them harden more, and within seconds he was suckling one in his mouth and holding the other in his hand, fondling it between his deft fingers.

Renee was unable to speak, unable to breathe. Everywhere that he could be, he was. Inside of her. On her. Kissing her. Rubbing her. Touching her. Screwing her.

Unable to take the constant bombardment of raw, hot sensations, she finally screamed out in ecstasy as her sex spasmed. But her recognition of her weakness only made Anatoly stronger. In long, coiling strokes, he moved in and out of her body, in and out of her wetness, pumping deeper and deeper into her. The sound of their bodies slapping together only drove him madder. He kept his own orgasm at bay, and continued to draw hers out.

"*Ty prinadlezhish☐ mne,*" Anatoly said in her ear. *You belong to me.*

She looked up at him in wonderment. It didn't take a linguist to know what he meant. It was in his eyes, in his kiss. Love.

The sheets were soaked. She moved against his body, feeling his sweat in between them. Knees buried into the bed, arms holding her thighs, he punished her body in a rhythmic pattern of passion.

The burn in her eyes fueled his passion. In one motion, he had pulled her to her side. He continued until she was nearly out of breath. Reaching for him, unable to put her hands in one position for more than a second, she grabbed the sheets and tore them from the mattress. Her cry intensified his desire. He reached back and slapped a burning, hot palm to her ample backside, then rubbed the pain into her skin. The sting left her panting.

Unable to control himself any longer, he buried himself deep inside her. With a hand full of her black hair in his hand and the other hand around her neck, he pulled her up to him.

She could smell his cologne as he slipped his finger in her mouth. His hot breath hissed at the back of her neck. Low whimpers became moans as he broke the walls of her tension, flooding his body with her thick liquid. She felt her body tensing, words forming on her lips to tell him that she was so close.

Knowing she had reached her point, he turned her around to see her face. Now, on top of her, he pumped into her body. Face-to-face, they both climaxed. Holding each other tight, kissing and moaning, they collapsed into each other's arms.

Anatoly looked over at her, wrapped in his embrace, exhausted and happy.

"I...I really do love you," he said again, trying to catch his breath.

She looked up into his eyes and smiled. "I love you, too."

Chapter Twenty-Three

Anatoly felt something licking his fingers beside the bed. His eyes opened slowly and focused on the empty space and disheveled sheets next to him. Sitting up, he looked around the room. No clothes. No shoes. No purse. No Renee.

Pulling himself out of the bed, he ran his hand over his dog's ears and looked around. The sun was cruelly bright this morning, shining through his window like a blazing alarm clock. The bed was a mess, and Renee was gone.

Deep inside, he hoped that she was downstairs fixing breakfast or at the boutique with the patrons, but he knew the truth. There was no need to look for her, and no need to call.

He had done this once. When he woke up in Prague next to Victoria, he too had felt the urge to flee. He imagined that he knew every emotion that Renee had felt that morning when she woke. But it wasn't until now that he knew how Victoria must have felt. The pain of waking up to being alone again. No note. No indication that he'd ever come back. No indication that he'd ever been there.

"The bitch is still getting me back," he said aloud of Victoria. "Still tormenting me from the grave."

***

Across town, two members of the Medlov Organized Crime family were meeting without their council and against the code. Over breakfast, Yuri and Oleg, two of the divine 16, were strategizing on what their counter measure would be now that Igor had been murdered. His death in Miami by Anatoly's hand had been a dreadful blow to their outside income streams.

"He was our man. We should have done more to protect him," Oleg said, eating his Bavarian pancakes. "How did that little shit ever find out anyway?"

"No one knows. Things were going great. We were cutting into the Cuban gun shipments to pay for the drugs from the Columbians. It was a perfect plan. Now we have to figure something else out or come out of our own pockets to pay for this little operation."

"If Anatoly knew about the guns, how are we not sure that he doesn't know about the drugs?"

"Because there hasn't been anything done about it yet. And we all know that Anatoly is very quick, almost impatient, to act. Otherwise, Igor would still be alive."

"This could still work, as long as we play it smart. We cannot have another incident like before," Yuri said quietly. "The last thing that we want is for Dmitry to take things over from Prague."

"I think he'd clean the entire council, at this point. There wouldn't be one of us left." Oleg shoved a pancake into his mouth with his boney fingers.

"We must develop plan," Yuri said. "There is one last shipment going out to the Cubans for guns. It's the final shipment of Anatoly's precious weapons from Sochi. This is going to be major. We must find someone that we can trust to do that last shipment and take our cut. If Anatoly gets his hands on it, our opportunity will be lost, and we will be stuck paying for Columbian's cocaine or risk waging war. We cannot afford either."

"Don't worry. We'll convince Anatoly to let us handle it. He's been so removed and wrapped up in whatever is going on in his family that he has little time to deal with these things. For now, we must work on distribution of the next shipment of drugs once they arrive here in three days."

"Did you secure the warehouse?"

"*Da, da*. It has all been arranged."

***

Gabriel put his arm around Briggy's warm body and nuzzled his head into her soft hair. *This is heaven*, he thought to himself. She slept peacefully beside him, curled into his naked body without a care in the world. He wanted to wake her, to see her eyes flit open and gaze at him the way she did to make his heart skip a beat. It had been the same for a week now. Intense love making at night and tutorials from his uncle during the day.

He was forgetting himself, forgetting why he was here. The DEA thought that there were drugs involved, but he had discovered none. They were like weapons of mass destruction at this point. Just a figment of the government's imagination. And he was here, with his family, setting them up like a snake. Like his father. The pain was ripping at him, tearing him apart. There was not a moment that passed that he wasn't in complete despair over his actions.

"Good morning," Briggy said, opening her eyes. She looked up at him and smiled. With a single finger on his lip, she pulled him to her kiss.

"Good morning, baby," he said, forgetting for a moment all of his woes. Planting his body on top of her, to cover her from the world, he moved her hair out of her face and kissed the side of her neck.

She giggled, biting her lip as she felt his hardness prodding at her leg.

"I have to get up and get breakfast ready for the house," she said regretfully.

"Do you want me to help you?" he asked, adjusting his long body to move inside of her.

"You'd do that?" she asked surprised.

"Why wouldn't I? Whatever it takes to get you back into my bed faster, I'll do."

"You're so different," she said with wonderment in her eyes. "So special." She trailed her hand over his face.

"I'm not special," he said, looking away.

"Of course you are. I love your family, Gabriel. But you are different from them. There is so much good in you. You're very much different from your cousin."

"Anatoly's alright," Gabriel said, dismissing her compliment. "But I don't want to talk about him right now." He sat on his knees, grabbed her waist and pushed inside of her.

Briggy closed her eyes and relaxed her body. Feeling Gabriel harden inside of her, she released a gasp. He was so amazingly huge until it was obscene. And he demanded so much of her. Every inch. He kissed her, licked her, pleased her with no end in sight. Lying on her back with her core locked to his lap, she forgot about breakfast and enjoyed making love to her perfect lover.

***

Dmitry couldn't sleep. He sat by the fireplace in his robe reading his newspaper while Royal snored lightly in the bed across from him. She'd only recently started to snore. Oddly, she only did it in the second and third trimester of her pregnancies. The doctors couldn't explain it, and he tried not to make a big deal out of it, because she was so emotional. Nonetheless, it often made nights unbearable, because he never could sleep with an ounce of noise in the room.

However, something else wasn't right. He could feel it, only he couldn't place where the problem actually was.

Checking his watch, he realized that it was already six in the morning. Unfortunately, he'd been up since four going over in his mind every intricacy of his life. Finances. Relationships. Business deals. He'd thought about it all.

He knew that it was imperative also that he send Gabriel to Anatoly soon. And while he appreciated young love, he knew also that he'd have to separate Gabriel and Briggy for a while.

It was strange to actually have Royal approve of anyone on her staff dating a family member, but she genuinely accepted Gabriel and Briggy. It could have been that once he told her about his role in the boy's life that she felt he deserved a great deal more leeway. It could have also been that she saw their own relationship in the young couple. Whatever it was, once she gave her stamp of approval on the two, Gabriel and Briggy had been inseparable.

In a way, he knew that it was also his doing. Many months ago, when Briggy was invariably torn apart by his son's quick dismissal of her after a short love affair, he had told her to find someone who wasn't ashamed of her. Ironically, she had found that in Gabriel. He took her out in public, treated her to nice gifts and always acknowledged her.

If Briggy was in the room, Gabriel could not keep his eyes off of her. If she was busy working, he'd offer to help. He'd disappear as soon as it was time for her to get off of work, and she hadn't spent a night in her room since their first date.

Dmitry thought they'd fallen in love, and he was sure of it after last night. At dinner, they had sat beside each other talking quietly as if no one else was in the room. After dinner, they'd disappeared up to his guest room. It was the way that young lovers behaved, he knew that. But he was worried. How would his young Briggy recover when soon her bliss was cut short? The tables would definitely turn and the women of the house would expect for him to do something about it, especially the one snoring in the bed.

There were also the many conversations between him and Gabriel to consider. The boy was growing on him. He was no longer a stranger. They had discussed in detail his childhood and college years. And it had all checked out with the Intel he'd gathered from his private investigators in New York.

At first, Dmitry did not trust the boy. But each day, he found himself growing closer to him. Maybe it was that he looked a great deal like his mother and in his mind he was mending relationships that had no other way of being fixed.

After all, Emma Hutton had long since passed and so had Ivan. There was no way to go back and help either one of them. But maybe he could help himself heal wounds that he secretly nursed for all three of them – four of them, counting Gabriel.

Royal had noticed their relationship. She too worried at first. However, over the last week, her conversations with him had eased her suspicions as well. *I like him*, she had said. *He's a good boy*, she had vouched. *You can trust him*, she had promised.

And while his wife's opinion meant everything to him, he knew that it must come down to what he felt. Only, he didn't know how he felt about the boy anymore. It disturbed him that he approved of him. It disturbed him that he admired him. It disturbed him that he saw things in him that he wished for his own son to have, like true integrity, like passion.

It was ironic that Ivan's son had turned out to be so graceful. He was intelligent, creative and hard working. He saw himself in Gabriel. And what of it? Could he really hold back a man who was his own blood and so much like him?

He knew the answer to that question. No, he could not hold the boy back, and the only way to allow him to thrive in their organization was to send him to his son.

He smirked to himself. That would be tricky. While the people here liked him, cared for him. Gabriel would truly start to cut his teeth in Memphis with Anatoly. And that would not be easy. His son was more like Ivan than he cared to admit. Anatoly was quick to kill, but it took him forever to feel for someone. He was always slow on emotions, unless it was hate. Anatoly could hate with the best of them. But he had to let men be men. He could not coddle Gabriel.

Excusing himself from the bedroom, he walked down the long corridor and opened Anya's door to find her sleeping. After sneaking in to kiss her on her forehead, he headed down to his office.

When he got there, a fresh pot of coffee and juice sat on his table in a tray. Evidently, Briggy was up and as always diligently working. He was proud of her. While it was small, it was very important to him that the people around him always remembered first their obligations.

Pouring a cup of coffee, he sat behind his desk, hit the button to open his blinds and called his son.

Anatoly picked up on the first ring.

"Hello," he said gravely.

"You sound like shit," Dmitry said, sipping out of his favorite mug.

"I'm alright." Anatoly put down his glass of vodka. "What's up, papa. It's barely six there. Why are you already about?"

"I've decided it's time to send Gabriel to you."

"So, you've seen what you need to see?"

"*Da*, he's a good boy."

"Where in this organization can I use a good boy?" Anatoly asked angrily. "I need men. I need killers. I don't need good boys." He sat in his office behind his desk brooding alone.

"How do you think that you started? I saw a good boy when you came to my door step. I didn't see killer or even a *man*. I saw a young boy who had potential."

Anatoly was silent.

"So, I'm sending him to you. He's agreed to set aside his obligations in New York. There are a few men who can run things there for him while he learns the ropes from you," Dmitry said, turning on his television to watch the news. He controlled his anger.

"Fine. Send him," Anatoly said shortly.

"I plan to," Dmitry sighed. "Something else has developed since you left."

"What?"

"It seems that Gabriel and Briggy have become an item." Dmitry waited for his son to explode. He'd always had territory issues.

"So, you want her to come too?"

"No. I want you to know this before he comes, so you can deal with your emotions before he arrives. This should be a non-issue, because you and Briggy are a non-issue. Am I making myself clear?"

"Papa, I don't give a fuck about your maid." Anatoly rolled his eyes.

"So I take it that you and my *shop girl*, Renee, are doing well then?" Dmitry asked, making his point about one woman's position over the other. To demean a woman for doing an honest job was like demeaning a priest for being holy - ridiculous. And he wouldn't have it.

"I haven't spoken to Renee in a week. She left the shop. She left my home. She left my life."

Dmitry knew that there was something wrong. And there it was; heart-break. He felt for the boy, but it was only a matter of time before he fell in love with someone. And it was only normal in their occupation that it wouldn't bode well.

"Give it time," Dmitry said softly. "I'm sure that you'll find a way to reach her and talk things over. These things do not fix themselves over night. If they do, they are not real."

Anatoly couldn't even bring himself to say anything clever. In fact, just the thought of her brought him pain. "Let us hope, papa."

"It's good that you know how to compartmental-ize these types of situations. Moving on, when Gabriel arrives, after you've introduced him to everyone, I want you to send him to Dallas to speak with Royal's mother and arrange a meeting in Jamai-ca for the family."

"Now, I'm responsible for family reunions? Papa, I'm boss. I'm not travel agent or..."

"I am asking you this favor as your father. Re-member always who I am to you and know that my requests are more important than even your biggest business deals." Dmitry's voice was harsh.

Anatoly quickly bit his tongue. "Of course, papa. Forgive me. I will arrange as soon as Gabriel ar-rives."

"Good. Now, if you'll excuse me, I'd like to get on with my day," Dmitry said, hanging up the phone.

Chapter Twenty-Four

Gabriel had only been to Memphis once. The first time that he had come, he had imagined pulling up to a rural speck of land with hogs and chickens running wildly about, but it was mildly impressive. The people seemed warm and there was a true appreciation for food, especially pork. Evidently, he'd landed in the Home of The Blues and barbeque.

Downtown Memphis was a busy little spot. Cars and trolleys littered the main thoroughfares. People walked up and down the streets in their suits with their heads attached to their cell phones. Cops stood on the corners. Pockets of homeless people hid in the alleyways, emerging only to beg for a few bucks or get something to eat. It was basically a little Manhattan. He shrugged, maybe not that similar, but the place had its own nice metro vibe.

Anatoly had put him up in the loft above his clothing store, *Dmitry's Closet*. Evidently, his ex-girl had lived here before him, because while he was unpacking his things and putting them away, he found a letter to Anatoly. The guy had been a complete prick to him until he showed him that little note. He lit up like a Christmas tree, though he tried to conceal it.

Gabriel could understand. He missed Briggy so badly until it literally felt like his heart would fall out of his body. They spoke daily, but it was hard to keep contact, because of the time difference. He knew the time would come when his uncle would send him off, but he was hoping for more time with her. She had cried for two days when he told her that he was leaving. She had said that she would quit and come with him, but he had talked her out of it. Knowing the previous relationship with Anatoly and knowing that he was undercover, there was no way in hell that he was going to drag her into this anymore than he already had.

Today, Gabriel was set to meet the council. This was a big step. He would know all the players in the Medlov crime family, and they would know him. This was by far the riskiest thing that he had done. There was no turning back now.

Vasily knocked on the front door and waited for him. Grabbing his coat, and putting on his guns, Gabriel quickly met him and was escorted over to the restaurant. They convened the meeting in the basement of *Mother Russia* amidst the largest group of heavily armed bodyguards that he'd ever seen. He knew from the briefing with the DEA that there was once a basement to this place, but after the bombings the entire building had been rebuilt and a lot of rooms had been restructured. However, one thing that was wrong in the reports was that the basement no longer existed. It did exist, and it was now heavily reinforced. It would take an army to get down into this place and many causalities to get out of it.

Anatoly evidently had a serious thing for guns and bodyguards, because there were more of them than council members. And none of the council members' bodyguards were ever allowed inside. They were completely vulnerable, if not under the boss's protection.

The 15 men sat at a table built from old wood that Gabriel imagined came from Russia considering the organization's nostalgic demeanor like kings at court. He also noticed that they were all a great deal older than Anatoly. Gabriel imagined that really pissed most of them off. These men were powerful, dangerous and notorious, yet a boy sat at the head of their table, and they had no choice but to either respect him or war with him.

However, Anatoly Medlov was no light-weight. Once Gabriel was seated in the corner, Anatoly came into the room with Vasily and three other men closely behind. He commanded their attention not with theatrics but with a scowl that rivaled Putin's. He looked ready to kill at any moment. It was obvious that he did not trust them, or at least some of them.

In jeans and a t-shirt, he sat down at the head of the table and looked around. With a sigh, he began the meeting, indicating either his frustration with the men or himself.

"Vasily, check the room, please," Anatoly said, pouring himself a glass of water.

Vasily quickly checked the room for bugs then nodded at his boss to begin.

"I have brought you all here to meet a very important member of my family," Anatoly said slowly, irritated. He gritted his teeth as he talked. "My father has blessed the...*existence* of my cousin Gabriel Medlov, who is the son of Ivan Medlov."

The room buzzed. They all turned to look at the stranger who had been escorted it the room. His familiarity was suddenly apparent.

Anatoly rolled his eyes. "It is my father's wish, and therefore my own, that you humbly accept our brother, a fellow thief-in-law into the Medlov Organized Crime Family. His role will be minimal to start. He has been assigned Igor's former position and will handle our trafficking efforts in South Florida. Once he has proven himself, he will be assigned other duties. Are there any questions?"

Gabriel could feel the angst and hesitation in the room. Anatoly may have been just a boy in years but his knowledge of the men and the organization was great and their knowledge of his brutality was evident. Anatoly stared them down as he sat quietly with the glass in his hand, waiting for them to say one unjust word against his father's decision. But no one was that careless. Instead, they posed the questions to be more susceptible to Anatoly's cooperation.

"Is there a file on this young man?" Khalid, the oldest and most respected of the council asked, turning towards Gabriel. "It is my request, Anatoly, that we all receive a little background knowledge on him. He is after all being allowed into the most sacred part of our lives. Know that I do not question the choice of my dear friend, Dmitry. I simply remember the boy's father, and I want to feel more comfortable with him even being alive."

Anatoly sat back in his chair. "You request is warranted, *brat*. A file will be provided to all 15 members of the council by the end of the day."

Yuri chimed in after seeing that Anatoly was open to conversation. "And what of our South Florida shipments? This is a major part of our business. If he proves to be unable to fulfill his obligation as the trafficker of our product then it leaves both the family and the client in peril."

"We don't need to exaggerate the value of the South Florida inventory. It only makes up two percent of our global shipments. However, I will assist Gabriel in this. Only because my father has asked me, will I lower myself to this responsibility. However," Anatoly looked at Gabriel, "he is my cousin. And he is of royal bloodline. So, while I completely understand your concern, I would ask that you know that I am more than capable of handling the South Florida shipments and all the others for that matter. And there is no need to worry if I am involved."

"Of course there is not," Yuri, bowing his head. "Knowing that you will be responsible for him and the shipments makes us all feel better about the situation. I'm sure." He looked at Oleg.

The men concurred.

Anatoly nodded at the council member for his concern and his graceful digression.

"Any other questions?" Anatoly asked.

"Why has the boy been in hiding?" Oleg asked at the far end of the table.

Anatoly sat forward in his seat. "The council's job is to ensure my father's interests. The council's job is to ensure the family's diversity, devotion to the code and the sustainability of the organization's financial foundation for perpetuity, *if possible*. The council's job is *not* to question my father, the founder of this family. I don't understand why a man of your age would not know this. But I do understand when my leadership is being questioned. Once a few years ago, my father allowed this council to be more than what it was founded to be, and it yielded bad fruit in the form of men thinking that they were bigger and greater than this organization. Since then, there have been modifications, and since then you all have agreed through blood covenant to that agreement. You were bound to it on that day. You are bound to the covenant still and until death. Do not forget it. Because I am not my father. I do not have *history* clouding my position. In fact, I do not forgive, gentlemen."

The room was silent.

"Are there any other questions," Anatoly asked, looking around the room at the men.

The room continued in silence.

Anatoly stood up from the table. "I extend my best wishes to you and to your families. Until our next meeting, be well."

***

The words rang in Gabriel's ears well after the meeting. *I do not forgive, gentlemen.* He could hear Anatoly say it over and over. He realized that while his cousin had not meant the words for him specifically, they had affected him most.

After the meeting, Gabriel had been brought to Anatoly's mansion by Vasily, while Anatoly went to take care of some other important business regarding another deal taking place in Israel later that month.

Evidently, his cousin handled many different business transactions on a daily basis and none ever took place in his home city. That had been the cardinal rule since the horrible show down almost four years ago with his father. The Medlov Organized Crime family had done a complete 180 since then. Rules had been put in place that could not be broken.

Anatoly was going to go over a few of those rules with Gabriel tonight over dinner. This would be the first intimate conversation he had held with him alone. And in truth, he was very nervous about it. While Dmitry was more interested in his background and all the things that he had missed growing up

away from the family, Anatoly would not be so
interested in anything but operations and how he
could use him.

At the very moment, Gabriel was alone at the
mansion with the exception of one of Vasily's un-
derlings and the maids and house staff. He had been
confined to the entertainment room and given a
remote.

He wasn't really a big television watcher. In
fact, he hardly ever turned the thing on except to
watch the news, but for now he calmed his thoughts
by watching ridiculous reality shows and eating the
candy in the bowl on the table.

Several hours later, after he had fallen asleep on
the couch, he felt his foot being kicked. He looked up
to realize that he was not back in Prague but in his
cousin's house. It was strange how lately he often
went to bed and forgot where he was all together.

"Wake up, I want to talk to you," Anatoly said,
sitting across from him on the opposite couch.

Gabriel stretched and looked at his watch. It was
almost eleven at night. The last thing he remembered
it was six in the evening. Now the day had completely gone and was giving way to midnight.

Anatoly coddled a glass of vodka in one hand and
rubbed his dog's head with the other. Under a scru-
pulous stare, he put his bare feet up on the ottoman
and motioned for Vasily to turn off the television.

"Are you comfortable in Renee's old place?"
Anatoly asked.

"Yes, it's a nice set up. Thanks." Gabriel answered, looking at his dogs.

"Well, you won't be spending much time there. Until I'm comfortable with you, you'll be expected to report here by seven in the morning. So, I hope that you're an early riser. You'll shadow me all day. You won't be allowed to sit in on any meetings until I'm certain that I want you there. You'll do what I say, when I say."

"Cool," Gabriel nodded.

Anatoly sat up a little and squinted. Pointing at him with the glass in his hand, he shook his head. "See that's what bothers me about you, Gabriel. You think that everything is *cool*. You supposedly built an entire organization yourself, and you have no problem running around doing my bitch work. Why is that?"

Gabriel didn't blink. He looked over at Vasily and raised his hand. "Hey bring me a glass of that vodka, will ya?" he said, turning back to Anatoly.

"To tell you that it doesn't bother me not to run my own shit would be a lie, but just like you had to start somewhere to get somewhere, I'm here. I'd rather be back in New York running my crew, but we're small fries. I know that if I ever want to sit at that table with those 15 men across from you, if I want my own money, if I want real power, then the best thing that I can do is to put in my time down here and learn something new."

Anatoly sat back in his seat and took a sip of drink. As he did, Vasily brought Gabriel a drink.

"Alright then. We'll talk about the way things work around here after I give you your first assignment," Anatoly said, letting whatever was on his mind fester.

Gabriel listened quietly.

"I want you to go to Dallas and find that woman that you said is Royal's mother. Without scaring the life out of her, I want you persuade her to go to Jamaica to see her daughter."

"Why me?" Gabriel asked.

"Well, for one thing, this all came to pass because of your nosy ass. So, it's only right for you to have to go up there. Secondly, I don't want to be bothered with it. I have a real organization to deal with here, and I need to keep my eyes on these men and my money."

"Fine, when do you want me to go?"

"Sooner than later. Set it up; let Vasily know what you need, and get it done." It was the first time that Gabriel had been given an unsupervised job since he arrived.

Gabriel happily took on the responsibility. "Done. Now, when will I get to chance to start working on this deal in South Florida?"

"We'll talk about that tonight," Anatoly said, glad that his cousin could stay focused. "We move at a very high tempo here. Nothing is done in a lax manner, nothing is done a second time. We do things right the first time. We are always thorough and always professional with our clients. Keep your emotions to yourself. If you see something you don't like, then deal with it. I don't deal well with people asking me to back off a thing, a person, a situation. If I tell you to shoot and kill, do it. I don't give a damn if it's a woman, a child, a dog. It doesn't matter. My final word is *the* final word. It doesn't go any higher than me, and my word doesn't change. So don't ask. I'm not God, but I'm ruler of this. We need to be clear, because I saw your hesitation in Italy. And I didn't like it. Killing is what we do. We supply guns to kill. We use guns to kill. We send people to kill. This is the industry that you want in – so if you don't like the core purpose, get on a plane and go back to New York."

Gabriel tried to control his impulse to cringe. "I understand completely. And I'll do exactly as you tell me to.

Anatoly smiled. He always gave the *kill speech*, because his father had given it to him. However, he had hardly been in a situation where a woman was involved. And he'd never imagined hurting a child. He just wanted to see the guy's face. "Though you probably will never see another woman killed. We don't normally do that shit –with the exception of your father. And trust me, Victoria had it coming," he said finally. He pulled out his cigarettes and lit one.

"If you don't mind me asking, how did she *have it coming*?" Gabriel could finally ignore the statements about his father. He understood that it was just Anatoly's way of giving him crap. And Gabriel already knew about Victoria. Briggy had told him the entire story from what she knew while he was back in Prague. However, to act as if he wasn't curious would only look more suspect.

"Victoria was trying to expose our entire organization, even after my father gave her chance after chance. She'd contacted the cops here of all places. I still don't know why she would call the local police department. Evidently, she saw all the press this one prick, Agosto, had received here."

"Yeah, I even read about him," Gabriel added. It was the truth. He had. The guy was a certifiable bad ass and had a lot of respect in the law enforcement community. Whenever anyone even mentioned Memphis, Agosto's name was brought up to certify credibility.

Anatoly took a puff of his cigarette and laughed. "Plus, she had already tried to seduce my father in his house after drugging his wife. *Big mistake.* Not to mention that she just aggravated the shit out of me. She was a fucking stalker and crazy as hell. That last move just proved to us all that she had to go."

Gabriel couldn't help but smirk. He had heard the same story from Briggy and a few other things from Dmitry. She was a piece of work. Plus, there was no way to trace her. He had called the wine estate

afterwards and asked for Victoria Jackson and someone had answered as her. It would be impossible for
him to know if he had been set up to see if he would
snitch or to know if someone was posing as Victoria
to cover the murder. He had been taught during his
training that an undercover agent couldn't save
everyone, and Victoria had been the one that he
couldn't save. Besides, if he had to save anyone at
all in this it would Briggy.

Chapter Twenty-Five

The days had turned to weeks and the weeks into nearly a month. Anatoly was going mad in his own brain, quietly trying to hide his mounting despair of being deprived of his best friend. He immersed himself in work, meeting and planning, never wanting to go to bed or even return to his bedroom. Every time that he did, he thought of her.

He had expected a call, an email, a text. But Renee had gone silent. When she said that she needed some time to think, he assumed that she would do it in the city. But she had cut out of Memphis and left him alone.

However, one something had been bothering him a great deal in the last few days. She had told him that she was used to a man *chasing her*. The words had awakened him out of his sleep and driven him out to the patio where he now was sitting with his dogs and smoking. Was he supposed to go after her? Was she waiting on him?

He'd never been as lonely as he was lately. There was no one to confide in, and in her absence he'd actually grown fond of Gabriel. The thought repulsed him. Day after day, he got to know the man a little better, and he actually proved to be somewhat efficient.

In fact, he'd started to mildly trust him, giving him more responsibilities than he originally planned.

"Hey, Anatoly," Gabriel said, knocking on the door.

Anatoly looked up from dogs, trying to hide his melancholy. "Yeah."

"The maid said that you were out here. I just wanted to let you know that the thing with Royal's mother has been arranged. I just need to head down there. I can leave in the morning, if you don't mind."

"Go, please. I need papa off my back," he said sighing.

"One other thing that may or may not be appropriate for me to bring up, but I know that you'd said you wanted better tabs on the council members. Have you considered bugging their homes and their businesses? I could set it all up in your office or a room here where you would be the only one with access. It would simplify things for you, if you know what I mean."

Anatoly thought that could be a good idea. He nodded. "You can bug their businesses. Hell, what Feds haven't? But you may not bug their homes. We are brothers. There are some lines that we do not cross. There are certain privacies that are meant to stay intact."

"Cool. You alright?" Gabriel asked, stepping outside and closing the door.

Anatoly looked up at the man and debated if he should cross the line, become personal with him.

Gabriel waited with a look of true sincerity on his face.

"Do you ever miss, Briggy?" Anatoly asked softly.

Gabriel shook his head. "Like crazy, man." He stuffed his hands down in his pockets. "I just...it's hard to be without her now that I know what life is like with her." He frowned, worried that he had shared too much.

Anatoly looked at him without any expression on his face. "Send for her." His eyes eased along with the tension in his shoulders. He slumped over, showing his utter defeat. "Before it's too late and all the right things are never said and all the wrong things are done."

"You mean like for a weekend or something?"

"No. I mean send for her for good." Anatoly shrugged. "Royal can find a new maid. My father will see to it. But you can't as easily find a woman who is willing to be discrete and caring. Briggy has been with the family for a long time. She is trust-worthy and a hard worker. She can also be of some use at *Dmitry's Closet*. I still haven't found anyone to fill Renee's spot and the assistant manager is completely clueless."

"Wow. Thanks. I'll call her," Gabriel said, moved. He knew this was a major step for his cousin. "Was Renee your girl?"

"Yeah. You could call her that, but it was over before it could begin. Hell, you went out on a date with her. You know how special she is. I just messed up. Man to man, I fucked up bad. And there isn't an amount that will buy her or a woman who can replace her. I'm screwed. She's probably out right now with some idiot."

Gabriel smirked. "It was a very *guarded* date with Renee, you know. She wouldn't even let me touch her hand. No kiss. Nothing. She barely looked at me all night. I think she did it to get back at you, because she talked about her *boss* all night."

Anatoly laughed. "Did she?" his deep voice lightened.

"Yeah, she was really into you. So, I doubt that much has changed in such a short period of time. She's probably just waiting...on you, I mean. That's the way that women are. They want you to stake your claim."

Anatoly nodded. He was proud of her, and it made him feel better about himself. "Do you think that before you leave in the morning for Dallas, you could get me an address of where she is in Atlanta?" he asked as an idea hit him.

"Sure," Gabriel said, turning to walk away. "I'll leave it in the kitchen for you on the island."

Anatoly nodded and turned his attention back to his dogs. "*Spasiba, brat.*"

Gabriel stopped in his tracks. Anatoly had never once thanked him. "D*obro pozhalovat* " Gabriel answered, closing the door behind him.

***

As Gabriel promised, there was green sticky note on the kitchen island when Anatoly came downstairs the next morning for breakfast. On it was Renee's home address and her new cell number. In his usual routine, he turned on the television to watch the morning news on CNN, fixed a bowl of Cheerios and grabbed a green apple.

Vasily came in minutes later, fully dressed and ready to work. He had been out all morning getting the hardware needed to bug all the men on the council's businesses, per Gabriel's suggestion.

"Boss, what you asked of me last night has been done," he said, going to the refrigerator to get a bottle of water.

"Good," Anatoly said, nodding at the maid who came in and began to quickly tidy up the kitchen behind him. He turned his attention back to Vasily. "Cancel all of my meetings for today," he said finally.

Vasily looked up confused. They had a major meet and greet at *Mother Russia* at one this afternoon.

"I'm going to Atlanta," Anatoly answered Vasily's frown.

"Should I make preparations for when the plane arrives back from Dallas?" he asked.

"No, it's only a six hour drive. I'll take the Bentley," he said, running his spoon around the rim of the bowl. "And before you ask, yes, I'm going alone."

"May I ask who you're going to see?" Vasily leaned against the door.

"You already know who I'm going to *get*," Anatoly said with a wicked grin. "I don't know how long it's going to take. So, cancel everything until I tell you otherwise. Anyone who is too important already has my cell."

"*Da, da*, boss. I'll go and do it now," Vasily said, excusing himself.

Anatoly looked up at the television and smirked. He was going to do it. He was going to chase Renee.

***

As Gabriel sat down for lunch after meeting with Royal's mother during an emotional conversation that ended with a vow of secrecy, he realized that he was both physically and mentally exhausted. Never in his history as an agent, or just as a human, had he seen a woman cry so much. His mother had been a rock, hard as nails. And his father was a sociopath, *enough said*. So often years went by before anyone showed any emotion other than anger and pride.

Now as he sat alone in the confines of an upscale steakhouse, as only expected in Texas, to enjoy a nice meal, he realized just how much of the human emotional spectrum he lacked. He had never once cried like that or loved like that or hurt like that...until now. As the woman heard that one of her daughters was alive and well in another country and was seeking her out, she exhaled a cry from deep within. There was happiness, joy and pain all wrapped into one mental breakdown. She almost pulled a tear out of him, especially with how torn he had been lately. He just didn't think he could take anymore...

"Welcome to Mitchell's Steakhouse. Today's special is Operation Family Raid. Have you given any thought to what you'd like to order?" the woman asked with her notepad in hand. She looked down her glasses at him, and motioned towards the bathroom door.

"That's cute," Gabriel said, putting down his glass of water. He pulled the napkin from his lap and put it on the table as he stood. "Bring me a steak or something. I'll eat it when I get back."

While looking around carefully, he strode over to the men's restroom. As he stepped inside, Agent Lee closed and locked the door behind him.

"It's hard as hell to get in touch with you these days, Agent Medlov. It is still agent, isn't it? Or maybe you've dropped off that title," Agent Lee said sarcastically.

Gabriel walked to each stall and opened it. Looking in, he still did not say a word.

"It's safe, agent," Lee said.

Gabriel went to the last stall and looked around then came back. "You can never be too sure." He swallowed hard and put his hands down into the pockets of his four-thousand dollar suit.

Agent Lee automatically noticed this clothes and his changed demeanor.

"You've changed," Lee said, pulling out a thumb drive.

"No, I haven't. I've been under a lot of stress lately with trying to set up my own family." Even the words left a sour taste in Gabriel's mouth. He felt like spitting at the man's foot but controlled himself.

"Your own family?" Lee asked with a flinch. "Let's get this straight. You volunteered for this. You convinced us to take you on. Now, you feel like what...because they let you in, you're suddenly one of the guys?"

"That's not what I said," Gabriel growled.

"Why haven't you checked in? It's been six weeks, Agent Medlov."

"This is the first time in six weeks that I've been trusted to go anywhere or do anything by myself. If I had blown my cover, I may have lost my life. But I know that docsn't matter to you fucking people." Gabriel looked at his Rolex. "I don't have much time. So here." He knelt down and pulled a thumb drive out of his shoe. "What I could get is on here."

"Maybe it's time that you come in, Gabriel," Lee said, moving out of the way.

"Because what? Because I'm working my ass off? Because doing this job means that you can't have your hands on me at all times?" Gabriel asked looking down to Agent Lee's face.

Agent Lee smirked and backed off the brooding giant. "No, it has nothing to do with any of that. It's because you're becoming what we sent you in to tear down," he said, touching Gabriel's suit. "Just remember this. You're supposed to be there to do a job. When it's done these people will go to jail for a long time, and don't think just because they're nice to you, that they don't deserve to burn."

Gabriel felt the heat rising from his collar. He looked down at the man and scowled. "Nice to me? Are you fucking insane. The Medlov Organized family is a lot of things, but nice isn't one of them."

"You know who you sound like right now?" Agent Lee asked.

Gabriel raised his brow. *Like he cared what this guy thought.*

"Anatoly Medlov," Lee said, shaking his head. "If you don't come up with some new Intel on where these drugs are very quickly, I'm pulling you off this."

"Like I said, this is my first time out in six weeks. It takes time."

"Time we don't have. Our source says that the last major shipment for this year will take place in three weeks. We need to be there for the drop – and on time, Agent Medlov. If we're not, this entire charade has been for nothing. Do you understand that?"

Gabriel grabbed the door handle. "I'll find your fucking drugs. Just back off me. Don't blow my cover."

"With all the money exchanging hands and the girls...don't forget whose side you're on," Lee reminded as the door closed.

Chapter Twenty - Six

Renee knew that she should have already gotten an apartment by now, but being away from Anatoly for the first time in years had made her lonely for companionship. So, she settled for the next best thing to having a pseudo-boyfriend and moved back in with Big Momma.

Everyone was surprised to see her pull up in her old car, considering she had bragged about the Hummer that she was given Christmas of last year as a work car. But they were still happy to see her just the same.

News had traveled fast up from Memphis a few years before when the Medlov family got into a nationally publicized gunfight that spanned half the city. Her entire family had expected her to move back then. But Renee had vouched for them and said that it was all a *big misunderstanding* and the Medlov's were *good people*.

No one had bought it, but they let her stay without throwing a fit. They knew there must have been a man involved.

Now, Renee was home. She had gotten a job working at a major clothing store downtown, but she hated it. For nearly four years, she had run her own shop, and now she was suddenly back to taking orders from someone else. The truth of the matter was that she had enough money in the bank not to work for a while, to get her head together. But Renee knew that an idle mind was the devil's work-shop. It was best for her to find something to do to while trying to mend her broken heart and to keep her from dragging herself back to Memphis.

Big Momma lived in the heart of Washington Park in North Atlanta on a corner-lot, white, two-story home built in the early 1940's. Everyone east of Ashbury knew her either from the church as head usher or the local babysitter. She had babysat hun-dreds of kids in the community and prayed for hun-dreds more. Plus, at some point, in between raising children and being a good wife to Big Daddy before he passed, Big Momma was a freedom fighter during the 1960's. So, she was extremely hard on her kids about higher-educational achievement and black love.

Renee had been one her favorite grandchildren. After her mother and Army father divorced early in her childhood, Renee was dropped off with Big Momma, and she stayed there until she graduated from Clarke Atlanta University and moved to Mem-phis. The rest was history.

***

It was the middle of the week, and Renee had one day off. She was using it to help weed Big Momma's garden for her, since she had been ailing from gout all morning. Out in the petunia patch, she worked in a pair of sweat pants and an old Clark Atlanta t-shirt with her I-pod buds planted deep in her ears. She just wanted to drown the rest of the world out. Every morning since she'd arrived, she'd cried. And every evening, since she'd arrived, she'd spent waiting. Anatoly never called and he never came for her. And something in her wouldn't let her call him.

If she knew anything about Anatoly, she knew that he thought that he was God's gift to women. He didn't respond well to constant affection or attention. It worked in spurts, when he was low, he would need a pick-me-up, and when he was too high, he needed someone to ground him. Other than that, the boy stayed somewhere in the middle all of the time. It had worked for them, however. Their strange relationship allowed her to go about her busy schedule with the shop and him to travel around the world, and they still have someone to come home to at the end of the day. Because from what she had seen, no one else cared for her schedule or her passion for clothes.

Renee knew that she had run the store better than Royal – better than anyone. And Anatoly knew it too, which was why he had begged her to stay.

The thought made Renee nearly cry again. She hadn't stayed.

Shaking her head, she dug her hoe down into the earth and tried to block more images of the man she'd run away from out of her mind.

On the porch, just a few feet from her, her cousins Angie and Rita sat talking to each other and watching all the cars as they went past. Many of them blew their horn, especially the men, because everyone knew Angie and Rita. They were the black sheep of the grandchildren or sisters-in-trouble as Big Momma called them.

Out of 12 grandchildren, Rita and Angie were the only ones who hadn't gone to college and had barely finished high school. They had seven children between the two of them and not one stable father. Of course, they hated Renee, because she was Big Momma's baby and had so many good things going for herself. So, they were thoroughly enjoying her serious depression.

"Girl, why don't you get up out them weeds before you get funky," Rita said, picking her teeth and leaning off the elevated porch.

Renee could hear her even though her ear buds were in, but chose to act as if she could not. She kept her eyes on the garden.

"She can't hear you," Angie said, rolling her eyes. "Oh...look. This is the hairstyle I told you I wanted you to do for me."

Rita sauntered over to the bench that Angie was sitting on and took the hair magazine. Smacking her lips, she hit the page. "Girl, you can't do that with your hair. That's for somebody who got *good hair*."

"There is no such thing as good hair," Renee said, looking up from her work. "It's all designed to keep you ignorant."

"I told you her stuck up ass could hear us," Rita said, rolling her eyes.

"Who is she calling ignorant?" Angie asked, standing up.

"I don't mean you, *necessarily*," Renee said shaking her head. "I mean...us...black women. If you want to get a perm – fine. Go for it. But do it because you want to do it and not because society tells you that it makes you more attractive. You're already beautiful."

"This bitch thinks she's Erykah Badu or something," Rita said, rolling her eyes.

They quickly turned to ignore Renee, who simply went back working, and this time turned up her I-pod where she couldn't hear them at all.

***

Anatoly had been to Atlanta on a couple of occasions, but he had flown in and out – never driven. As he pulled down the street that Renee's grandmother supposedly lived on, the hoards of people on the corners and on the various porches looked on curiously. He could see from the car, their many points, waves and stares.

Stopping at the corner, he rolled down his window and stuck his head out. Getting the attention of one of the guys talking by the stop sign, Anatoly waved him over.

"What you looking for, homey?" the man asked, hitting the tip of his nose with the knuckle of his index finger.

Anatoly took the sticky note off the dashboard and passed it to him.

"I'm looking for that place," Anatoly said in his thick Russian accent without a smile. He pulled his Aviator shades off and looked the man in the eye. "Can you help me?"

The man first surveyed the car, then Anatoly and the Glock in his passenger seat. Finally, he turned and pointed in the opposite direction. "You see that white house right there?"

Anatoly lifted his head. "*Da*," he said slowly.

"That's Big Momma's house. That's the address you're looking for."

"Does Renee live there?"

The man laughed. "Yeah, I think she just moved back."

Anatoly slipped on his shades and smiled. "Thanks...*homey*," he said, mockingly.

Angie and Rita spotted the Bentley before it could turn down the street. Standing up, they hit each other and made their way down the steps.

"Who in the hell is that white boy?" Rita asked, pulling down her shirt. "Damn, he's is so fine."

"Girl, I got dibs on this one," Angie said, patting her hair. "Oh...look. He's stopping right here, girl."

"Do you think he's one of those mission dudes that Big Momma be working with?" Rita whispered.

"I don't know. She be working with some really rich people, but he don't look like no saint," Angie said smiling.

Anatoly parked right in front of the house and looked at the sticky note again. This was right place. Turning the car off, he stepped out and made his way up to the fence where he saw two women on the steps of the porch and one burrowed down working in the garden. It didn't even take a second glance for him to know who that was.

As he walked up the narrow concrete walk-way that led to the steps of the house, he pointed towards Renee.

"Does she have those ear buds in?" he asked the women as he touched his own ears.

Rita was dumbfounded. Laughing and looking at Angie, she nodded her head. "Yeah, she's got'em on."

"Oh, I don't believe this shit," Angie said, shaking her head.

Anatoly walked up behind Renee as she worked. The music was up so loud until she could not hear anything going on around her. He knelt behind her, right on her back and watched her.

She felt his body heat and turned around. Surprised, she fell over into the dirt and on top of the flowers.

Anatoly laughed. He was so happy to see her, so happy to smell her again. She had on the perfume that he had bought her in Israel and the gold hoop earrings he had bought her in Istanbul. But it warmed his heart even more to know that she wasn't off with another man. She was here waiting on him.

"Ana, what are you doing here?" she asked, taking off her IPod. She looked around for Vasily and realized that he was alone.

"Chasing you, I guess," he said softly, helping her up.

They stood up, only inches away from each other. Renee looked away and wiped the dirt off her clothes, embarrassed that he had seen her looking so homely. But Anatoly quickly grabbed her chin and pulled her to him.

"Do you think I drove all the way down here to watch you wipe yourself," he asked.

Renee couldn't talk. With a grin, she wrapped her dirty arms around his white t-shirt and kissed his lips slowly. He met her with the same enthusiasm, taking her mouth hungrily, he wrapped his strong arms around her, exposing his many tattoos as he tightly held her.

"I missed you," he whispered on her lips with his eyes still closed, still savoring her taste.

"I missed you," she answered, kissing him again.

"Ain't this a bitch," Rita commented. "I'm gon' quit worrying about my hair and start doing yard work."

Angie laughed. "Shit, me too." She screamed out to Renee. "Hey, girl. Can I borrow your hoe?"

***

By dusk, everyone was at Big Momma's house for dinner. Renee's two uncles, who also lived with their mother, along with a host of cousins and aunts gathered in the backyard for a fish fry.

Anatoly had never seen so many family members in one place who were all happy to see each other or cordial to one another.

Big Momma had insisted that he stay the night in the guest bedroom, which was a box of a room down the hall from Renee painted in sea blue with a picture of a black Jesus above the bed. He agreed happily, interested to see what type of home Renee had come from. In truth, he envied her. He had never had a grandmother, especially one as grand as Big Momma. And while the family was poor in finances, they were richly rooted in love.

Anatoly sat by Renee in the lawn chairs out on the patio, talking and eating spaghetti, slaw and catfish while the men interrogated him, and the women swooned after him.

"So you own a clothing store?" Uncle Leman asked, cleaning his teeth with a toothpick after dinner.

Uncle Leman was a factory worker with an honest gambling habit. He was living with Big Momma to get up on his feet after a nasty divorce from his wife of twenty years. Still, he was grounded. He had spent four years in the military and had come back to Atlanta to open a barber shop, but things hadn't panned out for him after he developed an appreciation for game of craps. Still he was crazy about Renee and didn't necessarily like the element that she was around. He knew trouble when he saw it, and Anatoly Medlov was big trouble.

"*Da*, I own a clothing store among other things." Anatoly answered, trying to get comfortable in the chair.

"And you make enough to drive a Bentley?" Renee's other uncle asked. "You know, I used to know a pimp who had a Bentley."

"A pimp?" Anatoly raised his brow. "I am no pimp."

"Good," Uncle Leman said, opening his beer. "Cuz if you were *a pimp*, we were gonna have to kick your ass."

"Uncle Lee!" Renee gasped. "This is my friend."

"Boyfriend," Anatoly corrected.

Renee looked back at Anatoly and smiled. "My boyfriend. And he's no pimp. Now let it go."

"No, he's right. If I were him, I'd be concerned also," Anatoly said, touching her hand. "I'm a business man." He looked back at Uncle Leman.

"I Googled you on my new cell phone my daughter bought me, and it says here that you're a mobster," Uncle Leman said, raising his phone. "Is that true?"

Anatoly smirked. "You can't believe everything you read on Internet."

"I'm sure that there are things that are not on the Internet, Uncle Lee, that you wouldn't want people digging up about you. Now, let it go," Renee said, rolling her eyes.

Rita and Angie sat across from them, watching and whispering to one another. When Anatoly glanced their way, they waved. He waved back and raised his brow at Renee. "Your cousins are very colorful."

"Careful, you look at them too long, you'll get them pregnant," she said under breath.

Anatoly laughed. "You have a beautiful family." He moved her hair out of her face. "But I want you to come home."

Renee put down her plate. "You wanna take a walk?" she asked, standing up.

"Sure," Anatoly said, putting away his food.

They headed through the fence together, hand-in-hand. The street lights had come on and people walked up and down the sidewalks as they talked quietly.

"I've been doing a lot of thinking," Renee said, biting her lip. "And I have to have something of my own, Ana. I know that you don't understand, but the morning that I woke up in your bed, I realized that you were starting to be my everything. That frightened me, because I knew that it wouldn't be reciprocated. So, I left."

Anatoly looked down at her as she talked. *Her everything?* The words were only recently familiar to him, but he shared her sentiment. Suddenly, he knew that he had heard what he needed to hear.

"I have something for you," he said, reaching into his back pocket.

"Ana, I don't want any more gifts," she said protesting.

"It's not gift. Well, not really." He stopped walking and turned to her. Under the streetlight, he passed her a document.

Renee took the paper and unfolded it. As she read it, tears formed in the corner of her brown eyes and rolled down her hot cheeks. She looked up at him and sighed. "Is this for real, Ana?"

Anatoly shook his head. "I wanted to give you reason to stay in Memphis. Plus, it's yours. You...you've done well with it."

"What did Dmitry say?"

"He told me to sell it almost a year ago. I was just holding on to it, because you were there." He wiped her face. "But I have one *little* request."

"Anything," she said in a whisper.

"There is a girl coming from Prague who needs a job. Can you hire her? She's a family friend."

"Is she you ex-girlfriend?"

He looked up at the night sky and smiled. *Still the same old Renee.* "She's Gabriel's girlfriend." He avoided answering the question. *What was one minor secret?*

"Sure, she's hired." Renee looked down at the deed to the shop again and gasped. "I just can't believe that it's mine. Free and clear."

"It's yours. You have some paperwork you need to go over with the lawyers but.." Anatoly took her hand in his face. "So, I know that this is a bribe, but will you come home now?"

Renee laughed. "Yeah...I was coming home anyway the moment you got here. I guess," she sighed. "I guess I just needed it know that I was important enough for you to come for me. It may seem childish. In some ways, it is, but you've been given so much. I just wasn't sure if you valued me."

"I love you," Anatoly said seriously. "I know that I have a funny way of showing it, but I do. And I'll try to do so much better."

"No other women?" she asked, narrowing her eyes on him.

"No other women," he answered.

"No sex videos."

"Does that include with you?" he asked.

She rolled her eyes.

"Okay," he said, nodding. "No sex videos."

"Just us," Renee said, moving into him.

"Just us," Anatoly said, leaning down to kiss her.

***

Gabriel had to find a way to get to the bottom of this case before he got his cousin and his family into a world of trouble. Sitting down in Anatoly's office with Vasily back at the mansion, he looked over the new cameras that they had spent all day installing after he arrived back from Dallas and shook his head.

"Looks like we have everyone on here," Gabriel said, happy with their progress.

"This is good, *da*?" Vasily asked, looking at one of the monitors. "The boss will be happy."

"Fucking thrilled," Gabriel said, turning up the volume. "Make sure this thing continuously records. Change the tapes often. If I forget, I need you to have my back. This is too important to mess up on."

"What are we looking for?" Vasily asked curiously.

"A snake," Gabriel answered, looking at Vasily.

Chapter Twenty - Seven

Renee stepped out of the car after the long drive from Atlanta and looked at Anatoly's vast mansion the way that Royal must have looked at it the first time that she realized that she would be living there. It seemed massive all of a sudden.

As she went to the trunk to get her bag, Anatoly stopped her and pointed toward the house. "Go make yourself comfortable. Someone else will get your things."

"Is this where I start to get lazy?" she asked playfully.

"You live here now. You live the way that I live, and we don't carry our luggage." He grabbed her hands. "Come on."

The doors opened as they hit the step, and the maids moved out the way to greet them. Renee had never had that happen before. Normally, when she came over, she used her key.

"Good afternoon, Master Medlov" the maid said, passing him his mail.

"Hello Theresa," Anatoly said courteously. He looked down at his mail and waited for his dogs to appear. "Did Vasily make the arrangements as I told him."

"Yes, sir. Your room is ready for you both," she said, nodding at Renee.

Renee turned to the maid and smiled. "Just call me Renee, please. I mean, *Master* or *Mistress* – that is just too much for me."

"Yes ma'am," the maid said, excusing herself.

Anatoly put down his mail and shook his head. Just then, his dogs came running, scratching against the marble floor as they attacked him with licks and barks.

Renee walked towards the kitchen to give him a minute with his animals. "Are you hungry? I can fix us something to eat."

Anatoly stood up and put the mail back on the table. Slowly, he walked over to her and slipped his hand over hers. He lovingly kissed her forehead. "I have been trying to be a gentleman for the last twenty-four hours. And I think I did pretty good at it, but at this very moment," he ran his other hand down the side of her neck. "I'm only hungry for one thing."

Renee's eyes burned with fire. There was no way that they were going to make it upstairs. Following him quickly and quietly into his study, they burst through the door, kissing and stripping each other of their clothes.

Renee panted heavily as he pulled her pink bra strap down and bit her shoulder. In one quick motion, he had picked her up off the ground and pushed her against the wall while she struggled to unbuckle his pants.

"Umm…excuse me," Gabriel said, standing up from behind the desk. Vasily stood behind him unable to speak.

"Oh my goodness!" Renee exclaimed, trying to cover herself in front of the Vasily, and the guy she'd gone on the date with a few months ago. "What the hell is he doing here?" she asked, looking to Anatoly for an answer.

"Shit," Anatoly said, feeling his erection go down. He slid Renee carefully down to the floor and opened the door for her to slip out.

Turning to the men, he clasped his hands together and shook his head. "What the hell are you two doing in my office?"

"We're setting up the surveillance equipment and watching the council," Vasily explained. "Like you asked us to do, boss."

Anatoly forgot for a brief moment Renee's embarrassment and walked over to look at all the monitors. "This is all the businesses?" he asked, zipping up his pants.

"Every one of them," Gabriel answered. He moved out of the way so that Anatoly could see the equipment better.

Anatoly nodded, pleased with the men. He looked up from the monitors and smirked. "Good work."

"I take it that she didn't know about my little reconnaissance work?" Gabriel asked concerned.

"I forgot all about it. Now, I have to deal with that shit," Anatoly sighed and leaned against the table.

"I could go explain for you."

"I'm boss. No one explains for me."

Gabriel raised his brow. Sometimes, he forgot the duality of the man. One minute, he was just a guy trying to get a girl. The next minute, he was the boss of a multi-national crime syndicate.

Anatoly rubbed his head and got up. "Did you send for Briggy, yet?"

"I talk to her this morning. She's going to Dmitry and Royal about it."

Anatoly nodded. "I got her job at boutique."

"Thanks," Gabriel said, looking at the door as it opened. It was Renee – fully dressed. She crossed her arms over her chest and swallowed hard.

"Who is this for real, Ana?" she asked softly.

"This is my cousin Gabriel. I believe that you two already met under different circumstances."

Gabriel raised his hand. "Sorry about that, Renee. It was screwed up."

"You think?" she asked sarcastically.

Anatoly grinned and licked his lips. "Clear out of here," he said to the men. "I'll see you tomorrow."

The men quickly left Renee alone with Anatoly. As the door closed, she rolled her eyes at him. He had lied or hidden something again, before she could get through the door good.

Anatoly read her mind through her facial expression. He leaned his hands behind him on the desk and sighed. "I forgot to explain." He looked at her under heavy, hooded eyes.

"So is he like your buddy now?"she asked upset.

"Gabriel is useful." He reached behind him and grabbed the remote to turn off the monitors. The room became silent, and suddenly the two were back where they began. The rain beat against the outside of the windows and darkened the already cloudy skies. "Come here," Anatoly ordered, unbuttoning his jeans.

Renee knew when to let go. She obeyed his quiet command and walked over to him. His animal magnetism often drove her mad—like right now. He was leaning, muscles bulging, against the desk with his jean-clad, bow-legs spread wide. The rise in his pants imprinted from the bulging crotch down the inside of his thigh. The sensual look in his crystal blue eyes and the naughty curl of his lips willed her towards him.

Lifting her face to his, he leaned in and kissed her, stealing the wetness from them and creating new wetness in between her steaming thighs. His soft tongue stroked the inside of her mouth and made her forget all about Gabriel and Vasily.

Control spiraled away as he eagerly searched her swollen, hot mouth. Surrender on the horizon, she lifted one delicate, trembling hand to his rock-hard chest and planted it over his heart to feel the pound of it, beating like a lion.

From behind her, Anatoly ran his hand over her zipper and pulled it down. Hot skin of a firm backside cupped in his hand, he moaned as he pulled her against his throbbing erection.

Suddenly, he remembered his father doing this many years ago, taking Royal one night in this very room to tame her, to stake his claim upon her in a manner so carnal, no one would ever be able to come behind him. It was then that he decided that he must do the same.

He knew Renee would not understand it. In fact, she might think that he'd gone mad at first, but he committed to the action anyway. He had to dominate her.

The rain outside became violent. Heavy downpours of wind and water hit the windows and beat the house. It only drove him more to it. With the flick of a switch in reach, the lights were off and the fireplace turned on. Yellow-white flames colored the darkness and set the mood for his deed.

Still kissing her, he removed her silk skirt completely and pulled down her panties. Now bottomless, she clung to her silk, cream blouse as she tried to recognize the look in his eyes. He seemed changed, different.

Anatoly pulled her by her small waist in his powerful grip. Running his hands over her shirt, he unbuttoned it carefully and dropped it on the ground between them. As he did so, the strap of her pink bra fell down her arm. She tried to pull it up, but he stopped her.

"Let me help you," he said softly. With the flick of his wrist in the middle of her back, the bra fell down to the floor as well. Now completely naked, she stood vulnerable to his will, and he liked it.

His erection throbbed in his pants, dying to be buried inside of her. But he held his control.

Rubbing her shoulders, he slowly, lovingly, carefully, guided her down to her knees.

She looked up at him in shock. The first night, he had pleasured her without once indicating his own desires, but tonight, she could see in his eyes that all the things he had never asked of her before, he would ask in this room.

Anatoly caressed her face with his hand, then slipped a single digit into her wet mouth. She looked at him the entire time as she sucked it, making him feel a flush of sensations run through his entire body. Moving her thick locks of black hair from her face, he moved her up on her knees, closer to his groin.

As her warm, petite hands grasped his shaft, he closed his eyes for a minute to get his bearings before he guided himself inside her wet mouth. His own mouth started to water and his toes began to curl. Growling, he felt her suck the tip of him before devouring half of his length.

Snatching his shirt from his body, he pulled his jeans off quickly and lay down in between her shaking legs. She looked at him unsure if she had pleased him, but he quickly kissed her, taking away any discomfort that he might have caused through the act.

On the forty-thousand dollar rug, Anatoly splayed her body out in front of the fire. Licking his way from between her breasts down her belly button into her sex, he opened her legs wide and dipped below.

He gave equal amounts of pleasure for all that she had given. Sucking at her body, he felt her tense, and then tremble, but he would not give her any reprieve. A thousand thoughts assailed him. He drank in every detail of her body as he made her submit. She cried out in the room, and he was sure that it echoed down the hall, but he did not care. He was boss. She was his. Everyone would know it.

Slowly, he reached down to thread his fingers in her soaking sex. She clamored for him – in fact, begged for his merciful entry into her aching, burning body, but he denied her.

"Slow," he whispered as he rose to kiss her mouth. His hand cupped her breasts and tugged gently at their tips. With her legs wrapped around him, she tried to angle her body towards his hardness, but he pulled her down, running his hand over her sweating body.

"Please," she begged for him in a husky, needy whimper. "Please, Ana. Take me."

The deep darkness of her skin against the beige rug and the crackling fireplace turned him on more and more. Every muscle in her stomach showed as she bent her abdomen to pull him inside. Her long, trim arms, reached out to him. Her long neck begged to be kissed. Her hot thighs trembled and slicked with cream.

Breathing deep breaths, he clenched his jaw and bent to kiss her again. "Slow," he said again, this time hearing his own voice break.

She moaned louder as he slipped one of her tortured breasts into his mouth. With his palm placed in between her thighs, pushing down on her burning clitoris and the other very close to her inner buttocks, she began to pant uncontrollably. He reached back and lightly tapped her aching sex - the sound echoing through the room.

She twisted and turned her head on the floor, biting her lip and moaning his name. He reached back and carefully slapped it again. This time, she screamed out, feeling her body shake in despair. When he was certain that she had nearly expired from ecstasy, he bent to kiss her there again, feeling the heat and smelling scent of her body draw him in for the kill.

He knew it was a risky thing to do. As he watched her undulate under him, drunk with passion, blinded by love, he knew that there could be the possibility of no going back, but he did it anyway.

Pulling her legs apart, uncovered and exposed, vulnerable to only trust, he penetrated her body.

His searching hands dug into the carpet beside her shoulders as they made eye contact. With his knees planted below her and her legs around his waist, he pumped into her body unprotected. She let her head rest back, hot tears running down the sides of her face.

He quickly kissed them away, but continued to go deep and deeper into her. The slick feeling of her body connected to his through raw nerve endings that electrocuted their senses made him crazy. His muscled tensed, his body sweated, his eyes darkened.

Renee let out a helpless cry. Her body shook in pleasure as he lifted her hips and fought to go deeper into her heated center. Arching her back, she felt her body lift off the ground as Anatoly carried them both in his embrace. Still with his hand braced against the floor, his throbbing penis inside her, his knees planted, he heard her reach her climatic end. She screamed aloud, calling his name, his full name. Tears and sobs followed, but he continued on, continued until she was silent, then continued until she was moaning against the pool of heat re-emerging in between them. He continued until she was forced to look into his eyes and submit to his entire will; until the tears had gone and she had accepted that she was at his mercy, until he could take no more.

His body tensed to rigid rock, but he kept his gaze on her. The veins in his neck protruded out, his skin burned and flushed red. Then as he bent to kiss her, she felt it. The hot seed poured from his body into hers.

Collapsing to the ground, he pushed further into her body, rocking her hips to finish it. With one final pump into her body, he whispered into her mouth. "You're mine," he said, kissing her lips and looking into her eyes. "You're mine."

She nodded in agreement, unable to speak due to the pure shock of what had just happened. She had actually let him do what she said she would never allow him to, and he knew it.

Rolling over on her side, she felt him behind her, stroking her and resting. She looked into the fire and tried to catch her breath. What was she doing? This had all happened so fast. First, he just came to her out of the blue from Prague, then he had sex with her, then he drove to Atlanta to collect her, then he gave her a boutique, and now he was emptying himself into her—all of this in a matter of a month.

Renee swallowed hard. Before she knew it, she'd be pregnant too. And she would be just like Royal. She had judged that poor woman so harshly. She had thought her weak and cowardly, but now she knew. These men were overpowering. They had a way of making a person do exactly what they wanted regardless of the person's will.

Anatoly's arm slipped over her and pulled her into his body. Kissing her shoulder, he closed his eyes.

I do belong to you, she thought to herself of the man behind her. "But you belong to me too," she said aloud before she could help it.

Anatoly's eyes cracked open, and he looked at the back of her head. Smiling, he licked his lips and sighed. "I know," he answered in a low baritone, knowing without asking that she was brooding about his decision.

The truth of the matter was that he'd never use a condom with her again. He would not have to. If he ever denied her after this, she'd be the one to protest. He knew because she enjoyed it too much. She didn't fight it; she opened up to him, allowed him to fill her to the brim. She loved him as much as he loved her, only she was so stubborn, she was going to try her damndest to fight it.

Everyone always loses to a Medlov, he thought to himself. "Get some rest, baby," he said, stroking her exposed breast. "*YA lyublyu tebya*,"

"I love you, too," she said drifting off to sleep.

Chapter Twenty-Eight

Two weeks had passed and the day had finally come. Rushing out to the jet, Gabriel held his breath as the hatch opened and the staircase was put under her feet. He had never seen anyone so beautiful. She emerged into the crisp air wrapped in a delicate pink sweater with her golden locks around her face and her blue eyes set on him.   Briggy.

She ran down the stairs to him, eyes brimming with tears. He met her with a strong, loving embrace, pulling her up to his face and kissing her with the passion of a million missed moons. He felt alive again with her there, like his blood had finally begun to pump through his steely veins again.

Anatoly had given Gabriel the day off. "Take care of her," he had said. "Make sure that she gets situated before this all goes down."

And even though he didn't know the city well, Gabriel had an entire day planned for just the two of them.

Plus, since Anatoly had arrived back from Atlanta, they had worked every day making deals, preparing deliveries; and tomorrow, he was scheduled to head to South Florida for the major deal there with the last of Anatoly's personal stash of guns from the Sochi buy.

Briggy wiped her eyes and whispered *I love you* in French. Her beautiful lips found his again, kissing his full mouth and holding him close. Finally, he put her down, and he motioned for the bodyguards to get her things.

As he walked off the tarmac with her, he noticed a man in window of entryway. It was a startlingly familiar face. Agent Lee.

He didn't make contact with him, just let him know that he was there, that he was watching, and suddenly, just as he intended, Gabriel's joy had been stolen.

***

Gabriel knew that it was time to tell Briggy. After she had moved into the apartment with him, after dinner and after intense love making, he knew that one thing still had to be handled. Everything within him told him not to send for her. *But where was reason when a man was lonely?* Having been deprived for so long of human contact, he could not help his desire to be with her.

Then there was the issue of Anatoly and his own intense affair. Every moment that he wasn't working, he and Renee were together. Everyone noticed it, but no one had the balls to say anything about it. He guessed that it didn't matter much to the Vory as long as the money continued to come in, and they didn't marry.

Anatoly and Vasily talked about the code often, discussing men that he'd never heard of or ever imagined knowing. Anatoly knew them all - the ones no one knew were Vory and the ones that the FBI posted on every bolo around the country.

When Gabriel first began this adventure, he might have used the information, but the deeper he got, the more he found no desire to go digging in the family business. He saw the Medlov men for what they were, and he finally understood why everything had happened.

So much of what his father had taught him was true, only so much of it wasn't. It left him in a fury that often kept him up at nights and made him constantly hate himself.

He knew that his father had hated Dmitry, but as he infiltrated the organization, he saw that his father had been jealous of his brother's power, very much like he would be of Anatoly if he were a real Vor...if he were a real Medlov.

Briggy came out of the shower wrapped in a towel and crawled into bed with him. Her long blonde locks were pulled into a ponytail and her face free of makeup. Gabriel snapped out of his daze and glanced up at her. Touching her face, he adjusted his head on the headboard and turned off the television.

"What's bothering you, sweetheart," she asked, straddling his naked body.

"I have something that I need to tell you." He looked her in her eyes and smiled. "Over a midnight snack that is. So, get dressed. Let's go get some ice cream." Gabriel thought about what he was doing. If everyone on the council's business was bugged, he was certain that his own place might be. He could not get caught slipping up. With Agent Lee in Memphis and the drug bust looming, everything mattered.

"Alright," she said, wide-eyed. "I'll get dressed."

***

Before the sun could rise, Anatoly, Gabriel and Vasily were off on the jet headed to Miami to prepare for the drop. From what Anatoly had told Gabriel, no one wanted him on this job. It was too dangerous and a cardinal sin to allow a boss to do any grunt work. But Anatoly insisted that he show Gabriel the ropes.

By breakfast, amidst a beautiful seventy-degree day, the men were at the balmy docks exchanging money for the last of his precious shipment of military-grade weapons.

Anatoly had called in advance for an additional thirty men because of the shipment size and because of problems that they had previously with Igor. Likewise, the Cubans had done the same.

From the outside, it may have looked like over-kill, but Anatoly never bet small. He had learned from previous ambushes to take nothing for granted. It was a lesson that he was currently trying to teach Gabriel for future jobs.

A tall, Cuban man by the name of Adolfo with startling hazel eyes and a dark, mesmerizing tan stood with Anatoly smoking a cigar and talking about

the Riviera while Gabriel and Vasily saw to the
loading of the shipment on a freight boat off the
shore.

Evidently, Adolfo was the eldest son of Diego,
the restaurant owner that Anatoly had visited with
Destiny a few months back. Adolfo was a fearless
man with dominating features, a strong jaw, muscular
build, piercing eyes, deep voice and a thick Cuban
accent. While he was born in Miami, he had spent
his entire life fighting for his father's cause. The men
under Diego and Adolfo's charge were very much
against the Castro regime and funneled their brothers
out of the country as well as aide to their families
who were still in Cuba.

The guns were used to ensure their safety and to
fight the war that silently continued between the sons
of Cuba who wanted their people free.

Dmitry and Diego had been friends and business
partners for many years. Moneys were often trans-
ferred for various causes and meet and greets took
place in distant locales to serve both of their purposes.

When Diego retired from his post and stepped
aside, he had tapped Adolfo to take over. He had
done so happily and provided new energy and enthusiasm in recruiting men and resources.

Adolfo and Anatoly had become friends of sorts.
They both knew the perils of serving under the
command and then taking over the reign. Not many
young men of their age had been accountable for

such a terrifying responsibility, but they both had taken on their charge with fervor.

Gabriel watched the men all day, learning from them through their conversations that he had not been the only ones to have a hard father, a hard existence or many trials and tribulations. They all shared in the experience, each one taking something different from it.

When they were done, they set a date to come back to Miami and just *hang out*. Anatoly happily introduced his cousin and told him that Adolfo would be doing business with him in the future.

Adolfo seemed to like Gabriel, which surprised him. And like every experience with the Medlov men, Gabriel sincerely felt more in his element with them than with the DEA.

The flight back was relaxed. Anatoly popped a bottle of champagne to celebrate, and the men had dinner in the confines of the jet alone, enjoying conversation that didn't center on guns or the mafia. For that evening, they were just guys hanging out after a long day at work.

***

Oleg came into the office of his chemical plant on the outskirts of Memphis and hit the table, knocking papers to the floor. Yuri, his partner in crime, was already there waiting to figure out what they were going to do now that things had gone so terribly wrong.

With Anatoly and Gabriel handling the last load of the shipment to the Cubans today, there was no way to cut out their take. Now, they were faced with paying the Columbians out of their own money to a tune of $6 million dollars in cash in less than four days.

They had sent a group to highjack the load from their boss, but when the hired men arrived and saw how heavily armed both Adolfo's men and Anatoly's men were, they promptly cancelled the operation.

No one takes on Anatoly Medlov. That was the word that was sent to them only an hour ago, after they thought that they were rid of the troublesome boy and his entourage.

"Do you have six million dollars?" Yuri asked, rubbing his cold hands together. The arthritis in his body only seemed to flare more under stress, which lately was often enough.

"It will be very hard to acquire in four days. Between the two of us, I'm sure that we can liquidate and pay, but it puts us in a very complicated situation, *brat*. How are we to explain it away to banks, to IRS, to anyone?" Oleg shook his head and stared out the window at the men working below.

"Something has to be done," Yuri said in shock. "We must call the Columbians and ask for more time."

Oleg took a heart pill and drank the glass of water on the table. His hands shook. "There is no way to reverse this. The drugs are already on the way. We made a promise...It will surely get back to the council...to Anatoly...my God, it will get back to Dmitry in Prague, and we will surely be finished."

"This boy...no...this council and its rules are going to be the end of us. We must do something about it. We must *re-organize*," the man pleaded. "There must be someone we can hire to do it. With the boy out of the way, there will be less focus on us. We can blame it on any number of people. Then we can have time to fix it with the Columbians and cover our tracks." Yuri sat back in the chair and brainstormed.

"Anatoly informed us that he and his men must leave for three days. They won't return until the meeting the morning before the drop. That will be our only chance to hit him. It will be costly. There might be other sacrifices, but we must do it."

Yuri didn't care nearly as much for the other 14 council members as he did for his own life   not even their own sons who sat on the council with them.

"But who will stand against Anatoly?" Yuri asked with his shoulders shrugged. He leaned against his cane.

"We have two days to find someone and one day to prep them. Let's go for someone *not* local. I'll call my brother in Chicago and see what can be done. He stands to lose a lot of money in this as well. He can send down an *untraceable* favor."

"Well, we must. We have gone too far now, *brat*," Yuri conceded.

***

Gabriel got off the jet and nearly collapsed. The weight of the world was on his shoulders. It had taken everything in him to hide the job from Agent Lee, who was lurking around waiting for a signal, and Briggy had begged him to reveal his true identity to Dmitry before Anatoly found out who he was. "They will find out, Gabriel," she had warned. "They always do."

He was shocked at how forgiving she had been of his deception. She had cried for hours, holding on to him, asking him what he was going to do, if he was going to have to leave her, pledging her love and utter devotion. All those things had only made him worry more. He loved Briggy. He knew it deep inside of himself, and he knew now that bringing her here might have cost him her life as well.

"Are you alright, *brat*?" Anatoly asked, hitting him on his back. "Let's go to my house. Renee's cooking."

Gabriel tried to get out of it. "Can't. I promised Briggy..."

"Call her. Tell her to get ready and Vasily can go and get her," Anatoly said, not taking no for an answer.

The drive over to the house from the private airstrip was a short one, but still Gabriel had sweated through his clothes and was now ringing wet. Flushed red, he sat in the back of the car, looking out of the window and contemplating suicide.

"Are you sick?" Anatoly asked finally.

"Sometimes the plane messes with me," he said, explaining his anxiety away.

Anatoly reached down into the side of the car and pulled out a bottle of vodka. "Here, this gets rid of jet lag." He smiled but looked at him curiously.

As soon as they arrived at the mansion, Gabriel separated from the men and went to Anatoly's office. He prayed to God literally for an answer. He couldn't stomach the idea any longer of being a traitor. Only now, he wasn't sure which side he was deceiving.

He ran through the tapes quickly, looking for anything that might tell him where the drugs were.

Anatoly walked into the office a few minutes later and closed the door. "I know when something isn't right in my own camp, Gabriel. I know when there is a problem," he said, stuffing his hands down in his pockets past the guns that were shining in their holsters.

Gabriel turned around and faced him in the chair. Taking a deep breath, he wiped the sweat from his head and was about to confess to everything and beg for Briggy's life when he heard the replay at Oleg's office.

"Hold that thought," Gabriel said, turning up the volume.

They both listened to the entire conversation. With each statement from the men, Gabriel's heart lightened a little more. He finally, finally had found someone to take the fall. Resting his head on the desk, he laughed out loud and looked up at Anatoly, who was standing in shock and confusion.

"And you're happy about this why?" Anatoly asked, completely refocused on his council members instead of Gabriel's strange behavior.

"Because I'm right," Gabriel said, revealing the dimple in his jaw as he smiled. "Because my hunch was fucking right."

Anatoly smiled. "You're a lucky bastard."

Walking over to the monitor, Anatoly sat on the end of the desk. "Rewind it. I want to hear again," he said, looking at the door as Vasily came in with a gun in his hand.

"Everything alright, boss?" Vasily asked, looking at the two of them confused.

Anatoly smirked. "Everything is fine now. Put gun away. It seems that Oleg and Yuri are planning to assassinate me. Apparently, they've gotten involved with the Columbians and a nasty little $6 million coke deal that they can't afford. Gabriel found out for us. And he seems happy about it."

"There is no telling who else knows about this," Gabriel said, instantly covering his tracks. "For all we know, the feds could be listening to the exact same thing, because they don't clean their office."

Anatoly gazed nonchalantly at Gabriel and nodded. No expression was on his face. "Let's let them plan this entire thing. And when we get back from Royal's little reunion, we'll deal with them."

"You don't want to deal with them now?" Gabriel asked.

"No." Anatoly shook his head. "No, I don't. I want to go and have dinner with the girls and relax. Like I said, we can deal with them when we get back. Tomorrow, we go to Jamaica." Hitting Gabriel on the back, he stood up and rounded the corner of the desk. "Let's go eat, *brat*. Enough with these old-ass men and *your hunch*."

As Anatoly disappeared back out of the office, Gabriel let out a sigh of relief. He looked up to the ceiling and made the sign of the cross. "Thank you, God," he said aloud as he stood up.

He had to figure out a way to get a copy of this tape to Lee and get this entire investigation under his control right then.

Chapter Twenty-Nine

Anatoly did not lie to Renee when he told her a few months ago that he had a nice place in Jamaica. What he failed to tell her was that it was the size of a miniature resort. On a peninsula of Discovery Bay, the seven-bedroom, white mansion on a gentle hill sat above perfect white sand beaches with views of the Caribbean Sea. Anatoly called the place Jezebel, but Renee called it heaven.

They arrived at first dusk to a butler and staff, who waited on their every need. Food had already been prepared and the table was set for dinner, which would start as soon as all the parties had arrived.

From the breathtaking window views, beautiful hues of blue and gold skies danced across the horizon while the inside of the home was spectacularly designed for only the best living.

Renee was speechless, caught in the awe of pure beauty and decadence beyond her wildest dreams. But Gabriel and Briggy were used to the Medlov style after staying at their sprawling chateau outside of Prague.

Anatoly led everyone to their rooms, which matched the elegant, beach-style of the entire home and then took Renee to their room. He had forgone the suite, because he knew that his father was coming – hence his place as second in command.

Going into the restroom, he came back out and threw a box of Kleenex on the bed. As Renee unpacked her clothes, she looked up at him confused.

"What's that for?" she asked, picking up the purple box.

"For the crying," he said, lying on the bed. "I know how you women are. As soon as you see Royal and she sees you, you both will begin to cry. I just want you ready."

Renee laughed. "You may be right." Pulling out clothes, fresh off the racks from the boutique, she threw a black negligee over to Anatoly and raised her brow. "For after I'm done crying," she said seductively.

Anatoly lifted it with his thumbs and bit his lip. "Let's get this show on the road then, *eh*," he said, pulling her into bed.

***

Royal and Dmitry finally arrived at the mansion an hour later. Sauntering in with a large entourage of bodyguards and the entire family, minus her mother, Royal held on her husband's arm and tried to calm her nerves. She'd been crying the entire trip off and on and was only able to hide her hysterics with the large designer sunglasses that covered her bloodshot eyes.

Dmitry knew that Royal's pregnancy had a lot to do with her current emotional state and tried to be as understanding as possible.

"It's going to be alright," he assured her softly.

She looked up at him and nodded silently, but inside she was falling apart. This would be the first time in her life that she had ever seen her mother. No one knew how things would turn out. It could be a disaster or the best thing to happen to Royal. Still, everyone gave their support.

As they gathered in the foyer, Anatoly and Renee, followed by Gabriel and Briggy joined them. They quickly made their way down the stairwell to their waiting family, who welcomed them with open arms.

Anya automatically ran to Anatoly. As usual, she jumped up in his arms and kissed him profusely then interrogated him about where her presents were. Only this time, after getting hugs from her brother, she found her way to Gabriel.

He bent down to give her a hug and pulled out a small box. Inside of it was a golden locket with a picture that they had taken together while he was in Prague. Gabriel didn't know how long the good part of his history would last, but he wanted to leave his young cousin with something to remember him by.

The reunion was halted when Royal and Renee laid eyes on each other. Quietly, Royal took off her glasses and let go of her husband's arm to make her way over to her old friend. But Renee was stuck.

She stood trembling, watching the woman that she mourned laugh and smile in front of her.

"Hey," Royal said with tears in her eyes.

"Hey, girl," Renee said, looking down at Royal's bulging stomach, then to her daughter. Tears marked her face in flowing streams. "You look...alive."

They both laughed and then in one motion, they finally hugged. Holding each other tightly, they cried for everything that they knew about the lives that they had chosen and everything that they didn't know about each other. Sisters. True sisters together again at last.

The men watched, moved by the sincerity of the act. Briggy wiped her face and held on to Anya. No one said a word for a while, taking the moment in and appreciating how treasured it actually was.

Royal finally pulled away as the baby kicked. "We have so much to catch up on," she said, touching her tummy.

"You just don't know how happy I am right now," Renee said, wiping her face. She looked over at Dmitry, who nodded her way and smiled. "You better get over here and give me a hug," she said, reaching for him.

Dmitry laughed and bent down to hug her. Picking her up off the ground, he whirled her around. "Look at you! Two seconds from being a Medlov yourself," he laughed.

Anatoly instantly blushed. He knew it was true.

"I don't know about you guys but I'm starving," Royal said relaxing. "Have they already cooked?"

"Dinner is in the main dining hall," the butler said, stepping from out of the corner.

"Well, let's go that way," Renee said, grabbing Anatoly's hand. "Thank you," she whispered into his ear.

Anatoly looked at her, truly looked into her. It was then that he knew that his father was right. She would be his wife. He wasn't sure when or how, but he had to keep her.

As they all walked into the dining hall, a single person sat at the long table, behind a brilliant candelabras and food fit for a king. Nervousness was clearly present in her face. She stood quickly, smoothing out her yellow sundress.

Royal was the last to see her in the corner waiting. She walked in talking until she laid eyes on her.

She was the woman in the picture. Her mother.

"I figured that I'd have her wait in here for you," Anatoly said quietly. He looked to his father for approval, who nodded kindly.

Suddenly, everyone else in the room disappeared for Royal as if it were just the two of them. Their eyes were planted upon each other, waiting for approval, waiting for words, for some movement. But they both stood still.

Dmitry watched curiously. Feeling the need to say something, to help his wife, he touched her shoulder and cleared his throat.

"Thank you coming all of this way, Ms. Smith." His voice boomed in the quiet room, jolting everyone back to reality.

"Thank you for having me, Mr. Medlov," she answered.

"Please call me Dmitry. I am, after all, your son-in-law." He rubbed through Royal's coal black locks. "This is...well, this is your daughter." He put his large hands on her shoulders.

Feeling more self-conscious, Ms. Smith moved away from the table and slowly inched towards the beautiful woman. As she got closer, the tears flowed down her cheeks harder. *Royal...her oldest daughter. Her sunshine.*

"When I lost you, I thought for sure that they'd changed your name. I never imagined in a million years that you'd be able to keep it," her mother said, reaching out to touch her arm.

Royal wiped the tears that blanketed her face. "That was all they allowed me to keep," she said, wanting to run away.

Her mother sobbed. "I've been looking for you since you were put up for adoption. And I even hired a private detective, who finally came back three years ago and said that you were dead. But there wasn't a single night that I didn't pray for my girls, worry about you and miss you." Her voice faded as she cried.

Dmitry motioned towards the door and quietly excused the rest of the family so that Ms. Smith and

Royal could speak in private. Turning quickly as he ducked out of the room, Royal looked to him, begging him through her eyes to stay.

"Baby, you can do this. I'll be right in the next room. Why don't you two get familiar, and we'll join you in a little while," Dmitry said, holding Anya in his arms.

"Okay," Royal said, wiping tears.

***

While Royal got to know her mother, the men excused themselves and left Briggy, Anya and Renee to get familiar with the upstairs entertainment rooms. There were things to discuss that dealt with immediate life or death. And they knew that the senior Boss Medlov would want to weigh in on the matter.

Convening out on the deck in a secluded area by the cove and with drinks in hand, the three of them laid out the plan.

"Yuri has always been a slick *sonofabitch*," Dmitry said, sipping his scotch. "I should have known that he might do something like this as soon as I was out of the way."

"So what do you think that we should do?" Anatoly asked, enjoying in the warm breeze coming from the waterway.

"After this little reunion, you and I are going back to Memphis together," Dmitry said with a clever grin.

"Papa, you haven't been to the states since the *thing*," Anatoly said worried.

"I'm not a fugitive. I can come back whenever I like, and I'd *like* to go now. I can't wait to see their faces."

"You better not let Agosto find out," Anatoly said laughing.

Dmitry laughed with him. "I should probably give him a call...just to fuck with him." He turned to his son and sighed. "Did Adolfo happen to send any cigars with him?"

Anatoly stopped smiling and nodded. "*Da*, papa. He sent some."

"If you don't mind," Dmitry said, motioning towards the door of the patio. "Go and get one for me."

Anatoly turned and looked at Gabriel with a frown and stood up. "I'll be right back."

Gabriel watched quietly wondering what he had missed. Taking a deep, quiet breath, he took a sip of his scotch and sat back in the chair.

When Anatoly had gone, Dmitry turned to Gabriel and stared him down. He waited a minute, thinking thoughts in his head, calculating. Then, he gave a clever, summed-up smirk.

"Since we're all having our own little mini-reunions, I thought you and I might have one ourselves," Dmitry said, reaching into his pocket.

Gabriel waited for a gun to emerge from his uncle's pocket, but instead, he pulled out an envelope. Sliding it over to him as a gust of wind blew through, he looked his nephew in the eye. "This is for you."

"What is it?" Gabriel asked, taking the envelope.

"You mother was cut out of her family's estate, because she didn't see eye to eye with your grand-mother about me. That is the money that was sup-posed to go to her upon your grandmother's death. Now, I tried to give it to her shortly after you were born, but she wouldn't take a dime of it."

Gabriel opened the envelope to find a check for $35 million dollars. Shaking his head, he tried to give it back.

"I don't deserve this," Gabriel said, voice trem-bling.

"You do deserve it. It's yours. And I won't take it back or be refused," Dmitry said, sitting back in his chair. He bit his bottom lip and tapped the table with his large hand.

"Why now?" Gabriel asked, looking at the check.

"Because I have the distinct feeling that after this reunion of ours and after we return to Memphis, we won't be seeing each other anymore; that is after we both get what we came for. So, this is yours. And it won't bounce after the meeting. It'll never bounce. It's yours. You cash it when you're ready, when you can. You and Briggy can start over somewhere fresh where there are no extradition treaties." He smirked.

Gabriel sat quietly, fighting the tears and trying to catch his breath. He looked up at the night sky and nodded. His bottom lip quivered.

"Hey." Dmitry looked him in his eyes. "I want you to know that what happened to you was my fault. And I don't blame you. I don't fault you for what you have become as a result. And I made a promise to Royal after she found out our little story and after you reconnected her to her mother that I'd see after you. This...this should do just that."

Gabriel wiped his eyes. "Do you...do you know who I am?"

Dmitry smiled and raised his drink. "You're a Medlov."

The sound of the ocean waves beating against the rocks calmed the moment. They both stared at each other, both men from different sides of the same coin.

Anatoly came through the doors with three cigars in his hand and walked back over to the table. Sitting down, he noticed the mood change. Looking at his father, he shrugged. "What did I miss?" he asked, passing his father his cigar.

Chapter Thirty

A ferocious autumn storm ripped through Memphis as the Medlov jet landed. However, all the men on the plane were aware of the fact that things were going to get a lot worse in the city in just a minute.

Briggy and Renee were escorted in one car to an off-site location with no explanation of why; neither asked.

The men loaded up in six of Anatoly's bullet proof Land Rovers and headed to Mother Russia.

The meeting would take place in fifteen minutes. Suiting up, Dmitry rode in one car with his body-guard Davyd and three other men, fully strapped with his trusty Glock, a bullet-proof vest, two AK47s and a knife from his childhood.

Anatoly rode in a separate SUV with Vasily and three of his men, fully loaded and ready to attack. Cracking his knuckles as they rode, he smiled to himself, ready to finally taste blood again.

Gabriel rode in an SUV with a few men who had been tapped specifically for this job. As they drove, he finally texted Agent Lee the location of the drug warehouse and the time to meet him there. He had been in contact with him since the night of his uncle's talk and had arranged a swift attack.

Three additional SUVs ran protection around the convoy, each carrying men in tactical gear just in case things got out of control. Other men rode high-grade bikes through the rain on the convoy's flanks.

***

As the storm raged outside, Agosto sat at his desk with his feet up eating Chinese food with chop sticks and going over the notes to a file he was working on regarding three children who had come up missing. His worry was that he was dealing with a possible child-ring. Exhausted from being at the office all night, he popped a couple of caffeine pills and drank a protein shake.

The phone rang on his hip, pulling him away from his work. Frustrated, he answered.

"Yeah," he said quickly.

"Agosto. I just saw the biggest fucking Medlov convoy since the restaurant thing," the airport worker said, looking around him as he made the call on the pay phone.

Agosto jumped up. "Did you see Dmitry Medlov?"

"The big, seven-foot tall motherfucker. Yeah, I saw the dude. He was with like a hundred men. They loaded up and headed out of the airport about five minutes ago."

"Shit. Alright. Thanks." Agosto jumped up from his desk and grabbed his coat and pulled his drawer open to grab his extra clips. "Hey, Martinez!" he screamed.

"Yeah," the detective said, sticking his head through the door.

"Get your shit. Dmitry Medlov is home. Something big is going down. He's headed somewhere. I need someone out at the fucking restaurant..." He slammed his drawer shut and locked it. "And I need cars ready to rock when I give the word."

"Got it boss," Martinez said, walking off.

"Hey, Martinez..."

"Yeah," he said, coming back to the door.

"Call Harrison. Tell him that this might be the only chance to get that bastard Anatoly Medlov back for fucking his ex-fiancé."

"On it," Martinez said disappearing.

***

The convoy pulled up to the back of *Mother Russia* restaurant, and the men quickly flooded out, opening the doors for their bosses to escort them safely inside out of sight.

Since the restaurant had been rebuilt, there were several entry-ways that lead to the downstairs basement and several exits that led out.

Hitting the stairs, they opened the doors and cleared the halls as Dmitry and Anatoly made their way down to the meeting. The people eating out in the restaurant didn't have a clue that on the other side of the bullet-proof walls, and a few feet below them a war was about to ensue.

The council members sat waiting Anatoly to arrive. No one knew what was keeping him so long with the exception that maybe the conditions had gotten too bad to fly. Suddenly, they heard footsteps, only it sounded like more than normal.

The door swung open and in flooded men in tactical gear. Shortly after, Anatoly walked in and then Dmitry followed. The room silenced, gasps were held.

Dmitry walked in with a bright, devious smile. Showing the deep dimples in his square jaws, clenching his teeth and staring his council down, he smirked.

"Don't look so happy to see me," he said, walking over to the head of the table. Anatoly pulled the chair out for him and he sat down. Wiping the rain water from his face, he took a deep breath and poured himself a glass of water. "It's good to be home. Anatoly, check the room before we begin."

Anatoly did so quickly. He nodded when they were clear. "Ten minutes until they arrive," Anatoly said, checking his text from the detective Cory, who had actually gotten useful Intel to them on time.

"So, I guess that I'll make this short. You motherfuckers were supposed to support my son, not kill him. Not allow him to be killed." Dmitry's voice was a low, menacing growl. Looking like a predator stalking his prey, he set his knife on the table.

"We have done our jobs," Khalid answered confidently. "We have not forgotten the code."

Dmitry nodded and pointed his long finger. "Some of you *have* forgotten. Two of you at least." His point landed on Oleg and Yuri.

"Eight minutes." Anatoly said, counting down the time they had before the police arrived.

"Let this be a lesson to you who may have forgotten. This is my house. I built it!" Dmitry screamed, hitting the table with his fist. "And there isn't a thing that either of your sons of whores can do about it. As long as I live, as long as I draw breath, my son will not be removed from this table as boss, will not be over-thrown by anyone on this council and will not be plotted against by the very men that I put in charge to protect his interests. And each and every time that I have to come here to make that point, it will be a motherfucking, bloody damned massacre."

Standing up as the chair fell behind him, Dmitry pulled his Glock and shot Yuri and Oleg in the head. He then pulled out his knife. The serrated edge gleamed. Walking over to them, he bent down on his knee and snatched their head back. Their dead eyes looked up at the ceiling. Pulling their shirt open, he cut off the stars on their chest, indicating their status in the Vory. Throwing the pieces of flesh on the ground, he looked around.

Breathing heavily, he wiped the blood on his shirt. "Are there any questions?" he asked.

The men shook their heads, mortified by what they had just witnessed, specifically Oleg and Yuri's sons - who were spared for some reason. They sat in complete shock as they watched their fathers murdered. Still, they felt relieved in some ways that Dmitry had been merciful than expected.

Spitting, Dmitry looked at his son.

"Four minutes," Anatoly said, looking at his watch.

"Vasily, I want every man in both of these men's camp dead by dusk. Do you understand? Take Roman and Alesky to a safe house until it's over. I don't want them harmed. I'm sure that they've been through enough watching what has happened to their fathers."

"*Da*, boss," Vasily answered quickly.

Dmitry looked at both of the quivering men and smiled. "Don't worry. I don't have any plans to kill you."

"Let's go, papa" Anatoly said, opening the door. "Council members *still standing*, let's go."

Wiping the blood off his face, Dmitry walked back out of the basement and was guided back out into the rain by his bodyguards. Two men stayed behind to get rid of the bodies.

Everyone knew that they would have plenty of time to clean up the mess and get rid of the bodies before the police department could get a warrant to search.

Within five minutes, everyone was gone. Sirens blared behind them in the thunderstorm. The trucks split off in different locations, going unnoticed as they disappeared into traffic. Dmitry headed in one direction. Anatoly headed in the other.

***

"Damn this is a lot of coke," Agent Lee said, hitting Gabriel on the back. "Good job, man. I was worried about you, but you did it. You brought the bastards down."

"Yeah, we didn't get Anatoly or Dmitry, but we got the people responsible for it. Between the tapes and this, I'd say this investigation was successful."

"There is always next time for them. And you say that these warehouses belong to Yuri and Oleg?" Lee asked, watching the warehouse being emptied by the undercover agents.

Gabriel nodded. "Not just them. Their two sons are on the council as well. Roman and Alesky. Those are the only men that I really got a chance to ever meet, but they were supposed to be here. I don't understand where they went to."

"We'll get them," Lee said, holding up the umbrella to protect himself from the fierce storm. "They all can't run forever, right?"

Gabriel smirked. "I'm sure that they'll pop up. I just doubt that you'll get anything out of them. Vor don't talk to cops. They'll do their time quietly."

"We don't need them to talk with all of this evidence. They can sit in jail and rot."

"Alright, well, I'm out of here."

"I need you back at the office to debrief tomorrow," Agent Lee reminded.

"About that," Gabriel said, pulling out his badge. "I've been through enough. I did what I came to do." He passed his badge and gun to Agent Lee and nodded. "I won't be needing that anymore."

"You're going to take the girl and run?" Agent Lee asked.

"Yeah, I am," Gabriel said, walking way. "Take care of yourself, man."

As the rain beat against his face, Gabriel walked away, feeling free for the first time in his life. He stood straighter, saw things clearer. Even in the storm, everything finally made sense.

***

Dmitry was back on a private plane headed on a long journey back to Prague out of Tunica, Mississippi by night fall. Still in his bloody clothes, he sat back and enjoyed a glass of vodka knowing that his family was safe and his point had been made. It was definitely worth the trip. Now, he could return to his family, to his wife, to his twin boys, to his daughter, to his wife. He smiled at the thought. Everything was just as it should have been.

***

Fifty miles away, Gabriel and Briggy were loading into a car and heading far away. He didn't get a chance to say goodbye to Anatoly, possibly because his father had already told him about who he really was – possibly because it would be too painful for his cousin to see him go, but he knew for once that he had their blessings. And more than anything, he knew who they were and they know who he was. Kissing Briggy's hand, he headed out on the dark highway with no luggage and just one envelope. He had no idea where they were going to start their new life, but he would take his uncle's advice and make sure that it was somewhere that did not extradite.

***

The rain beat against the windows with a definite fury at Anatoly's mansion. He stood looking out of the windows of his solarium and drinking a glass of vodka straight. He needed something to take the edge off of a very long day.

Reflecting, he thought about the men who were headed off in to the world with his last name. His father had risked everything to protect him again, and he had risked everything by protecting his cousin even though he was a cop.

Anatoly had found out the truth of Gabriel's identity through Aldolfo at the docks. He'd tipped him off as soon as he saw him. Considering that the Cuban's dealings had them in contact very often with DEA, he had run across the man unbeknown to him.

Anatoly had made up his mind to protect Gabriel when they were in his office after the job. He could see that his cousin was torn, hurting. It was then that he had called his father and asked him what to do before the trip to Jamaica.

"Let him fly," Dmitry had said quickly. "We owe it to him." Anatoly had taken his father's advice. He knew that Gabriel was looking for anyone to take the fall to protect them. So, it was only fair that he do the same. Now, they had all settled up.

In the morning, Aleksey and Roman would be found holed up in a hotel by the DEA and take the fall for their fathers. And he would start to rebuild the council based upon his own choices.

He was actually grateful for this adventure, every part of it. Victoria had taught him the meaning of lust. Destiny had taught him the meaning of revenge. Renee had taught him the meaning of love. And Gabriel had taught him the meaning of family.

"Baby, are you coming to bed?" Renee asked, walking into the room.

He turned to her and smiled. "In a minute," he said, licking his lips. His blood began to burn at the thought of what he was going to do her tonight.

I was made for this, he thought to himself of his life. *And hopefully, she was made for me.*

Dmitry's Closet (2010)

From author Latrivia S. Nelson, author of the epic romance *Ivy's Twisted Vine*, comes a story about Memphis, TN, a deadly faction of the Russian mafia and an innocent woman who dismantles an empire. Orphaned virgin Royal Stone is looking for employment in one of the country's toughest recessions. What she finds is the seven-foot, blonde millionaire Dmitry Medlov, who offers her a job as the manager of his new boutique Dmitry's Closet. After she accepts his job offer, she soon accepts his gifts, his bed and his lifestyle. What she does not know is that her knight in shining armor is also the head of the Medlov Organized Crime Family, a faction of the elite Russian mafia Vory v Zakone. Falling in love with the clueless Royal makes Dmitry want to break the code, leave his empire and start a life far away from the perils of the Thieves-in-Law. Only, his brother Ivan comes to the Memphis from New York City bent on a murderous revenge. With the FBI and Memphis Police Department working hard to build a case against Dmitry and his brother trying to kill him, he is forced to tell Royal of his true identity, but Royal also is keeping a secret - one that changes everything. Who will win? Who will lose? Who will die? Watch all the skeletons as they tumble out of the urban literature sensation Dmitry's Closet.

www.dmitryscloset.com

Dmitry's Royal Flush: Rise of the Queen

(2010)

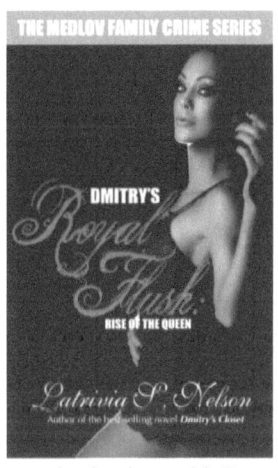

From the popular multicultural author, Latrivia S. Nelson, comes the highly anticipated second installment of the Medlov Crime Family Series, Dmitry's Royal Flush: Rise of the Queen. For Dmitry and Royal Medlov, money doesn't equal happiness. Forced to leave Memphis, TN and flee to Prague after a brutal mafia war, the couple nestled into the countryside to raise their daughter, Anya, and lead a safe, quiet life. But when Dmitry's son, Anatoly, shows up with an offer he can't refuse, Dmitry is forced to go back to the life he left as boss of the most feared criminal organization in world. Consequently, the deal could not only destroy the Medlov Crime Family but also Dmitry and Royal. Royal hasn't been the same since she was attacked three years ago. Where she used to be a sweet, innocent girl, she's now the jaded, bitter mistress of the Medlov Chateau. However, a reality check is in store for the pre-Madonna when Anya's new teacher shows up with her sights set on stealing Dmitry, and Ivan's old ally shows up with his sights on killing him. Can Royal save them all? Will she? With a family in such turmoil, the only way to survive is to stick together. Read the gripping tale of a marriage strong enough to stand the test of time as Dmitry realizes that he has the best cards in the house as long as he has a Royal Flush.

www.dmitrysroyalflush.com

The Medlov Crime Family Series

Dmitry's Closet
www.dmitryscloset.com
(January 2010)

Dmitry's Royal Flush: Rise of the Queen
www.dmitrysroyalflush.com
(Summer 2010)

Anatoly Medlov: Complete Reign
www.latrivianelson.info
(January 2011)

The Medlov Family: Saving Anya
www.latrivianelson.info
(Fall 2011)

About the Author

Latrivia S. Nelson is an urban fiction and interracial romance author. Her first novel, Ivy's Twisted Vine (2008), is the largest interracial novel in its genre. Dmitry's Closet is her first urban fiction/interracial romance novel and a bestseller.

Currently, Nelson is working on her next book and pursing her Ph.D. in criminal justice. She lives in the suburbs of Memphis with her husband (Adam) and two children (Tierra & Jordan) and is a senior specialist for The Carter Malone Group, a full-service public relations firm.

"Typically, I write about untraditional, unconventional and taboo relationships in contemporary society. I give them a voice, and they give me inspiration. So far, I've never conformed, and I probably never will."

-Latrivia S. Nelson
www.latrivianelson.com

Bold Authors. Bold Statements.

www.riverhousepublishingllc.com